Pawing Through the Past

RITA MAE BROWN
& SNEAKY PIE BROWN

ILLUSTRATIONS BY ITOKO MAENO

Pawing Through the Past

WHEELER
PUBLISHING, INC.
ROCKLAND, MA

★ AN AMERICAN COMPANY ★

Published in Large Print by arrangement with Bantam Books, a division of Random House, Inc., in the United States and Canada.

Wheeler Large Print Book Series.

Set in 16 pt Plantin.

Illustrations by Itoko Maeno

Library of Congress Cataloging-in-Publication Data

Brown, Rita Mae.
  Pawing through the past/ Rita Mae Brown & Sneaky Pie Brown; illustrations by Itoko Maeno.
      p. (large print) cm.(Wheeler large print book series)
    ISBN 1-56895-134-5 (hardcover)
    1. Haristeen, Harry (Fictitious character)—Fiction. 2. Murphy, Mrs. (Fictitious character)—Fiction. 3. Women postal service employees—Fiction. 4. Women detectives—Fiction. 5. Women cat owners—Fiction. 6. Class reunions—Fiction. 7. Cats—Fiction. 8. Virginia—Fiction. 9. Large type books. I. Title. II. Series

[PS3552.R698 P36 2001]
813'.54—dc21
                                                          00-068663
                                                              CIP

Dedicated to
Cindy Chandler

In a dog-eat-dog world,
she hands us our napkins

Cast of Characters

Mary Minor Haristeen (Harry), the young postmistress of Crozet. She won double senior superlatives in high school: Most Likely to Succeed and Most Athletic.

Mrs. Murphy, Harry's gray tiger cat, calm in a crisis and sassy, too.

Tee Tucker, Harry's Welsh corgi, Mrs. Murphy's friend and confidante, is a solid, courageous creature.

Pewter, Market Shiflett's shamelessly fat gray cat, who now lives with Harry and family. Her high intelligence is usually in the service of her self-indulgence.

Pharamond Haristeen (Fair), an equine veterinarian, formerly married to Harry. He wants to get back together again with Harry.

Susan Tucker, Harry's best friend. She tells it like it is. She won the Best All-Round senior superlative in high school.

Olivia Craycroft (BoomBoom), a buxom dilettante who constantly irritates Harry. Her senior superlative was Best Looking.

Cynthia Cooper, a young deputy in the sheriff's department, who is willing to use unorthodox methods to capture criminals.

Sheriff Rick Shaw, a dedicated, reliable public servant. He may not be the most imaginative sheriff but he is the most persistent.

Tracy Raz, the former All-State football player, who comes home for his fiftieth high-school reunion and rekindles his romance with Miranda.

Chris Sharpton, a newcomer to Crozet, she jumps right into activities hoping to make friends.

Bitsy Valenzuela, a socially active woman who includes Chris in her circle.

Marcy Wiggins, an unhappily married woman, who looks forward to her outings with Bitsy and Chris. She needs the diversion.

Big Marilyn Sanburne (Mim), the undisputed queen of Crozet, who can be an awful snob at times. She knows the way the world works.

Little Marilyn Sanburne (Little Mim), a chip off the old block yet quite resentful of it.

Charlie Ashcraft, a notoriously successful seducer of women. Voted Best Looking by his high-school class.

Leo Burkey, was voted Wittiest.

Bonnie Baltier, was voted Wittiest.

Hank Bittner, was voted Most Talented.

Bob Shoaf, was voted Most Athletic later playing cornerback for the New York Giants.

Dennis Rablan, voted Best All-Round and now a photographer. He squandered his inheritance and is regarded as a failure.

Miranda Hogendobber, last but not least on the list: A woman of solid virtue, common sense, she works with Harry at the post office.

1

The huge ceiling fan lazily swirled overhead, vainly attempting to move the soggy August air. Mary Minor Haristeen, Harry to her friends—and everyone was a friend—scribbled ideas on a yellow legal pad. Seated around the kitchen table, high-school yearbooks open, were Susan Tucker, her best friend, Mrs. Miranda Hogendobber, her coworker and good friend, and Chris Sharpton, an attractive woman new to the area.

"We could have had this meeting at the post office," Susan remarked as she wiped the sweat from her forehead.

"Government property," Miranda said.

"Right, government property paid for with my taxes," Susan laughed.

Harry, the postmistress in tiny Crozet, Virginia, said, "Okay, it is air-conditioned but think how many hours Miranda and I spend in that place. I have no desire to hang out there in my free time."

"You've got air conditioning at your house." Miranda stared at Susan.

"I know but the kids are having a pool party and—"

"You left the house with a party in progress? There won't be a drop of liquor left," Harry interrupted.

1

"My kids know when to stop."

"Congratulations," Harry taunted her. "That doesn't mean anyone else's kids know when to stop. I hope you locked the bar."

"Ned is there." Susan returned to the opened yearbook, the conversation clearly over. Her husband could handle any crisis.

"You could have said that in the first place." Harry opened her yearbook to the same page.

"Why? It's more fun to listen to you tell me what to do."

"Oh." Harry sheepishly bent over the yearbook photo of one of her senior superlatives, Most Likely to Succeed. "I can't believe I looked like that."

"You look exactly the same. Exactly." Miranda pulled Harry's yearbook to her.

"Don't compliment her, it will go to her head." Susan turned to Chris. "Are you sorry you volunteered to help us?"

"No, but I don't see as I'm doing much good." The newcomer smiled, her hand on her own high-school yearbook.

"All right. Down to business." Harry straightened her shoulders. "I'm in charge of special categories for our twentieth high-school reunion. BoomBoom Craycroft, our fearless leader"—Harry said this with a tinge of sarcasm about the head of the reunion—"is going to reshoot photographs of our senior superlatives with us as we are today. My job is to come up with other things to do with people who weren't senior superlatives.

"That's only fair. I mean, there are only

twelve senior superlatives, one male, one female. That's twenty people out of one hundred and thirty-two, give or take a few, since some of us were voted more than one superlative." Harry paused for a breath. "How many were in your class, Miranda?"

"Fifty-six. Forty-two are still alive, although some of us might be on respirators. My task for my reunion is easier." Miranda giggled, her hand resting on the worn cover of her 1950 yearbook.

"You all were so lucky to go to small high schools. Mine was a consolidated. Huge," Chris remarked, and indeed her yearbook bore witness to the fact, being three times fatter than that of Harry and Susan or Mrs. Hogendobber.

Susan agreed. "I guess we were lucky but we didn't know it at the time."

"Does anyone?" Harry tapped her yellow wooden pencil against the back of her left wrist.

"Probably not. Not when you're young. What fun we had." Miranda, a widow, nodded her head, jammed with happy memories.

"Okay, here's what I've got. Ready?" They nodded in assent so Harry began reading, "These are categories to try and include others: Most Distance Traveled. Most Children. Most Wives—"

"You're not going to do that." Miranda chuckled.

"Why not? That one is followed by Most Husbands. Too bad we can't have one for Most Affairs." Harry lifted her eyebrows.

"Malicious," Susan said dryly.

"Rhymes with delicious." Harry's eyes brightened. "Okay, what else have I got here? Most Changed. Obviously that has to be in some good way. Can't pick out someone who has porked on an extra hundred pounds. And—uh—I couldn't think of anything else."

"Harry, you're usually so imaginative." Miranda seemed surprised.

"She's not at *all* imaginative but she *is* ruthlessly logical. I'll give her that."

Harry ignored Susan's assessment of her, speaking to Chris, "When you're new to a place it takes a long time to ferret out people's relationships to one another. Suffice it to say that Susan, my best friend since birth, feels compelled to point out my shortcomings."

"Harry, being logical isn't a shortcoming. It's a virtue," Susan protested. "But we are light on categories here."

Chris opened her dark green yearbook to a club photo. "My twentieth reunion was last year. One of the things we did was go through the club photos to see if we could find anyone who became a professional at something they were known for in high school. You know, like did anyone in Latin club become a Latin teacher. It's kind of hokey but you do get desperate after a time."

Harry pulled the book toward her, the youthful faces of the Pep Club staring back at her. "Which one are you?"

Chris pointed to a tall girl in the back row. "I wasn't blonde then."

"I can see that." Harry read the names below the photo, finding Chris Sharpton. She slid the book back to the owner.

"What we also did which took a bit of quick thinking on the spot was, we had cards made up with classmates' names written on them in italics. They were pretty. Anyway, if the individual hadn't fit into some earlier category we did things like Tom Cruise Double—anything to make them feel special."

"That's clever," Miranda complimented her.

"The other thing we did was make calls. As you know, people disperse after high school. Each of us on the committee called everyone we were still in contact with from our class. We asked who they were in contact with and what they knew about the people. This way we gathered information for things like Most Community Service. After a time it's a stretch but it's important that everyone be included in some way. At the last minute we even wrote a card up, Still the Same."

"Chris, these are good ideas." Harry was grateful. "You're wonderful to come help us. I mean, this isn't even your reunion."

"I'm not as generous as you think," Chris laughed. "Susan bet me she'd beat me by three strokes on the Keswick golf course. The bet was I'd help you all if I lost."

"What would you have gotten if you'd won?"

"Two English boxwoods planted by my front walkway."

5

Since moving to Crozet four months ago, Chris had thrown herself into decorating and landscaping her house in the Deep Valley subdivision, a magnet for under-forty newcomers to Albemarle County.

An outgoing person, Chris had made friends with her neighbors but most especially Marcy Wiggins and Bitsy Valenzuela, two women married to men who were classmates of Harry's.

"Good bet," Harry whistled.

"I told you my golf game was improving." Susan gloated. "But Miranda, I don't think we've done one thing to help you."

She smiled a slow smile. "Our expectations are different than yours. At your fiftieth high-school reunion you're thrilled that all your parts are moving. We'll be happy to eat good food, share stories, sit around. I suppose we'll pitch horseshoes and dance. That sort of thing."

"Are you in charge of the whole thing?" Chris was incredulous.

"Pretty much. I'll need to round up a few people to help me decorate. I'm keeping it simple because I'm simple."

Before anyone could protest that Miranda was not simple, Mrs. Murphy, Harry's beautiful tiger cat, burst through the animal door.

"What have you got?" Harry rose from the table expecting the worst.

Pewter, the plump gray cat, immediately followed through the animal door and Tee Tucker, Harry's corgi, burst through behind her, bumping the cat in the rear end, which brought forth a snarl.

Susan focused on the animals. "I don't know what she's got but everyone wants it."

Mrs. Murphy blew through the kitchen into the living room, where she crouched behind the sofa as Pewter leapt onto the large stuffed curving arm.

"Selfish!"

The tiger cat did not answer her gray accuser because if she did, the mole she had carefully stalked would have popped out of her mouth and escaped.

Harry knelt down. "Say, Murphy, good job. That's a huge mole. Why, that mole could dig to China."

"She didn't catch it by herself," Pewter complained loudly. *"I blocked off the other exit. I deserve half of that mole."*

"I helped." The corgi drooled.

"Ha!" Pewter disagreed.

"Thank you for bringing me this prize." Harry carefully reached behind the sofa, petted Murphy, then grabbed the limp mole by the scruff of its neck.

The tiger cat opened her jaws. *"Moles are dangerous, you know. William of Orange, King of England, was killed when his horse stepped in a mole hole. He broke his collarbone and then took a fever."*

"Show-off." Pewter's pupils narrowed to slits.

Mrs. Murphy sashayed into the kitchen, ignoring her detractors.

"Excuse me, ladies." Harry walked outside, depositing the mole at the back of the

7

woodpile. The minute it was on the ground it scurried under the logs. "That's Murphy for you. She didn't even break your neck, little guy. She was bringing me a present. Guess she expected me to dispatch you."

When Harry returned, Chris said, nose wrinkled, "I don't know how you could pick up that mole. I could never do that. I'm too squeamish."

"Oh, when you grow up in the country you don't think about stuff. You just do it." She pointed to Chris's yearbook. "Lake Shore, Illinois, must be a far cry from the country."

"That it is." Chris laughed.

Susan, flipping through her yearbook, bubbled. "I'm getting excited about this reunion. October will be here before we know it. Time flies."

"Don't say that. I'm nervous enough about getting organized for the damn thing," Harry grumbled.

"Maybe you're nervous about seeing all those people," Chris said.

"I'm as nervous about them seeing me as me seeing them. What will they think? Do I look like a..." Susan paused. "Well, do I look older? Will they be disappointed when they see me?"

"You look great," Harry said with conviction. "Besides, half of our class still lives within shouting distance. Everyone knows what you look like."

"Harry, we hardly even see the people who moved to Richmond—like Leo Burkey. Shouting distance doesn't matter."

Harry cupped her chin in her hand. "Leo Burkey will be just like always, handsome and B-A-D."

"Hey, I'd like to meet this guy." The single Chris smiled.

"Is he between wives?" Harry asked Susan.

"BoomBoom will know."

"Of course she will." Harry laughed. "Miranda, we really aren't doing a thing for you but I'm glad our reunions are at the same time. We can use a skateboard to go up and down the halls to visit."

"I'll bet you think I can't even use a skateboard," Miranda challenged her.

"I never said that!"

"You didn't have to." Miranda winked. But just you wait, Miranda thought to herself, smiling.

"*It's not fair that Murphy gets all the attention,*" Pewter wailed as she jumped on the kitchen counter.

"*I don't get all the attention but I did bring in a fresh mole. Jealous.*"

"*I am unloved,*" Pewter warbled at a high-decibel range.

Harry got up, opened the cupboard, and removed a round plastic bowl of fresh catnip. She rolled it between her fingers, releasing the heavenly aroma. Then she placed the bits on the floor where Pewter dove in, quickly followed by Murphy. Harry handed Tucker a Milk-Bone, which satisfied her.

A little coo from Pewter directed all human eyes to her. Blitzed on catnip, she lay on her back on the heart pine floor, her tail slowly swishing. Mrs. Murphy was on her side, her paws covering her eyes.

"Bliss." Miranda laughed.

"I love the whole world and everyone in it," Pewter meowed.

Murphy removed one paw—*"Me, too"*—then she covered her eyes up again.

"That ought to hold them." Harry sat back down after pouring everyone iced tea. Mrs. Hogendobber had brought homemade icebox cookies, cucumber sandwiches, and fresh vegetables.

"Do you know that some schools now regard senior superlatives as politically incorrect?" Susan reached for a sandwich.

"Why?" Miranda wondered.

Susan pointed to the senior superlative section, one full page for each superlative. "Elitist. Hurts people's feelings."

"Life is unfair." Harry's voice rose slightly. "You might as well learn that in high school if you haven't already."

"You've got a point there." Chris shook her sleek blonde pageboy. "I can remember crying hot tears over stuff that now seems trivial but I learned that disappointments are going to come and I've got to handle them. And all that surging emotion going through you for the first time. How confusing."

"Still is." Harry sipped her tea. "For me anyway."

"Is everyone in your class still alive?" Chris asked Susan and Harry.

"We've lost two," Susan answered. "Aurora

10

Hughes." She turned the page to Most Talented and there a willowy girl in a full-length dress was in the arms of a young man, Hank Bittner, wearing a top hat and tails. "She died of leukemia the year after graduation. We were all in college and you know, I still feel guilty about not being there. Aurora was such a good kid. And she really was talented."

"Who was the other one?" Chris asked.

"Ronnie Brindell." Harry spoke since Susan had just stuffed a cookie in her mouth. "They say he jumped off the Golden Gate Bridge in San Francisco. He left a note. I still can't believe he did it. I liked Ron. I can't imagine he'd—well—what can you say about suicide?"

"Here." Susan flipped to the senior superlative for Most Popular. A slender, slightly effeminate young man sat on a merry-go-round with Meredith McLaughlin, her eyes sparkling with merriment.

"He doesn't look depressed." Chris studied the picture.

"People said he was gay and couldn't handle it." Harry also studied the picture. "He was a nice boy. But the bruiser boys used to pick on him something terrible. I bet it was rough being a gay kid in high school but back then no one said anything like that. The gay kids must have gotten roughed up daily but it was all hidden, you know."

"I do, actually. We had the same thing at Lake Shore. I guess every school did. It's sad really. And to think he jumped off the bridge." Chris shuddered.

11

"May the Lord be a tower of strength for the oppressed." Mrs. Hogendobber cited a verse from Psalm Nine and that closed the subject.

"Who knows what secrets will pop up like a jack-in-the-box?" Susan ruminated. "Old wounds might be opened."

"Susan, it's a high-school reunion for Pete's sake. Not therapy."

"Okay, maybe not therapy but it sure is a stage where past and present collide for all to see."

"Susan, I don't feel that way. We know these people."

"Harry, when was the last time you saw Bob Shoaf?" Susan mentioned the star athlete of their class, who became a professional football player.

"On television."

"You don't think he'll have the big head? Those guys snap their fingers for girls, cars, goodies...and presto, they get what they want. He won't be the same old Bob."

"He sounds fascinating, too." Chris's eyes widened.

"He thinks so. He was always conceited but he is good-looking and I guess he's rich. Those people pull down unreal salaries." Harry sighed, wishing a bit of money would fall her way.

"Maybe he blew it all. Maybe he's suffering from depression. Maybe he's impotent." A devilish grin filled Susan's face. "Secrets!"

"She's right, though. At our twentieth

people who had crushes on one another in high school snuck off, marriages hit the rocks, old rivalries were renewed. It was wild, really. I had a good time, though." Chris shyly grinned.

Susan wheeled on Harry. "Charlie Ashcraft!"

"Not if he were the last man on earth!"

"You slept with Charlie. That's your secret."

"Is not," Harry protested.

"Girls." Mrs. Hogendobber feigned shock. She'd spent enough time around this generation to know they said things directly that her generation did not. She still couldn't decide if that was wise or unwise.

"You know, Harry, it will all come out at the reunion if what Chris says holds true for us."

"You're one brick shy of a load." Harry considered flicking a cucumber at her face. "Anyway, a woman has to have some secrets. People are boring without secrets."

Mrs. Murphy raised her head, her mind clearing somewhat from the delightful effects of the homegrown catnip. *That depends on the secrets.*

2

Canada sent down a ridge of cool dry air which swept over central Virginia, bringing relief from the moist, suffocating August heat.

That evening Harry, on her knees weeding her garden, rocked back on her heels to inhale the light, cool fragrance. With the mercury dipping to sixty-five degrees Fahrenheit, she had put on a torn navy blue sweatshirt.

Mrs. Murphy stalked a maple moth who easily saw her coming; those compound eyes could see everything. The yellow and pinkish creature fluttered upwards, fixing on the top of the boxwoods. From this lordly perch it observed the sleek cat, who, intelligent as she was, couldn't climb a boxwood.

The pile of weeds grew to a mound.

"Better toss this before it gets too heavy." Harry lifted the pitchfork, wedged it under, and in one neat motion picked up the debris. She walked past to the compost pile some distance from the manure spreader.

"Dump it on the manure spreader," Murphy suggested.

"You don't have to come along," Harry replied to her cat, who she thought was complaining. She walked to the edge of the woods where she chucked the weeds. Murphy caught up with her.

"If you'd put it in the manure spreader, Harry, it would have been a lot easier."

Harry leaned on her pitchfork and looked out over the hay field. The bees were heading back to the hives as twilight deepened. Even the nasty brilliant yellow digger bees headed to their labyrinthine underground nests. The bats stirred overhead, consuming insects.

"Farmer's friend," Harry said. "Did you

know, Mrs. Murphy, that bats, black snakes, praying mantis, and owls are some of the best partners you can have among the wild animals?"

"I did. I forgot to tell you that the black snake that winters in the loft is now close to four and a half feet long and she's on the south side of the garden. Her hunting territory is a giant circle and she moves counterclockwise. The sight of her is a fright. 'Course, the sight of Flatface, the barn owl, is a fright, too. She's grown twice as tall as last year. Thinks she's better than the rest of us."

Harry reached down, picked up her little friend, and kissed the top of her head. "You are the most wonderful cat in the world. Have I told you that lately?"

"Thank you," Murphy purred, then wiggled to get down. The night creatures emerging were too tempting. She wanted to stalk a few.

Harry grabbed the pitchfork which she'd propped against a hickory: "Come on, time for supper."

The sweet smell of redbud clover filled their nostrils as the thin line of ground fog turned from seashell pink to mauve to pearl gray. A bobwhite called behind them. The magnificent owl of whom Mrs. Murphy had just spoken, flew out from the barn cupola on her first foraging mission of the evening.

Part of the rhythm of this place and these animals, Harry placed the pitchfork on the wall of the small storage shed. The night air cooled the temperature considerably. She put her hands in her jeans pockets as she hurried into the house.

"What took you so long?" Pewter complained. *"I thought you two were weeding the garden."*

"We did but we had things to talk about." Mrs. Murphy brushed past her, then quickly turned as she heard the can opener. *"Hope it's tuna tonight. I'm in the mood for tuna."*

A bark outside and then a whap on the doggie door announced Tucker's presence.

"Where were you?" Mrs. Murphy asked from the counter as Harry spooned out the tuna into the two cat dishes, one marked Her Highness and the other, Upholstery Destroyer.

"Blair Bainbridge's." The dog mentioned Harry's nearest neighbor to the west. *"Bought starter cattle and I had to help him herd them. He doesn't know beans and he's still moving a little slow after his injuries from last year. Wait until you see the calves. Weedy, spindly legs and thin chests, not good specimens at all but at least they've been wormed and had their shots. Wait until Mom sees them. It will be interesting to see how she manages to praise him without telling him these are the worst heifers she's ever seen."*

"She'll find a way."

"Tucker. You've been busy. You're getting lamb bits in gravy." Pewter sniffed the distinctive mutton aroma.

"Yeah!"

As the three ate, Harry popped a pasta dish in the microwave. She wasn't very hungry but she ate it anyway since she had a tendency to lose weight in the summers.

Afterward they all sat on the sofa while Harry tried to read the newspaper but she

16

kept rattling it, then putting it down. Finally, she got up, threw on her jacket, and walked outside.

"*What's she up to?*" Pewter, quite comfortable, wondered.

"*I'll go.*" Tucker roused herself and followed.

"*Me, too.*" Murphy shook herself.

"*Damn,*" Pewter grumbled. She flicked her tail over her gray nose, finally got up to stretch, and tagged along.

Harry walked to the paddocks behind the barn where she leaned against the black three-board fence to watch her horses, Gin Fizz, Tomahawk, and Poptart, enjoying the refreshing air.

They looked up, said hello, and returned to grazing.

Overhead the evening star appeared unreal, it was so big and clear. The Big Dipper rolled toward the horizon and Yellow Mountain was outlined in a thin band of blue, lighter than the deep skies.

"Kids, I couldn't live anywhere else. I know I work fourteen to sixteen hours a day between the post office and the farm, but I couldn't work in an office. I don't know..." Her voice trailed off. Pewter climbed up one fence post, Mrs. Murphy climbed up on another one while Tucker patiently sat on Harry's foot. "I kind of dread this reunion. I went to the fifteenth—still married then. It's a lot easier when you're married—socially, I mean. The ones from far away will look at me, then look at BoomBoom. I guess it's pretty easy to see why Fair hopped on her in a hurry. Wonder if he'll come? He was in the class ahead. But of course he will, he knows everybody. He's a good man, guys. He went through a bad patch, that's all, but I couldn't endure it. I just couldn't do it."

"He's over that now," Tucker stoutly replied. The corgi loved Fair Haristeen, DVM, with all her heart and soul. *"He's admitted he was wrong. He still loves you."*

"But she doesn't love him." Pewter licked her paw and rapidly passed it over her whiskers.

"She does love him," Mrs. Murphy countered, *"but she doesn't know how much or in what way. Like she wouldn't want to marry him again but she loves him as a person."*

"It's awfully confusing." Tucker's pretty ears drooped.

"Humans make such a mess," Pewter airily announced.

"They think too much and feel too little," Murphy noted. *"Even Mom and I love her, we all love her. It's the curse of the species. Then again I sometimes reverse that and believe they feel too much and don't think enough. Now I'm confused."* She laughed at herself.

"You all have so much to say tonight." Harry smiled at her family, then continued her musings. "I watch television sometimes. You know, the sitcoms. Apart from being the same age, I have nothing in common with those people. They live in beautiful apartments in big cities. They have great clothes and no

18

one worries about money. They're witty and cool. A drought means nothing to them. Over-seeding is a foreign word. They drive sexy cars while I drive a 1978 Ford half-ton truck. My generation is all those things that I am not." She frowned. "Not too many of us live in the country anymore. The old ways are being lost and I suppose I'll be lost with them but— I can't live any other way." She kicked the dewy grass. "Damn, why did I get so involved in this reunion? I am such a sucker!" She turned on her heel to go back to the house.

Mrs. Murphy gracefully leapt off the post while Pewter turned around to back down. No need to jar her bones if it wasn't absolutely nec-essary. Tucker stayed at her mother's left heel.

As they passed the front of the barn, Simon, the possum who lived in the hayloft, peered out the open loft door.

The animals greeted him, causing Harry to glance up, too. "Evening, Simon."

Simon blinked. He didn't hurry back to his nest, and that was as close as he got to greeting them.

"You want marshmallows, I know." Harry walked to her screened-in porch and opened the old zinc-lined milk box that her mother had used when Monticello Dairy used to deliver milk bottles. She kept marshmallows and a small bag of sunflower seeds for the finches there. She walked back with four marshmallows and threw them through the hayloft door. "Enjoy yourself, Simon."

He grabbed one, his glittering black eyes merry. *"I will."*

Harry looked up at Simon, then down at her three friends. "Well, I bet no one else in my class feeds marshmallows to their possum." Spirits somewhat restored, she trotted back into the house to warm up.

┌─────────┐
│   3   │
└─────────┘

After sorting everyone else's mail, Harry finally sorted her own. If the morning proved unusually hectic she'd slide her mail into her metal box, hoping she'd remember it before going home.

Sometimes two or three days would pass before she read her own mail.

This morning had been busy. Mrs. Hogendobber, a tower of strength in or out of the post office, ran back and forth to her house because the hot-water heater had stopped working. She finally gave up restarting it, calling a plumber. When he arrived she went home.

Fair stopped by early. He kissed his ex-wife on the cheek and apologized for delivering four hundred and fifty postcards to mail out. Each containing his e-mail address. He had, however, arranged them by zip code.

Susan stopped by, grabbed her mail, and opened it on the counter.

"Bills. Bills. Bills."

"*I can take care of that!*" Mrs. Murphy swished her tail, crouched and leapt onto the counter. She attacked the offending bills.

"Murphy." Harry reached for the cat, who easily eluded her.

"Murphy, you have the right idea." Susan smiled, then gently pushed the cat off her mail.

Mrs. Hogendobber came through the back door. "Four hundred and twenty dollars plus fifty dollars for a house call. I have to buy a new hot-water heater."

"That's terrible," Susan commiserated.

"I just ordered one and it will be here after lunch. I can't believe what things cost and Roy even gave me a ten-percent discount." She mentioned the appliance-store owner, an old friend.

"Hey." Susan opened a letter.

"*What?*" both Harry and Mrs. Murphy asked.

"Look at this." She held open a letter edged in Crozet High's colors, blue and gold.

It read, "You'll never get old."

"Let me see that." Harry took the letter and envelope from her. "Postmarked from the Barracks Road post office."

"But there's no name on it," Susan remarked.

"Wonder if I got one?" Harry reached into her mailbox from behind the counter. "Yep."

"Check other boxes," Susan ordered.

"I can check but I can't open the envelopes."

"I know that, Harry. I'm not an idiot."

Miranda, ignoring Susan's testiness, reached into Market Shiflett's mailbox, a member of Harry and Susan's class. "Another."

Harry checked the others, finding the same envelope. "Well, if someone was going to go to all that trouble to compliment us, he ought to sign his name."

"Maybe it's not a compliment," Mrs. Murphy remarked.

Pewter, asleep, opened one eye but didn't move from the small table in the back of the post office. *"What?"*

"Tell you later," Mrs. Murphy said, noticing that Tucker, on her side under the table, was dreaming.

"Oh, whoever mailed this will 'fess up or show up with a face-lift." Susan shrugged.

"We aren't old enough for face-lifts." Harry shuddered at the thought.

"People are doing stuff like that in their early thirties." Susan read too many popular magazines.

"And they look silly. I can always tell." Miranda, still upset about her hot-water heater bill, waved her hand dismissively.

"How?" both women and Mrs. Murphy asked.

Miranda ran her forefinger from the corner of her cheekbone to the corner of her mouth. "This muscle or ligament, whatever you call it, is always too tight, even in the very, very good ones."

"Like Mim's?" Susan mentioned Crozet's leading citizen.

"She won't admit to it." Harry liked Mim but never underestimated the woman's vanity.

"Cats are beautiful no matter how old we are," Mrs. Murphy smugly noted.

Harry, as if understanding her friend, leaned down. "If I had a furry face I wouldn't care."

Susan tossed the mailing in the trash. "You'll never get old. Ha!"

Ha, indeed.

4

"Now what?" Harry, hands on hips, sourly inspected her truck.

"Battery," Tucker matter-of-factly said.

Harry opened the hood, checked her cables and various wires, kept the hood open, then got back in the driver's seat and turned the ignition. A click, click, click rewarded her efforts.

"Damn! The battery."

"That's what I said." The corgi calmly sat, gazing at the hood of the old blue truck.

The truck, parked in the alleyway behind the post office, nose to the railroad tie used as a curb bumper, presented problems. Many problems. With over two hundred thousand miles on the 1978 V-8 engine, this machine had earned its keep and now had earned its rest. Harry had investigated rebuilding the engine. She might squeeze another thirty thousand miles out of the truck with that. She'd gone through eight sets of tires, three batteries, two clutches, but only one set of brakes. The upholstery, worn full of holes, was covered by a plaid Baker horse blanket Harry had Mrs. Martin, the town seamstress, convert into a bench seat cover. The blue paint on the truck was so old that patches glowed an iridescent purple. The rubber covers on the accelerator and clutch were worn thin, too.

Mrs. Hogendobber, having changed into her gardening clothes, including a wonderful goatskin apron, walked across the alley from her backyard to the post office. Apart from singing in the choir and baking, gardening was her passion. Even now—being the end of a hot summer—her lilies, of all varieties, flourished. She misted them each morning and each evening.

"Miranda, do you have jumper cables?" Harry called to her.

"Dead again?" Miranda shook her head, commiserating. "And this such a beautiful afternoon. I bet you want to get home."

Just then Market Shiflett stuck his head out of the back door of the store. "Harry, Pewter—half a chicken!"

"Uh-oh. I'll pay for it, Market. I'm sorry." Secretly, Harry laughed. The fresh chickens reposed in an old white case with shaved ice

and parsley. Pewter must have hooked one when Market opened the case. She was clever and she knew Market's ways, having spent her earlier years as his cat. "Did you see Mrs. Murphy?"

"Oh, yes." Market nodded. "Aiding and abetting a criminal! I often wonder what your human children will turn out to be should you have them."

"From the sound of it—chicken thieves." Out of the corner of her eye she saw Pewter valiantly struggling to haul the half-chicken to the truck. Mrs. Murphy tugged on the other side of the carcass.

"Let me help." Tucker gleefully leapt toward them.

"No, you don't," Mrs. Murphy spat, then saw Market. *"Pewter, quick, into the crepe myrtle!"*

The two cats dragged the chicken under the pinkish-purple crepe myrtle.

"Here." Harry dug into her pocket, handing Market a ten-dollar bill.

"It's not a gold-plated chicken." He fished in his pocket for change.

"Forget it, Market. You do plenty for me and I'm sorry Pewter behaved so badly."

"Breathed her last?" He turned his attention to the truck.

"No, just the battery."

"You've got cables, don't you?" Miranda smiled at Market, who was getting a little thick around the middle.

"I do."

"Well, if you don't mind, I'll let you two

recharge Old Paint here. I am determined to dust for Japanese beetles. And I'm enduring a grub attack, too. Maybe I should get some chickens. That would take care of that." Then she saw the two cats crouched under the crepe myrtle, passionately guarding the plucked corpse. "Then again, I think not."

Harry laughed. "Go on, Miranda. Market and I will fix this."

As Miranda walked back to her lawn, Market hopped in his Subaru, next to a large new dumpster, backed out, maneuvering his car so that its nose was at a right angle to the blue truck. This saved Harry from attempting to coast backwards.

"The cables will reach." He clipped the tiny copper jaws onto the battery nodes. "Off?"

"Yep."

He switched on his ignition. "Just give it two minutes. Did you check for a loose connection?"

"I did."

Market slid out from behind the wheel and came over to lean on the truck. "Harry, it's time to bite the bullet. You'll never get through another winter with this baby."

"I know," Harry mournfully agreed.

"Call Art."

"I can't afford a new truck."

"Who said you had to buy a new one? Buy a used one."

"Market, the bank won't give me a loan on a used truck."

"They will if it's a recent one, like two or three years old."

"Yeah, but then the price will be way up. It's damned if I do and damned if I don't."

Market, hearing the distress level in Harry's voice, put his arm around her shoulder. "Chill out, honey. Art is one of our buddies. He'll help. He makes enough money off everyone else. Go talk to the man."

"Well..." Her voice weakened. "I don't want to be disappointed."

"There are worse disappointments than that and we've both had them," Market genially encouraged her.

He was right, too. They'd both had a few hard knocks along the way—his divorce being more acrimonious than hers, but no divorce is happy. He had one beloved daughter, now in college. Poor Market had married the day he graduated from high school. His senior superlative was Friendliest and that friendliness meant his daughter was born seven months after the wedding.

"You know, time forges bonds of steel, doesn't it?" Harry said.

"What do you mean?"

"You, me, Miranda, Herbie, the gang. We know everything about one another—almost." She smiled.

"Yep. I can't believe we're having our twentieth. I'm"—he hummed a minute, a habit—"half-excited and half-apprehensive. How about you?"

"Same."

"Well, let's see if this baby is fired up."
He walked back and cut his motor. "Crank her up."

Harry hopped in. The engine turned over, then rumbled. "I think I'd better let her run for a few more minutes."

"Good idea. How are you coming along with ideas for the reunion?"

"Okay. We had our first meeting yesterday. I've gotten everything written out for the calendars of local newspapers for all the major towns in the state. And I've written up ads to run the week before the reunion—ads with photos. I'll have to fight BoomBoom for the money. The publicity part I can do with no problem. It's coming up with some special moniker for everyone that's driving me crazy."

"Speak of the devil," he said under his breath as BoomBoom, in a new 7-series BMW—to replace one wrecked during a theft attempt—rolled down the alleyway. She pulled over. The electrical windows purred as she lowered them.

"Hi." BoomBoom's voice purred like her windows.

Marcy Wiggins, Chris Sharpton, and Bitsy Valenzuela said "Hi" along with her.

Harry returned the hellos of the trio, all neighbors in the Deep Valley subdivision. Bitsy had married E.R. Valenzuela, a classmate who'd worked in Silicon Valley and moved back home last year to establish a cellular phone business. Since E.R. worked all the time no one ever saw much of him, including his wife.

Marcy, a somewhat withdrawn woman, had married Bill Wiggins, who'd gone to medical school in upstate New York, returning to the University of Virginia Hospital for his residency in oncology. No one saw much of Bill either, but he was congenial when they did.

"How'd you do?" Market asked the ladies, who all wore golf clothes.

"Not bad. We played in the Cancer Society tournament, captain's choice, and we each won a sleeve of balls. We came in seventh out of a field of twenty teams," BoomBoom bragged.

Chris leaned out the back window. "I've never played at Waynesboro Country Club. It's fun. I don't think I'll ever win boxwoods from Susan, though."

"Keep trying. Anyone roped into working on our reunion deserves boxwoods," Harry replied. "Do you all need mail?"

"No, everyone's husbands did their duty."

"Except for me," Chris laughed.

"Stay single, girl, believe me. Marriage is work," Marcy grumbled.

"Need your mail?" Harry inquired of Chris.

"No, I'll get it tomorrow. We're on our way to the big sale at Fashion Square," Chris answered. "Next time you see any of us— complete makeover." She crinkled her freckled nose.

The ladies waved and drove off.

"Cute, that Chris." Market winked.

"Yes. She reminds me of someone but I can't place it."

"Meg Ryan in a pageboy."

"You have made a study, haven't you?" Harry poked him.

"Hey, she's living in one of those new houses. She isn't going to look at a guy who owns a convenience store. I'm realistic. She's a stockbroker. Stockbrokers don't date grocers."

"The right man is the right man. Doesn't matter what he does."

"Bull. Especially from you."

"You trying to say I'm not romantic?"

"You're as realistic as I am and you always were. The Minors are solid people." He referred to Harry's paternal ancestors. She'd kept her married name, Haristeen.

"I wish someone in our family had had a head for business. Solid is good but a little money would have been wonderful."

"Mim Sanburne's got enough brains and money for the whole town, I guess." He folded his arms across his chest. "This morning a lady came in as Mim was picking up a big rack of lamb, beautiful piece of meat. She's having another one of her 'dos.' Anyway, these two ladies come in, tourists. They'd crawled over Monticello and Ash Lawn and they'd driven up to Orange to see Montpelier. They were on their way to Staunton to see Woodrow Wilson's birthplace and they needed gas. Anyway, they wound up right here in the middle of Crozet. The tall one says, 'This is kind of a dumpy town, isn't it?' The short one, maps under her arm, replies, 'Yes.' Then she looks at me and says,

'Is there anything of interest here?' Before I could open my mouth, Mim says, 'Me.' Gives them the freeze stare"—he rubbed his hands when he said that—"then opens the door, gets into her Bentley Turbo R, which these two ladies had no appreciation for, and drove off. 'Well, who does she think she is?' says the short one. 'The Queen of Crozet,' says I." He chuckled. "Guess they complained all the way to Fisherville. By that time they were probably consulting their maps again."

Harry laughed. "Crozet isn't exactly picturesque, but I think the painting the kids did on the railroad underpass is pretty nice." She leaned next to Market, shoulder to shoulder. "I guess we aren't much to look at but the land is beautiful. That's what counts. Buildings fall down and so do we. Can't be but so bad." She changed the subject abruptly, a habit of hers. "How do you get a name like Bitsy?"

"Probably the same way you get a name like Harry. You do something when you're little and it sticks. You picked up more injured animals than anyone I know. You were and remain dappled with an interesting assortment of animal sheddings."

"Which reminds me—give me a plastic bag so I can take that chicken home and boil it for them."

He fetched a beige plastic bag from the store. They both approached the two cats and Tucker, squatting before them, making them crazy.

"All right, girls, hand it over."

"Death to anyone who dares touch this chicken!" Pewter growled.

"Don't be melodramatic." The dog salivated.

Pewter lashed out, catching one of the corgi's long ears. Tucker yelped.

"Pewter, hateful thing." Harry knelt down. "Market, want your cat back?"

"Hell, no. She ate me out of my profit." He knelt down beside Harry. "Pewter, you're a bad cat."

"Put one over on you."

"Don't brag, Pewter, let's see if we can make a bargain." Mrs. Murphy swept her ears forward. *"Harry, if you don't throw the chicken away, we'll come out."*

"I'm going to cook the chicken."

"She understood!" Tucker was ecstatic.

The cats, equally amazed, released the chicken from their fangs and claws. Harry scooped it into the plastic bag.

"Come on."

They slunk out from under the bush just in case Market was going to take a swat at them.

Harry put the chicken on the seat, which meant three animals gladly scrambled into the truck. "Market, ask that Chris out. She'll say yes or she'll say no. And you've heard both before."

"I don't know."

"Hey, before I leave I forgot to ask you. Did you get a letter saying 'You'll never grow old'?"

"Yeah. In Crozet colors."

"I checked the envelopes. Each of our class-

33

mates living here got the same envelope, but that doesn't guarantee the same content. Thought I'd ask."

"No name." He stepped back from the driver's window. "I thought it was a joke because it's our twentieth reunion. Thirty-seven or thirty-eight, most of us, you know. I figured someone was panicking about turning forty."

"I didn't think of that. Susan thought it was a compliment. We look good. I guess." Harry smiled her beguiling smile.

"I'll take it." Market smacked the door of the truck like a horse's hindquarter and Harry drove off.

5

"Call to question." BoomBoom, sitting behind a long table, raised her voice.

"What are you talking about?" Harry, failing at hiding her irritation, snapped.

"Robert's Rules of Order. Otherwise we'll descend into chaos."

"BoomBoom, you're full of shit," Harry blurted out. "It's just us. Susan, Market, and Dennis."

Dennis Rablan, voted Best All-Round, volunteered to be in charge of the physical plant. That meant cleaning the gymnasium at Crozet High School, setting up the sound system for taped music, and working with the decorating committee. He'd gotten only one volunteer, Mike Zalaznik, to help him. Dennis was lazy as sin so Mike would wind up doing most of the work.

Dennis had learned to ignore the whisperings behind his back about how he had squandered away the large nest egg his father had left him. He owned a photography studio in downtown Crozet. Weddings, anniversaries, high-school graduation, red-haired Dennis was always on hand toting two or three cameras. He was the one classmate who saw the other local classmates during the turning points of their lives.

The small group sat in a history classroom at Crozet High, the windows wide open to catch the cool breeze since that wondrous Canadian high still hung around.

"Harry, don't lose your temper," Susan admonished her best friend. "BoomBoom"—she turned to the chair sitting opposite them—"you don't need to be so formal about this meeting. I don't like it any more than Harry does. Let's discuss ideas without the hoopla."

"What do you think, Dennis?" BoomBoom smiled at Dennis, her big eyes imploring him.

"Well, I never learned Robert's Rules of Order, I doubt I could contribute much, but then I might not be able to contribute much anyway." He brushed a bright forelock back.

"Aren't you going to ask me?" Market folded his arms across his chest.

"You'll vote with Harry. You always do."

"Because she has good sense." Market laughed. "Look, you want to reshoot our senior superlative pictures and have them blown up life-size to place around the auditorium. I'm not opposed to the idea but how are you going to get the superlatives from out of town to duplicate the photograph?"

"Easy." BoomBoom loved showing up Harry, although she told all who would listen that she bore Harry no ill will. After all, she had cavorted with Harry's husband after they separated but were not yet divorced, so, morally Harry was in the right. BoomBoom thought that by recognizing this she'd be absolved of her misdeeds. But small-town memories were long.

"Well?" Susan leaned forward in her seat.

"We shoot the original locations, ask the away people to duplicate their pose in a studio, and we superimpose it on the location photograph. Dennis knows how to do it. Right, Dennis?"

"Right."

"For how much?" Harry asked.

"Seven hundred dollars." BoomBoom smiled broadly, as though she'd scored a coup.

"Mostly that's for gas, chemicals, paper. There's not much in there for me," Dennis quickly added.

"You'd better not take it out of my publicity budget," Harry warned.

"You don't have a publicity budget." BoomBoom dismissed the idea.

"Oh, *yes,* I do. I worked it out over the weekend and I've made copies for everyone. If you want a bang-up reunion then you've got to cast wide your net." She handed out budget copies as Mrs. Murphy walked into the room, sitting down under the blackboard. "And don't forget, the day after Labor Day weekend I have to send a mailing with details to each class member. That's in the budget, too."

The school, built in 1920 out of fine red brick with a pretty white four-columned main entrance, exuded a coziness that Mrs. Murphy liked. Pewter and Tucker peeped around the doorjamb.

"Are they finished yet?" Pewter had found nothing in the hallway to entice her.

"No," Murphy replied. The other animals came in and sat next to her, watching the humans as humans watch animals in a zoo.

"Harry, we can go over your budget later. We need to nail down this superlative idea first." BoomBoom barely glanced at the paper. BoomBoom herself had been voted Best Looking.

"I think it's a good idea. And I assume you will blow up the original senior superlative photograph and put it next to the new one." Susan nodded.

"Exactly! Won't it be wonderful?"

"Not if you're going bald," Market moaned.

BoomBoom pounced on him. "If you'd take the herbs I drop off for you it would help, and if that doesn't give you results fast enough, then get those hair transplants. They really work."

"You'd look adorable," Dennis teased, "with those plugs in your scalp. Just like cornrows."

"I'll get you for that, Dennis. You know why God made hair? Because not everyone could have a perfect head."

"Three points for Market." Harry chalked up the air.

"Are you going to agree with my plan or not?" BoomBoom folded her hands, staring at Harry.

"Yes. There, bet that surprised you, didn't it?"

"Kinda." BoomBoom sighed with relief. "Dennis, when can you start?"

"The sooner the better. How about this week?"

"Fine," everyone said in unison. They wanted to go home. The weather was good and everyone had things to do.

"Let's go." Pewter shook herself.

"Not yet," Tucker sighed as BoomBoom plucked another paper off her pile.

"We still don't have a ball chairman. So many of us live in the central Virginia area—you'd think someone would volunteer."

"People are overcommitted," said Susan, a shining example.

"If I can't buttonhole someone soon, we'll have to do it," BoomBoom announced.

"No, we won't." Harry put her foot down.

"BoomBoom plucks Mom's last nerve. Beyond that, what is it about people sitting in a meeting?

Everything takes three times as long. Big fat waste of time," Murphy commented.

"Passing opinions is like passing gas. They can't help it," Pewter giggled.

"Harry, are you still our liaison person with Mrs. Hogendobber so we don't have any conflicts with their reunion?" BoomBoom ignored Harry's small rebellion.

"Liaison person? I see her five or six days out of the week."

"Thought I'd ask."

"BoomBoom, what's your idea for the decorating committee?" Susan had visions of a bare auditorium save for the senior superlative photographs.

"Marcy Wiggins and Bitsy Valenzuela have volunteered to help us if we help organize the Cancer Ball fund-raiser in December. I think Charlie Ashcraft will head the committee."

"You can't be serious," Harry blurted out. "Charlie is such a womanizer."

"He's all we've got. Plus"—BoomBoom lowered her voice conspiratorially—"he's already putting the moves on Marcy."

"I hope you've warned her." Susan frowned.

"She's a big girl." BoomBoom tidied the few papers on her desk.

"Boom, he's one of the handsomest men God ever put on earth and utterly irresponsible. His idea of going slow is to ask a woman to bed after being introduced to her instead of before. Come on." Harry leaned forward.

"She's married." Market waved off the subject, feeling Marcy's wedding ring offered protection—sort of like garlic against a vampire.

"Unhappily," BoomBoom demurred.

Dennis finally spoke. "Remember Raylene Ramsey and Meredith McLaughlin getting into a fight over Charlie at our fifteenth reunion?"

"I thought they'd kill one another." Market checked his watch.

"I'd rather hoped they'd kill Charlie," Harry laughed.

"I never could see what you girls saw in him." Dennis laughed, too.

"Don't look at me. I think he's an asshole." Harry held up her hands.

BoomBoom, having seduced Charlie in their youth, or vice versa, kept silent on this.

Susan jumped in. "I don't mind that he had sex with both of them at our fifteenth. I do mind, however, that he saw fit to do it in the pool at the Holiday Inn. Just because it was three in the morning didn't mean we weren't awake." Susan shook her head in disgust.

"Back to the subject. Charlie as head of decorating?" BoomBoom tapped the desk with her pencil. "And Marcy Wiggins and Bitsy Valenzuela," she added.

"But they didn't go to high school with us," Market protested.

"Who cares, Market? We need workers. Chris was a big help at our meeting at my house." Harry punched him lightly. "Anyway, they married into our class. That counts for something."

"Chris says maybe she'll meet some men.

40

It's hard for new people to fit in. We were born here. We never think about breaking into a new place," BoomBoom replied.

"Did she really say she wanted to meet men?" Market whispered.

"Yes," Harry whispered back.

"She's not half bad," Dennis whispered as he overheard them. This earned him a stern glare from Market.

"Are we okay on Charlie then?" Boom-Boom pressed on.

The others looked at one another, then reluctantly raised their hands in agreement since no one could think of a substitute.

"One last item of business before we adjourn." BoomBoom couldn't help but notice how fidgety her classmates had become. "I received a bordered letter, run off at Kinko's or KopyKat, I think. Anyway, it said, 'You'll never get old.' Harry, did you send that out?"

"Why me?" Harry was surprised.

"You're the postmistress. I thought you might be playing a practical joke on us."

"No. It wasn't me."

BoomBoom looked from one to the other as each one shook his or her head. "Well, I think it's in bad taste."

"Boom, what are you talking about?" Susan asked.

"Yeah," Market and Dennis said.

"'You'll never get old.' I should think it would be obvious. We'll never get old if we're dead. Here I am trying to create the best reunion ever and someone is sending out a sick joke."

"I didn't take it that way." Susan frowned since she didn't like BoomBoom's interpretation.

On that note the meeting broke up.

"It is odd," Mrs. Murphy mused to no one in particular.

6

"Are you really going to buy a truck?" Fair Haristeen asked his ex-wife as he picked up his mail the next morning.

"Gonna try."

"She's taking a two-hour lunch to visit Art Bushey." Miranda helpfully supplied him with information.

"Serious." He rubbed his chin.

"She cruises the lot at night, looking at trucks, but this is the first time she's going over in the day," Mrs. Murphy told Fair, who pulled a metal foil wrapper out of his pocket and gave it to her.

"Here, Houdini, open this." His deep voice rumbled.

Mrs. Murphy surreptitiously looked around. Pewter, asleep in the mail cart, remained unaware of the gift which Murphy inspected and then tore open. The aroma of moist fish tidbits caused one chartreuse eye to open down in the mail cart.

"Don't you have anything for me?" Tucker implored.

Fair reached into his other pocket, bringing forth a foil packet with a plum-colored edging marked Mouth-Watering Dog Divine Treats. He pulled open the pouch, spilling the contents on the floor.

"Thank you!" Tucker gobbled up the round meat treats.

Pewter, on her back, rolled over. She crawled out of the cart to join Mrs. Murphy, who wasn't wildly happy about it but she wasn't selfish either.

"Are you going to add a small-animal practice to your equine practice?" Mrs. Hogendobber laughed.

"No. I get freebies from feed companies. Which reminds me, I've got a bag of rich alfalfa cubes. I'm wondering if you'd help me, Harry? If I give you a feed schedule, three cubes per day along with your standard timothy, will you keep weight charts for me?"

"Sure," Harry happily agreed.

"You don't put your horses on a scale, do you?" Mrs. Hogendobber, not a horse person, inquired. "That would be awfully difficult, wouldn't it?"

"Miranda, the easiest way to keep track of gain is a tape measure. Just the kind you'd buy from the five-and-dime."

"Except there are no more five-and-dimes."
Miranda wrinkled her forehead. "When I
think of the times I ran into Woolworth's
with a quarter as a child and thought I was
rich..."

"You were." Fair smiled, which only made
him more handsome. He strongly resembled
the young Gary Cooper.

At six feet four inches, with blond hair, a
strong jaw, kind eyes, and broad shoulders,
Fair was a man women noticed. And they
usually smiled when they noticed.

"Those were the days." The older woman
rolled up the blue nylon belts used to hold large
quantities of mail. "Do you know, Fair Haristeen, that this year is my fiftieth high-school
reunion. I have to pinch myself to realize it."

"You don't look a day over thirty-nine and
no one in Crozet can hold a candle to your gardening powers."

She smiled broadly. "Better not say that in
front of Mim."

"If I had three gardeners I'd be on the
garden tour, too." He tossed catalogues in the
garbage can. "You do it by yourself."

"Thank you." She was mightily pleased.

"Almost lunch hour." Harry flicked two
letters into Susan Tucker's mailbox.

Fair glanced at the clock. "Want me to go
with you to Art's?"

"Why, you think I can't make a deal?"

"No. I think you'll cry if you part with that
heap out back."

"I will not." Color came to her cheeks.

44

"Okay." He winked at Miranda when Harry couldn't see him, walked to the door, then turned. "I'll drop the alfalfa cubes off tonight."

"I don't know if I want to talk to you. I can't believe you think I'd cry over a truck."

"Uh-huh." He pushed open the door and walked into the breezy air. It felt more like late September than the tail end of August.

"He gets my goat," Harry mumbled as she rolled up lingerie catalogues and slid them in Little Mim's mailbox. "Why does she get all these underwear wishing books?"

"Because she's wishing," Miranda answered.

Little Mim, divorced a few years back, was lonesome, lonesome and carrying a torch for Harry's neighbor, Blair Bainbridge.

"Oh." Harry blinked. She never thought of stuff like that.

"It's noon. Are you going to the Ford dealer, or not?"

"I'm going. I said I was going. I know none of you think I can count beans much less make a deal."

"I never said that."

"You didn't have to."

"Harry, calm yourself. I think you have a good head for figures. I admire your frugality. After all, I'm still driving my husband's Falcon and how many years has my poor George been called to heaven? Really now, I'm on your side."

Harry regretted her crabby moment. "I know you are, Miranda. I don't know what made me cross."

45

"Your ex."

She shrugged. "I think I can do better without the three musketeers. Mind letting them work through lunch hour?"

"Take me?" Tucker wagged her nonexistent tail.

"I'm staying right here." Pewter put one paw on the collapsed foil packet.

"I'll stay, too. Good luck, Mom."

Twenty minutes later Harry rolled down Pantops Mountain, for she'd driven down on I-64, turning left on Route 250 at the Shadwell exit. The Ford dealership, spanking blue and white, covered the north side of the road just before the river. In the old days there had been a covered bridge over the Rivanna River, called Free Bridge, since there was no toll to use it. A big storm would find horse and buggies lined up in the bridge waiting for the worst to blow over. Today such chance encounters and sensible acceptance of Nature's agenda had been pushed aside. People thought they could drive through anything. The covered bridge gave way to a two-lane buttressed bridge, which in turn gave way to a four-lane soulless piece of engineering. People zoomed across the river with never a thought for stopping and looking down or having a juicy chat with a friend while the thunder boomed overhead.

Harry pulled in front of the plate-glass windows at the older part of the Ford building.

Art Bushey walked out to see her. "Hi, beautiful. Did I ever tell you, I have a thing for postmistresses. I like that word 'mistress.' Just gives me chills."

"Pervert." Harry punched him, then hugged him.

"Knew you were coming. Half of Crozet called me, including your ex-husband. Still loves you, Harry. But hey, men fall all over you."

"You are so full of it."

"Love hearing it, though, don't you? You're a good-looking woman. I want good-looking women driving Ford trucks." He ducked his head into the 1978 truck to look at the speedometer. "How many times has this thing turned over?"

"Over two hundred thousand."

"We build 'em good, don't we?" He patted the nose of the blue truck. "Come on, let me show you what I've got and Harry, don't panic about the money just yet. Let me show you what's here. You drive them. I'll work something out. I want your money, now, don't misunderstand me. I love money. But Busheys, Minors, and Hepworths"—he mentioned her mother's maiden name—"go back a long way. I remember when your father bought this truck."

"I do, too. His first new truck. You still had your mustache." Harry recalled the flush on her father's lean face when he told his wife and daughter he'd bought a brand-new truck.

"Come on." He opened the door to a red half-ton 4 x 4. "Thinking about growing my mustache back."

"I guess you were expecting me—got the

plates on and everything." She smiled. "About the mustache: do it. Makes you look dangerous."

Art liked that. "They're all ready for you and I've got two used ones for you to look at as well."

She hopped in the cab, turned the motor over as he clicked on his seat belt in the passenger seat.

"Now this truck is maxed out. AC over here, tape deck and CD, speakers everywhere, captain's chairs—nice on the back—plush interior, which your cats will enjoy. Cats are fussy."

"Yeah, I'd hate to disappoint them." Harry hit the accelerator, they backed out, and in a minute they were heading toward Keswick. "Jeez, this thing drives like a car."

They roared down the road and as she touched the brakes, the machine glided to a smooth stop.

By the time they returned to the dealership she was amazed at how the truck felt. One by one they got into the different trucks, different trim packages.

After an hour of driving new and two very nice used trucks they repaired to Art's office. "What do you think?"

"I'm scared of the cost," she forthrightly replied.

He punched in a mess of numbers. "Look." He yanked out the computer printout. "I can get you an F250 HD 4 by 4 for twenty thousand, four hundred and seventy-eight dollars. That's stripped and doesn't figure in your trade-in, which I will know in a minute because while we were out cruising, one of my guys was going over your truck."

"It's in good shape."

"I know that. You take care of everything including yourself." He pointed to figures on the right-hand column. "Add in your tags, title transfer, documentation service—and I don't know whether you want the extended service plan or not but figure another five hundred. Hold that number in your head. Round numbers are easier to remember. If you buy this now, I can give you a six-hundred-dollar rebate. That expires September fifteenth. Don't ask me why. Ford makes those decisions and the dealer has nothing to say about it. Good for you, though. But here"—he punched in some more numbers—"I can get you the XLT package for another fifteen hundred. If you buy things piecemeal like the tape deck and AC it doesn't make sense. I know this sounds crazy but if you spend money you can save money on the payments. I'm figuring you'll finance for five years. Look, I can get you the bells and whistles—" He pointed to a figure on the bottom of a new page he pulled out of the computer.

Her eyes grew large. "But that's almost four thousand more dollars."

"It is. But if we spread it over the five years it means about another thirty in your payment schedule. And Harry, this isn't the final figure. Aren't you going to badger me about the price?"

49

"Uh..."

The phone rang. "Yeah," Art said. "Great." He punched the button. "One thousand five hundred dollars on your 1978. And here's what I'll sell you the F250 HD 4 by 4 for." He scrawled numbers.

"That's almost twenty percent less." She scooted to the edge of her seat.

"That's right. You're paying what I pay plus the paperwork. What color do you want?"

"Red."

"What interior?"

"Beige."

He pointed to a red truck sitting on the lot. "You got it. Now Harry, I know you don't make a lot of money. I also know you'll drive this truck for twenty years. Why don't you take the truck home? If you don't like it, bring it back but don't go telling everyone what the cost is or everyone will want the same deal and then I'd go broke."

"Art?"

"Hey." He threw up his hands. "Like I said, I've got a thing for postmistresses. Go on, get out of here before Miranda calls and says she's overloaded."

Harry drove the new machine along I-64 feeling certain that everyone on the highway was admiring the beautiful truck. She'd done her sums at home and knew she could carry, with care, about four hundred and fourteen dollars a month.

When she drove to the front of the post office instead of the back, Miranda, Mrs.

50

Murphy, Pewter, Tucker, and Market—in picking up his mail—ran out.

"Wow!" Market whistled.

"*Open the door!*" Mrs. Murphy excitedly demanded, and as the door swung open for everyone to see the plush interior, the cat jumped up on the floor and then on the seat.

"O-o-o." She dug her claws in the upholstery just a tiny bit.

Within seconds, Pewter sat next to her. "*Snuggly.*" She patted at the divider between the two seats, a console with trays, cup holders, all manner of niceties to make the truck a little office. "*Even a place to store catnip.*"

"*I want to see!*" The dog whined as the humans opened the door on the other side.

"Here." Harry picked up Tucker, a heavy child, putting her on the seat after wiping off her paws.

"*Neat.*" The dog smiled.

"*Not bad.*" Pewter squeezed next to Tucker.

"Did you buy it?" Miranda eagerly asked.

"I think I did. I have to call my banker. I didn't give Art a firm yes."

"You can put the fifth wheel in the back—haul your horses. The old half-ton was straining," Market counseled.

"What saved me was I only hauled one at a time." Harry laughed because it did make life that much harder not being able to take two horses in her two-horse trailer.

Chris Sharpton drove up and parked. "*This is new.*"

Harry smiled. "I haven't bought it yet."

"BoomBoom called me"—Chris pulled her mailbox key out of her purse—"asking me to come up with more ideas for the 'welcoming committee.' That's what she's calling you guys now. I told her I wouldn't mind but I hoped you wouldn't mind. After all, it's your reunion and your committee."

" 'Course, I don't mind."

Chris smiled. "The Boom is getting desperate—not so much about the work for this thing but because she wants to make certain that *she* is *perfect* by homecoming—head to toe."

"Big surprise," Harry giggled.

"Can we meet tomorrow night?" Chris walked into the post office as Harry nodded yes.

Later that night, Harry turned off the lights in the barn, walked across to the house, and burst into tears. She'd lived with her old truck for so many years she couldn't imagine living without it.

No sooner had she walked into the house then Tucker barked, *"Intruder!"*

Harry walked back outside.

Fair was driving her old 1978 blue truck, followed by Art Bushey in a new silver Jeep.

"Hi," she said as they both got out of their vehicles.

"Here's your truck." Fair handed her the keys.

"Huh?" She was confused.

"Fair put up the down payment on the

F250 so you don't have to trade in your dad's truck." Art crossed his arms over his chest and leaned against the silver Jeep. "I told him he's nuts. You still aren't going to take him back but he did it anyway."

"Art, you're awful." She burst out laughing as the cats hopped into the bed of the old blue truck. The vantage point was better.

"Fair, I can't take your money."

"A late divorce settlement." He shrugged. "Now do you want the F250 or the F350 dually?"

"I'd better stick to the F250 HD."

"Doing it my way it's twelve hundred more for the dually. So you have everything you've ever wanted—your half-ton and a dually," Art said. "Big F350 in red with a beige interior just like the 250 here. And those extra wheels in the back are what you need when you're hauling weight."

"Deal!" She shook his hand.

"Red." Fair slapped his baseball cap against his thigh. "I bet Art a hundred bucks you'd buy another blue truck."

"Gotcha." Art smiled.

"Hey, wait." Harry ran into the barn, returning with a paper. "Here's the figures on the horses. I measured them tonight."

"Damn, I knew I forgot something. I'll drop off the alfalfa cubes tomorrow."

"Fair."

"Huh?"

"You're a good man." She put her hand behind his neck, drew him down, and kissed him.

"What about me?"

"How could I forget?" She kissed Art, too.

"All right, buddy, drive this back." Art shepherded Fair to the Jeep. Art would drive back in the F250. "You can pick up your dually tomorrow unless you want me to send it to Cavalier Camper for the fifth wheel."

"That's a good idea," Harry agreed.

As they drove off, Pewter asked Mrs. Murphy, *"How'd he know she'd never part with her father's truck?"*

Tucker called from the ground, *"He's very sensitive."*

"But it's metal," Pewter protested, finding the emotion around the 1978 truck silly.

"Metal but it has so many memories."

"A cruise down Memory Lane." Tucker walked back toward the house.

"If she got this worked up over a truck, what's she going to be like at her high-school reunion?" Pewter gingerly stepped onto the back bumper and thence to the ground.

"A big smile. There. Cover of People magazine." Dennis Rablan clicked away, his black Nikon camera covering his face. "Boom, get your face closer to the steer. You, too, Charlie, get in there."

"Yuk." Charlie grimaced. "I didn't like this the first time we did it, twenty years ago."

"Least it's not a horse's ass," Harry quipped. She had been conned by Susan to help with the first superlative shoot.

"No, I've got Boom for that."

"You know, Charlie," she hissed through clenched teeth, "you won Best Looking but you sure didn't win Best Personality and you never will."

"Like I care." He beamed to the camera.

Susan stood to the side holding up a reflector, which the steer distrusted. Crouched beside the large animal were Fair Haristeen on one side and Blair Bainbridge, equally tall, on the other.

Although Blair was a professional model, Charlie Ashcraft held his own. He was a strikingly handsome man, with curly, glossy black hair, bright blue eyes, and a creamy tan. At six foot one with a good body, he bowled women over. He knew it. He used it. He abused it. He left a trail of broken hearts, broken marriages, and broken promises behind him. Despite that, women still fell for him even when they knew his history. His arrogance added fuel to the fire. He was loathed by those not under his spell, which was to say most men.

Her shoulders ached, her deltoids especially, as Harry held the silver reflector behind Denny Rablan. She thought, *How like Boom-Boom to take her own photo first. No matter what, her visage will be plastered all over the gym.* Instead she said, "Denny, I'm putting this down for a minute." The heat was giving her a headache, or was it the reunion itself? She wasn't sure she had improved with the passage of time.

Click. He said without looking at her, "Okay. All right, take a break, especially Hercules here."

Fair stepped up and put a small grain bucket in front of Hercules, whose mood improved considerably.

Marcy Wiggins in her candy-apple red Taurus GL drove down the farm lane followed by Chris Sharpton and Bitsy Valenzuela in Bitsy's Jaguar XJR, top down.

"Oh no, are we late?" Chris wailed, opening the car door.

"No, we're taking a break. Harry's arms are tired," BoomBoom answered.

"I'll hold the reflector," Chris eagerly volunteered.

"Great. You've got a job." Harry handed her the floppy silver square.

"Boom, you look fabulous—professional makeup job, I bet," Bitsy cooed.

"Oh..." BoomBoom Craycroft had no intention of answering that question.

Charlie glided over. "I don't believe I've had the pleasure."

"You have, too." Bitsy laughed. "I met you at the Foxfield Races. My husband is E. R. Valenzuela, the president of 360° Communications here in town. You let me know if you need a cell phone in your car, you hear now?"

"Foxfield, well, that is a distracting environment." He smoothed his hair, which sprang back into curls. "I had no idea E.R. had such good taste in women."

Then brazenly, Charlie swept his eyes from the top of Chris's head to her toes. "A model's body. Tall and angular. Have I ever told you how much I like that?"

"Yes." She laughed. "Every time you see me."

He beamed at each lady in turn. Marcy turned beet red. "I'll call you the three Amuses. Good, huh?"

"Brilliant." Chris's eyelids dropped a bit, then flickered upward.

"God, Charlie, I hope you don't say that to my husband." Marcy swallowed hard.

"Do you know what I say to any woman's husband? 'If you don't treat her right, some other man will. Just because you're married doesn't mean you can relax. A woman's got to be won over each and every day.' " He smiled from ear to ear.

"Good Lord," Marcy whispered.

"I think I'll help Boom," Bitsy brightly said as she skipped past her friend.

Bitsy wiped the shine from BoomBoom's nose, adding a dab of lipstick to her mouth.

Denny clapped his hands, which disturbed Hercules, who let out a bellow. "Let's go."

Harry, arms crossed, watched Charlie stoop down, Hercules on one side and BoomBoom on the other.

"Harry, why don't you take away this bucket?" BoomBoom pointed at the bucket.

"You crippled?" Harry turned on her heel, striding to her old Ford truck. "*Adios.*"

"You're not going to kiss me good-bye?" Charlie called out. He puckered his lips.

"I wouldn't kiss you if you were the last man on earth," Harry said, as Susan's jaw nearly dropped to her chest.

"Hey, I love you, too."

"Charlie, is this a command performance?" Marcy asked, voice wavering.

He winked at her, then called after Harry, "I understand you called me a body part at the reunion meeting."

"I should have called you an arrogant, empty-headed, vainglorious idiot. 'Asshole' showed a lack of imagination." She smiled a big fake smile, her head throbbing.

"You've been divorced too-o-o long," he said in a singsong voice.

She stopped in her tracks. Fair's face froze.

Susan covered her eyes, peeking out through her fingers. BoomBoom squared her shoulders, ready for the worst.

"You know what, Charlie? My claim to fame is that I'm one of seven women in Albemarle County who hasn't gone to bed with you."

"There's still time." He laughed as Marcy Wiggins' face registered dismay.

"You'll die before I do." Harry turned, heading back to the truck.

This icy pronouncement caught everyone off guard. Charlie laughed nervously. Dennis took over, rearranging the principals except for Hercules, who was firmly planted close to the grain.

Then Charlie yelled after her, "I knew you sent that letter about me not growing old."

"Dream on." Harry kept walking. "I wouldn't waste the postage."

"Susan, you aren't going, too?" Boom-Boom's voice, drenched in irritation, cut through Hercules' bellow as he cried for his grain bucket. Susan left with Harry.

Susan leaned over to Harry as they walked away. "You got a wild hair or what?" she said, *sotto voce.*

"I don't really know. Just know I can't take any more." Harry rubbed her temples. "Susan, I don't know what's happening to me. I have no patience anymore. None. And I'm sick and tired of beating around the bush. Hell with it."

"M-m-m."

"I don't want to be rude but I'm fresh out of tolerance for the fools of this life."

"Your poor mother will be spinning in her grave. All the years of cotillion, the Sunday teas."

Harry put her hand on the chrome door handle of the 1978 truck. "Here's what I don't get: where is the line between good manners and supporting people in their bullshit? I'm not putting up with Charlie for one more minute." She opened the door but didn't climb inside. "I've turned a corner. I'm not wearing that social face anymore. Too much time. Too much suppressed anger. If people are going to like me they can like me as I am. Treat me right and I'll treat you right."

"Within reason."

"Well...yes." Harry reluctantly conceded.

Susan breathed in the moist air. The heat had finally returned and with it the flies. "I know exactly how you feel. I'm not brave enough to act on it yet."

"Of course you are."

"No. I have a husband with a good career and two teenagers. When the last one graduates from college—five more years—" She sighed, "Then I expect I'll be ready."

"*Tempus fugit.*" Harry hopped in the truck. "Charlie Ashcraft has not one redeeming virtue. How is it that someone like him lives and someone good dies? Aurora Hughes was a wonderful person."

"Pity. He is the most divine-looking animal." Susan shrugged.

"Handsome is as handsome does."

"Tell that to my hormones," Susan countered.

They both laughed and Harry drove home feeling as if the weight of the world had been lifted off her shoulders. She wasn't sure why. Was it because she had erupted at Boom-Boom? At Charlie? Or because she had gotten tired and left, instead of standing there feeling like a resentful martyr? She decided she wasn't going to help with any other senior superlative photographs and she wasn't even sure she'd go through with her own. Then she thought better of it. After all, it would be really mean-spirited not to cooperate. They were all in this together. Still, the thought of BoomBoom hovering around... Of course, knowing Boom she'd put off Harry's shot until last and then photograph her in the worst light. Harry thought she'd better call Denny at the studio tomorrow.

After the chores, she played with Mrs. Murphy, Pewter, and Tucker. They loved to play hide 'n' seek.

The phone rang at nine P.M.

"Har?"

"Susan, don't tell me you just got home."

"No. I just heard this instant—Charlie Ashcraft was shot dead in the men's locker room at the Farmington Country Club."

"What?"

"Right between the eyes with a .38."

"Who did it?"

"Nobody knows."

61

"I can think of a dozen who'd fight for the chance."

"Me, too. Queer, though. After just seeing him."

"Bet BoomBoom's glad she got the photograph first," Harry shot from the hip.

"You're awful."

"No, I'm your best friend. I'm supposed to say anything in the world to you, 'member?"

"Then let me say this to *you*. Don't be too jolly. Think about what you said this afternoon. We have no idea of who he's slept with recently. That's for starters. He was gifted at hiding his amours for a time, anyway. I'm all for your cleansing inside but a little repression will go a long way right now."

"You're right."

After she hung up the phone she told Mrs. Murphy, Pewter, and Tucker, who listened with interest.

"A jilted husband finally did what everyone else has wanted to do," Tucker said.

"Tucker, you have the sweetest eyes." Harry stroked the soft head.

"Weren't there any witnesses?" Mrs. Murphy asked.

"Right between the eyes." Pewter shook her head.

8

Farmington Country Club glowed with the patina of years. The handmade bricks lent a soft paprika glow to the Georgian buildings in the long summer twilight. As the oldest country club in Albemarle County, Farmington counted among its members the movers and shakers of the region as well as the totally worthless whose only distinguishing feature was that they had inherited enough money to stay current on their dues. The median age of members was sixty-two, which didn't bode well for Farmington's future. However, Farmington rested secure in its old golf course with long, classic fairways. The modern golf courses employed far too many sharp doglegs and par 3's because land was so expensive.

Charlie Ashcraft, a good golfer, had divided his skills between Farmington and its challengers, Keswick and Glenmore. At a seven handicap he was much in demand as a partner, carrying pounds of silver from tournaments. He also carried away Belinda Harrier when he was only seventeen and she was thirty and had won the ladies' championship. That was the first clue that Charlie possessed unusual powers of persuasion. Charlie's parents fetched him from the Richmond motel to which they had fled and Belinda's husband promptly divorced her. Her golf game went to pot as did Belinda.

Rick Shaw, sheriff of Albemarle County, and his deputy, the young and very attractive Cynthia Cooper, knew all this. They had done their homework. Cynthia was about twenty years younger than Rick. The age difference enhanced their teamwork.

The men's locker room had been cordoned off with shiny plastic yellow tape. The employees of the club, all of whom had seen enough wild stuff to write a novel, had to admit this was the weirdest of the weird.

The locker room, recently remodeled, had a general sitting room with the lockers and showers beyond that. The exterior door faced out to the parking lot. An interior door was about thirty feet from the golf shop with a stairway in between which first rose to a landing and continued into the men's grill, forbidden to women. If a man walked through the grill he would wind up in the 19th Hole, the typical sort of restaurant most clubs provide at the golf course.

Getting in and out of the men's locker room would have been easy for Charlie's killer. As the golfers had come and gone, the only people around would have been those who'd been dressing for dinner in the main dining room or down in the tavern way at the other end of the huge structure. There would be little traffic in and out of the locker room. The housekeeping staff cleaned at about eleven at night, checking again at eight in the morning since the locker rooms never closed.

Charlie Ashcraft had been found by a local attorney, Mark DiBlasi. The body remained as Mark had found him, sitting upright, slumped against locker 13. Blood was smeared on the locker. Charlie's head hadn't slumped to the side; blood trickled out of his ears but none came from his eyes or his mouth. It was a clean shot at very close range; a circle of powder burn at the entry point signified that. The bullet exited the back of his head, tore into the locker door, and lodged in the opposite wall.

Mark DiBlasi had been dining with his mother and wife when he left the main dining room to fetch his wallet from his locker. He'd played golf, finished at six-thirty, showered, and closed his locker, but forgot his wallet, which was still in his golf shorts. The moment he saw Charlie he called the sheriff. He then called the club manager. After that he sat down and shook like a leaf.

"Mark, forgive me. I know this is trying." Cooper sat next to him on a bench. "You think you came back here at eight?"

"Yes." Mark struggled for composure.

"You noticed no one."

"Nobody."

She flipped through her notebook. "I think I've gotten everything. If I have other questions I'll call you at the office. I'm sorry your dinner was disturbed." She called to Rick, "Any questions?"

Rick wheeled around. "Mark, who was Charlie's latest conquest?"

Mark blushed and stammered a moment. "Uh—anyone new and pretty?"

Rick nodded. "Go on. I know where to find you. If you think of anything, call me."

"Will do." Mark straightened his tie as he hurried out.

"He'll have nightmares," Cynthia remarked.

"H-m-m." Rick changed the subject. "Charlie's four ex-wives. We'll start there."

"They all moved away, didn't they?"

"Yeah." He whistled as he walked through the men's locker room to fix the layout in his mind.

A knock on the door revealed Diana Robb, head of the Crozet Rescue Squad. "Ready?"

"I didn't hear the siren," Cynthia said.

"Didn't hit it. I was coming back from the hospital when you called, not more than a mile away." She looked at Charlie as she walked back into the lockers. "Neat as a pin. Even his tie is straight."

"Mark DiBlasi found him."

Diana called over her shoulder, "Hey guys, bring in the gurney and the body bag." Her two assistants scurried back out for the equipment.

"Mark said he was warm when he found him," Rick informed her.

"Fresh kill."

"We've already dusted. He's ready to go." Cynthia watched as the gurney was rolled in; the quarters were a bit tight.

"Put on your gloves and let's lift him up, carry him out to the sitting room," Diana directed. "Sucker's going to be heavy."

"Any ideas?" Cynthia asked Diana.

"Too many."

"Yeah, that seems to be the problem." Rick smiled.

"I do know this." Diana wiggled her fingers in the thin rubber gloves over which she pulled on a pair of heavier gloves. "Charlie always was a snob. If you didn't have money you had to have great bloodlines. There were no poor people involved."

9

The post office buzzed the next morning. As it was the central meeting point in town, each person arrived hopeful that someone would have more news than they had. Everyone had an opinion, that much was certain.

"Can't go sleeping with other men's wives without expecting trouble," Jim Sanburne, mayor of Crozet and husband of Mim, announced.

As Jim, in his youth, had indulged in affairs, the elegant Mim eyed him coldly. "Well said."

"This is getting good." Mrs. Murphy, whiskers

67

vibrating, perched on the counter between the mailroom and the public room.

Pewter, next to her, licked her paw, then absentmindedly forgot to wash herself. Tucker, mingling out with the people, believed she could smell guilt and anger.

"Will even one person lament his death?" Mim asked.

Jim Sanburne rubbed his chin. "Whoever he was carrying on with at the time, I reckon."

The Reverend Herb Jones growled, "He was a rascal, no doubt. But, then again, he was a young man in his prime—never forget redemption."

Miranda nodded her head in agreement with the Reverend.

"Something wrong with that boy." The massive Jim leaned over the counter so close that Pewter decided to rub against his arm to make him feel loved.

"Male version of nymphomania," Big Mim said as her daughter, Little Mim, blinked, surprised at her mother's boldness.

Fair, who'd walked in the door, picked up the word "nymphomania." "I came just in time."

Marcy Wiggins and Chris Sharpton also pushed open the door. Fair stepped aside. The small space was getting crowded.

Chris shyly blinked. "It's so shocking. I mean, we were all watching the superlative shoot and then this."

"Chris, don't waste your time feeling sorry for that s.o.b.," Susan Tucker told her. "You didn't know him well enough to be one of his victims—yet. He would have tried."

"Charlie should have been shot years ago," Fair laconically said, then turned solemn. "But still you never think something like this would happen to someone you know."

Noticing the look on Marcy's face, Harry added, "We're not as cold as you might think, Marcy. But ask E.R. about Charlie's past. He upset too many applecarts without giving a thought to what he was doing to people's lives. He remained unacquainted with responsibility for his entire life."

"Oh," Marcy replied, looking not at all comforted.

" 'The way of a fool is right in his own eyes, but a wise man listens to advice.' Proverbs. Twelfth chapter, fifteenth verse," Mrs. Hogendobber quoted. "Charlie Ashcraft was told many times in many ways by many people that he had to change his habits. He didn't. Someone changed them for him; not that that's right. No one has the right to take a life. That power belongs only to God."

"Tucker, smell anything?" Murphy called down.

"No, although Jim Sanburne has dog pee on his shoe. Bet Mim's dog got him and he doesn't even know it," the corgi gleefully reported. *"Of course, I haven't sniffed everyone yet. There's too much coming and going."*

BoomBoom flounced through the door, breathlessly put her tiny hand to her heart. "Can you believe it? Right after our superlative shoot."

"Aren't you glad you shot yours first?" Harry dryly commented. "As it is we'll have two people missing in our shoots. This way you would have had three."

"Harry, I can't believe you said that." BoomBoom folded her arms across her chest. "Do you really think I would be more concerned about our senior superlative photographs than a man's life?"

"In a word, yes." Harry also folded her arms across her chest.

"This is getting good," Pewter purred with excitement.

"Our classmate is dead," BoomBoom nearly shrieked. "After that damned letter you sent."

"I didn't send that stupid letter!" Harry lowered her voice instead of raising it.

"Harry would never do anything like that," Fair curtly said.

"She likes to stir the pot."

"Look who's talking." Harry squared off at BoomBoom.

"Pipe down," Big Mim commanded. "You aren't solving anything. This is about Charlie's murder, not your history with one another." She turned to her ex-husband. "If every man in Crozet were shot for infidelity, who would be left?"

"Now, honey, let sleeping dogs lie." His *basso profundo* voice rumbled.

"It's not sleeping dogs we're talking about," Mim snapped.

Little Marilyn tugged at the ends of her white linen jacket and suppressed a smile.

"We're all upset." Herb smoothed the waters. "After all, everyone of us here, with the exception of the two lovely young additions to our community"—he nodded toward Chris and Marcy—"have known Charlie since childhood. Yes, he was flawed, but is there anyone standing here who is perfect?"

A subdued quiet fell over the room.

"I'm perfect," Pewter warbled as the humans looked at her.

"Oh la!" Mrs. Murphy laughed.

"Girls, this is serious." The corgi frowned. *"You know sooner or later the murderer will pop up and what if he pops up here?!"*

"You've got a point," Mrs. Murphy, stretching fore and aft, agreed.

"Doesn't change the fact that I am perfect."

"Harry, what do you feed them?" Chris lightheartedly said, which broke the tension in the room.

The chatter again filled the room but the acrimony level died down.

Herb leaned over to Harry. "What's this letter business?"

"I'll show you." She walked back to the small table where she'd left three days' worth of mail. She returned, handing it over the counter.

He read it. "Could mean a lot of things."

"Exactly," Harry agreed.

"But it is creepy," BoomBoom intruded.

"Now it is, but we're viewing it through the lens of Charlie's death," Herb sensibly replied.

Fair put one elbow on the counter divider.

"I wouldn't make too much of this unless something else happens—something, uh, dark."

Chris joined in as Marcy was tongue-tied and uncomfortable. "I agree, but reunions are such loaded situations. All those memories."

"My memories are pretty wonderful." Fair winked at Harry, who blushed.

"You were the class ahead. Our memories might be different." BoomBoom sighed.

"I thought you had a great time—a great senior year," Harry said.

"I did."

"Well, then, Boom, what are you talking about?"

Mrs. H., fearing another spat, left the Sanburnes and Marcy Wiggins to go back behind the divider. "Let me tell you about memory. It plays tricks on you. The further I get from my youth the better it looks and then some sharp memory will startle me, like stepping on a nail. It might be a fragrance or a ring around the moon at midnight, but then I remember the swirling emotions—the confusion—and you know, I'm quite glad to be old."

"You're not old," Fair gallantly said.

Jim, overhearing, agreed. "We're holding up pretty good, Miranda, and of course, my bride"—he smiled broadly—"is as beautiful as the day I married her."

As the friends and neighbors applauded, Marcy slipped outside.

"*Odd.*" Tucker noticed as did Chris, who also walked outside.

"*Marcy?*" Mrs. Murphy knew her friend's mind.

"*Yes...such a little person with such a heavy burden.*" The dog put her paws on the windowsill.

Jim checked his gold watch. "Meeting at town hall." He kissed Mim on the cheek. "Home for dinner."

One by one the old friends left the post office.

"When's the next shoot?" Harry asked BoomBoom as she slipped the key into her mailbox. She was beginning to regret her anger at the high-school shoot and she really regretted saying she'd outlive Charlie even though she loathed him.

"Saturday."

"Who is it?"

"Bonnie Baltier and Leo Burkey. She's driving down from Warrenton and he's coming over from Richmond. I promised them dinner as a reward."

"Better do the shoot soon. I mean, you never know who else will die." Harry rolled the full mail cart over to the counter.

"That's ghoulish," BoomBoom indignantly replied.

"You're right." Harry sighed. "But I couldn't resist. I mean I could keel over right here. We're all so...fragile."

"Prophesy." Fair raised an eyebrow and Harry whitened.

"Don't say that. That's worse." Boom-Boom, an emotional type, crossed herself.

"I didn't say it was a prophecy. I said *prophesy*."

"I'm a little jangled." Boom's beautiful face clouded over.

"Your affair with Charlie was in high school," Harry snapped. "That's too far back to be jangled."

"That is uncalled for, Harry, and you're better than that," Miranda chided.

"Don't know that I am." Harry stuck her jaw out.

"Charlie Ashcraft was a big mistake. That was obvious even in high school. But I had to make the mistake first." Boom's face was pink. "I know you think little of me, Harry Haristeen, and not without just cause. I've apologized to you before. I can't spend my life apologizing. I am not promiscuous. I do not go around seducing every man I see and furthermore when my husband died my judgment was flawed. I did a lot of things I wouldn't do today. When are you ever going to let it go?"

Harry, amazed, blurted out, "It's easy to be gracious now— I even believe you. But it wasn't your marriage that hit the rocks."

"That was my fault." Fair finally spoke up. He'd been too stunned to speak.

"Why don't you three go out back and settle this?" Miranda saw more people pulling into the parking lot. "I know this is federal property and you have a right to be here but really, go out back."

"All right." Harry stomped out, slamming the back door behind her.

"I think we're on duty." Mrs. Murphy jumped down, then scooted across the back room.

Pewter followed. Tucker walked out the front door when Fair held the door for Boom-Boom. She tagged at their heels as they walked between Market Shiflett's store and the post office to the parking area in the rear.

In the parking lot by the alleyway they stood mutely staring at one another for a moment.

"Come on, Mom, get it out. Get it over with," Mrs. Murphy advised.

"I'm being a bitch. I know it." Harry finally broke the silence.

Fair said, "Some wounds take a long time to heal. And I am sorry, truly sorry. Harry, I was scared to death that I was missing something." He paused. "But if I hadn't made such a major mistake I wouldn't have known what a fool I was. Maybe other people can learn without as much chaos, but I don't think I could have grown if I hadn't gone through that time. The sorrow of it is, I dragged you through it, too."

Harry leaned against the clapboard side of the post office, the wood warm on her back. All three animals turned their faces up to her. She looked down at them, opened her mouth, but nothing came out.

"Go on," Mrs. Murphy encouraged her.

Harry picked up the tiger cat, stroking her. "I don't guess there is another way to learn. I don't know if it's worse being the one who goes or the one who stays. Does that make sense?"

"It does, sort of," BoomBoom replied. "We're so different, Harry, that if this hadn't happened we still wouldn't be best friends. I'm driven by my emotions and you, well, you're much more logical."

"I apologize for my rude remarks. And I accept your apology."

"Mom is growing up at last." Tucker felt quite proud of her human.

Before more could be said, Mrs. Hogendobber opened the back door. "Cynthia Cooper here to see all three of you."

They trooped back in, feeling a bit sheepish.

Cynthia noticed their demeanor and after a few pleasantries she asked them about the shoot, if they noticed anything un-usual about Charlie, if they had any specific ideas.

Each person confirmed what the other said. Nothing was different. Charlie was Charlie.

Cooper stuck her notepad in her back hip pocket. "Harry, I need to see you alone." She shepherded Harry out to the squad car. Mrs. Murphy and Pewter watched through the window. They could clearly see from their perch on the divider.

"What's going on?" Tucker, intently staring out the window, asked.

"Mother is frowning, talking, and using her hands a lot."

"I can see that. I mean what is really *going on?"* the dog snipped.

"H-m-m." Pewter blinked, not pleased with the turn of events.

The air conditioning hummed in the squad

car. Empty potato chip bags lay on the seat. Harry removed them to the floor.

"Whatever possessed you to tell Charlie Ashcraft he'd die before you'd sleep with him?"

"Coop, I don't know. I was mad as hell."

"Well, it doesn't look good. Because of that outburst I have to consider you a suspect. It was a dumb thing to say."

"Yeah..." Harry bent over, picked up the potato chip bags, and folded them lengthwise. "I hated that guy. But you know perfectly well I didn't kill him."

"Can you account for your whereabouts from six-thirty to eight last night?"

"Sure. I was on the farm."

"Can anyone corroborate this?" Cooper wrote in her steno pad.

"Murphy, Pewter, and Tucker."

"That's not funny, Harry. You really are a suspect."

"Oh come on, Cynthia."

"You are a member of the country club. It wouldn't have been difficult for you."

"No, I'm not," Harry quickly spoke. "Mom and Dad were but after they died I couldn't afford the dues. I'm allowed to go to the club once a month, which I usually do with Susan if she needs a tennis partner."

"But your presence at the club wouldn't seem unusual. Everyone knows you."

"Coop, let me tell you: there are old biddies, male and female, who have nothing better to do than cast the searching eye. If I had been there, you can be sure someone would have reported me because I've already played with Susan this month. I've used up my allotted time."

Cynthia flipped her book closed. "Do you think you could kill?"

"Sure, I could. In self-defense."

"In anger?"

"Probably," she replied honestly.

"He sexually baited you."

"He'd been doing that since high school."

"You snapped."

"Nope." Harry folded her arms across her chest.

Cynthia exhaled through her nostrils. "Rick will insist on keeping you an active suspect until better shows up. You know how he is. So don't leave the state. If an emergency should arise and you need to leave Virginia, call me."

"I'm not leaving. Now I'm insulted. If you don't find the killer, I will."

"What I'd advise you to do, Harry, is watch your mouth. That's why we're sitting in my squad car on a hot August day."

"I suppose BoomBoom couldn't wait to tell how I lost my temper."

"Let's just say she performed her civic duty."

"That bitch."

"Yes, well, if that bitch winds up dead you are in trouble."

"Coop, I didn't kill Charlie Ashcraft."

Relenting, dropping her professional

demeanor, Cynthia replied, "I know—but shut up. Really."

Harry smoothed the folded potato chip bags on her thigh. "I will. I don't know what's come over me. It's like I just don't give a damn anymore." She stared out the window. "You think it's this reunion? I'm getting stirred up?"

"I don't know. Your high-school class seems, well, volatile." She paused. "One more question."

"Sure."

"Do *you* think this murder has anything to do with your high-school reunion?"

10

"Nah. How could it?" *"Have you ever seen anything like it?"* Tucker inquired of Mrs. Murphy and Pewter as the animals watched Harry fall in love with her new truck.

"She's read the manual twice, she's crawled under the truck, and now she's identifying and playing with every single part she can reach in the engine. Humans are extremely peculiar. All this attention to a hunk of metal," Pewter said.

A little breeze kicked up a wind devil in front of the barn door where the animals crouched in the shade. Harry worked in the fading sun-light.

"It's a perfect red." Mrs. Murphy felt more people would notice her riding in a red truck than in any other color. *"Look who's rolling down the road."*

They heard the tire crunch a half mile away, saw the dust and soon Blair Bainbridge's 911 wide-body black turbo Porsche glided into view, a vastly different machine than the dually but each suited for its purpose.

Harry put down the grease gun she'd been using and wiped her hands on an old towel as Blair stopped. "Hey, had to see the new truck. I didn't believe it when Little Mim told me, but when Big Mim said you truly had a new truck, one that could haul your trailer, I had to see it."

"Big Mim is interested in my truck?" Harry smiled.

"The only topic of conversation hotter than your red truck is the end of Charlie Ashcraft. Everyone has a suspect and no one cares. Amazing." He stretched his long legs, unfolding himself from the cockpit of the Porsche. "It seems like everyone knew Charlie but no one *really* knew him."

"You could say that about a lot of people."

"Yes, I guess you could," he agreed.

She lingered over the big V-8 engine, admiring the cleanliness of it, touching the fuel injection ports, which meant she had to stand on an old wooden Coca-Cola box to lean down into the compact engine. "Blair, men talk. What are they saying?"

"Oh," he waved his hand, "I'm not in the inner circle." He took a breath.

"You know I value your judgment. You were born and bred here and, uh..." He stopped for a moment. "I find myself in a delicate situation."

"Too many women, too little time." Harry laughed.

He laughed, too. Harry relaxed him. "Not exactly, but close. Over the years we've become friends and I think I would have committed more blunders without you. I'm afraid I'm heading for a real cock-up, as the Brits say."

"Little Mim."

"Yes." He glanced up at the sky. "See, it's like this: women accuse men of being superficial over looks. Trust me. Women are equally as superficial."

"You would know." She smiled at the unbelievably handsome model.

Blair flew all over the world for photo shoots. The biggest names in men's fashions wanted him.

"You're not going to put up a fight? You're not going to tell me men are worse than women?"

"Nope." Harry jammed her hands in her back pockets. "Now tell me what's going on."

"Little Mim has a crush on me. Okay, I've dealt with crushes before and I like her. Don't get me wrong. But over the weekend I was at a fund-raiser and, of course, the Sanburnes were there. Big Mim pulled me away from the crowd, took me down to the rathskeller, and closed the door."

"This is getting serious," Harry remarked. The rathskeller was a small stone room in the basement of the Farmington Country Club.

"She offered me cash if I would stay away from Marilyn. She said modeling was not a suitable profession for her son-in-law."

"No!" Harry blurted out.

"I make a lot of money, but let's just say my business is timesensitive. I'd be a liar if I said I'm immune to a big bribe. And I've had enough scrapes and breaks to my body to wake me up to that fact. My Teotan Partnership Investment is doing very well, though. But really, I was shocked that the old girl would try to buy me off."

Through various twists and turns Blair wound up sole director of a corporation originally set up to sell water to Albemarle County. However, he'd begun bottling it and selling the mountain water—purified, of course—in specialty stores. This proved lucrative.

"You don't need her money." Harry thought to herself that it must be nice.

"No. But the Sanburnes control Crozet. If I spurn Little Mim, I'm cooked. If I ignore Big Mim's wishes, I'm cooked."

"M-m-m." Harry removed her hands from her pockets and rubbed them together absent-mindedly. "Do you like Marilyn?" She called Little Mim by her Christian name.

"Yes."

"Love?"

"No. Not yet, if ever. That takes time for me." He pursed his lips.

"Well, squire Little Mim around to local functions, spend some time with her and her family. Sometimes when you really get to know someone things look different. You look different, too."

He paused and rephrased his thoughts. "If I'm up-front about getting to know her daughter, the family, Mim will take it better if I choose to spend my life with her daughter?" he questioned, then quietly added, "If the relationship should progress, I mean."

"He is a Yankee." Mrs. Murphy laughed because Blair missed the subtlety of Harry's suggestion.

"Because he's only thinking of his feelings about Little Mim." Pewter had gotten a spot of grease on her paw, licked it, and spit.

"Go drink water," Tucker told her.

The gray cat scampered into the barn, standing on her hind legs to drink out of the water bucket in the wash stall.

"He's missing the point, that this gives Little Mim and Big Mim plenty of time to assess him." Tucker stood up and shook. *"Mom's betting on Little Mim getting the stars out of her eyes."*

"No. I think Mom is giving everyone a chance to draw closer or gracefully decline. If he walks away from Mim's offer she'll be furious. And if he took it he'd be held in contempt by her forever."

"He's in a fix. You don't think Little Marilyn knows?"

"Tucker, it would kill her."

"Yeah."

Pewter mumbled back, *"Let's drag that grease gun into the woods."*

"You'll have even more grease on you."

Pewter eyed the dog. *"I hate it when you're smarter than I am."*

All three animals laughed.

"...no hurry," Harry continued. "If you go slow and be honest, things will turn out for the best."

"I knew you'd know the right thing to do."

"And pay court to Big Mim even if she's cold to you. She loves the attention."

"Right." He folded himself back into his car. "Glad you finally got a new truck."

"Me, too."

He drove back down the driveway without fully realizing that now he really wanted Little Mim precisely because her mother refused him. Suddenly Little Mim was a challenge. She was desirable. People are funny that way.

As soon as he was out of sight, Harry raced for the phone in the tackroom.

"Susan."

"What?"

"I was just thinking about how people say one thing and do another—sometimes on purpose and sometimes because they don't know what they're doing."

"Yes..." Susan drew out the yes.

"Well, I was just talking to Blair about another matter but it made me think about people concealing their true intentions. Like

Charlie's behavior toward Marcy Wiggins at the shoot."

"He didn't pay much attention to her at the shoot." Susan thought back.

"Exactly," Harry said.

"H-m-m." Susan thought it over.

"Let's raise the flag and see who salutes." Harry's voice filled with excitement.

"What do you mean?" Susan wondered.

"Leave it to me." Harry almost smacked her lips.

"*She's incorrigible.*" The tiger cat sighed.

$$11$$

By eight-thirty the next morning, they had all the mail sorted and popped in the mailboxes.

Harry and Mrs. Hogendobber felt wonderful. Their job was easier in the summer. The catalogue glut diminished—only to return like a bad penny in the fall. A rise in summer postcards couldn't compete with the tidal wave of mail from Thanksgiving to Christmas.

Harry enjoyed reading postcards before sliding them in the boxes. Maine, an excellent place to be in mid-August, claimed four Crozetians. Nova Scotia, that exquisite appendage of Canada, had one. The rest of the postcards were from beach places, with the occasional glossy photo of a Notre Dame gargoyle from a student on vacation dutifully writing home to Mom and Dad.

Miranda had baked her specialty, orange-glazed cinnamon buns. The two women nibbled as they worked. Miranda swept the floor while Harry dusted down the backs of the metal mailboxes.

"*Why do humans have flat faces?*" Pewter lazily inquired, made tired by this ceaseless productivity.

"*Ran into a cosmic door.*" Mrs. Murphy cackled.

"*If they had long faces it would throw them out of balance,*" Tucker said.

"*What do you mean?*" Mrs. Murphy didn't follow the canine line of reasoning.

"*They'd be falling forward to keep up with their faces. Flat faces help them since they walk on two legs. Can't have too much weight in front.*"

"*You know, Tucker, you amaze me,*" Mrs. Murphy admiringly purred as she strolled over from the back door.

Harry had put an animal door in the back door so the kids could come and go. Each time an animal entered or left a little flap was heard. Mrs. Murphy was considering a stroll in Miranda's garden. Insect patrol. She changed her mind to sit next to Tucker.

The front door opened. Susan came in carrying a tin of English tea. "Hey, girls, let's try this."

"Darjeeling?" Harry examined the lavender tin.

"Miranda, tea or coffee?"

"This is a tea day. I can't drink but so much coffee when it's hot unless it's iced. Don't know why." She bent over to attack the dust pile with a black dustpan.

"Let me hold that, it's easier." Susan bent down with the pan as Miranda swept up.

"Have you made your morning calls?" Harry asked. Susan liked to get all her calls and chores done early.

"No, but Boom called bright and early, a switch for her. She wants to shoot the Best All-Round photo after Wittiest and I told her no. I need a month to lose seven pounds."

"Susan, you look fine."

"Easy for you to say." Susan felt that Harry would never know the battle of the bulge, as both her parents were lean and food just wasn't very important to her.

"She have a fit?"

"No, she asked again if I would help with Wittiest."

"Will you help?"

"Yes." Susan sighed. "What about you?"

"No!" Harry said this so loudly the animals flinched.

"One hour of your time," Susan cajoled.

"BoomBoom wanted to be the chair of our reunion, let her do it. I'm doing my part."

"Okay..." Susan's voice trailed off, which meant she was merely tabling her agenda until a better time.

The front door opened, and a well-built man of average height stood there, the light behind him. He had thick, steel-gray hair, a square chin, broad shoulders. He opened wide his arms as he walked toward the counter.

"Cuddles!"

Miranda squinted, looking hard at the man, thrust aside the broom, and raced to flip up the divider. She embraced him. "Tracy Raz!"

"Gee, it's good to see you." He hugged her, then held her away for a moment, then hugged her again. "You look like the girl I left in high school."

"What a fibber." She beamed.

Mrs. Murphy looked at Pewter and Tucker as the tiger cat whispered, *"Cuddles?"*

12

"How many of us are left?" Tracy reached over for another orange-glazed bun.

Harry, upon learning that Tracy Raz was a "lost" member of Mrs. Hogendobber's high-school class, forced her to take the day off. Miranda huffed and puffed but finally succumbed. She took Tracy home, setting out a sumptuous breakfast—homemade buns and doughnuts, cereal with thick cream, and the best coffee in the state of Virginia.

"Forty-two out of fifty-six." Miranda munched on a doughnut. "Korea accounted for two of us, Vietnam one—"

"Who was in Vietnam?"

"Xavier France. Career officer. Made full colonel, too. His helicopter was shot down near the Cambodia border."

"Xavier France, he was the last kid I would have picked for a service career. What about the others?"

"The usual: car accidents, cancer—far too much of that, I'm afraid—heart attacks. Poor Asther Dandridge died young of diabetes. Still, Tracy, if you think about it, our class is in good shape."

"You certainly are."

"You haven't changed a bit."

"Gray hair and twenty more pounds."

"Muscle." And it was. "How did you hear about the reunion? We'd given up on ever finding you."

"It was a funny thing." His movements carried an athlete's grace as he put the cup back on the saucer. "Naturally, I knew this was our fiftieth year. I hadn't much interest in attending the other reunions and I'll come to that later. I remembered that Kevin McKenna worked for Twentieth Century-Fox. I'd see his name in the papers. He's director of marketing. Got to be worth a bundle. I called and got the usual runaround but I left a message with my phone number and damned if he didn't call me back. He sent me a copy of the invitation. I was footloose and fancy-free so I came early. Thought you might need an old fullback to help you."

"Where do you live?"

"Hawaii. The island of Kauai. After high school I enlisted, which you knew. Well, in our day, Miranda, you enlisted or you were drafted. I figured if I enlisted I'd get a better deal than if I let myself get drafted. Army. Got good training. I wound up in intelligence, of all the strange things, and once my tour was up I re-enlisted but I made them promise to put me through Ranger school. Now it's Green Berets but then it was Rangers. They did. I stayed in for ten years. Left after being recruited by the CIA—"

"A spy?" Her kind eyes widened.

He waved his hand to dismiss the notion. "That's TV stuff. I had a wonderful job. I was sent all over the world to see events first-hand. For instance, during the oil crisis in the seventies I was in Riyadh. Worst posting I ever had was Nigeria. But basically I was a trou-bleshooter. I'd be the first one in, scope the situation and report back. They could make of my data what they wished—everyone in Washington has his own agenda. My God, Miranda, bureaucracy will ruin this country. That's my story. Retired and here I am."

"Did you ever marry?"

He nodded. "A beautiful Japanese girl I met in Kobe in 1958. That's when I bought

90

a little land in Kauai. Li could get back to her family and I could get to the States."

"I hope you'll bring her to the reunion."

He folded his hands. "She died two years ago. Lymphatic cancer. She fought hard." He stopped to swallow. "Now I rattle around in our house like a dried pea in a big shell. The kids are grown. My daughter, Mandy, works for Rubicon Advertising in New York, John runs the Kubota dealership in Kauai, and Carl is a lawyer in Honolulu. They speak fluent Japanese. I can carry on a conversation but the kids are fluent, which makes them valuable these days. They're all married with kids of their own." He smiled. "I'm kind of lost really." He slapped his thigh. "Here I am talking about myself. Tell me what happened to you."

"I married George Hogendobber, he became the postmaster here, and we lived a quiet but joyful life. He died of a heart attack, nearly ten years ago. Sometimes it seems like yesterday."

"I don't remember George."

"He moved here from Winchester."

"Kids?"

"No. That blessing passed me by, although I feel as though Mary Minor Haristeen is a daughter. She's the young woman you just met."

"Miranda, you were the spark plug of our class. I've thought of you more than you'll ever know, but I never sat down to write a letter. I'm a terrible letter writer. You'll always be my high-school sweetheart. Those were good times."

"Yes, they were," she said simply.

"I wanted to see the world and I did. But here I am. Back home."

"I feel as though I saw the world, too, Tracy. I suppose my world was within. I've drawn great strength from the Bible since George died. Harry calls me a religious nut."

"Harry?"

"The girl in the post office."

"Yes, of course. Minor. The people out on Yellow Mountain Road. He married a Hepworth."

"Good memory. She's their daughter. They're gone now."

"Whatever happened to Mim Conrad? Did she marry Larry Johnson?"

"No." Miranda's voice dropped as though Mim were in the next room. "Larry was four years older than we were. Remember, he was finishing college as she was finishing high school? Well, he did go to medical school. They dated and then the next thing I knew they weren't dating anymore. He married someone else and she married Jim Sanburne."

"That oaf?"

"The same."

"Mim marrying Jim Sanburne. I can't believe it."

"He was big and handsome. He runs to fat now. But he's a genial man once you get to know him."

"I never tried. Larry still alive?"

"Yes, he practiced medicine here for decades. Still does, although he sold his practice to a young man, Hayden McIntire, with the provision that Larry'd work just one more year, get Hayden settled with the patients. That was several years ago. Still working, though. Hayden doesn't seem to mind. Larry's wife died years ago. He and Mim are friendly."

"They were such a hot item."

"You never know how the cookie will crumble." She giggled a little.

"Guess not. Here I am. Miranda, it's as though I never left. Oh, a few things are different, like that old-age home by the railroad underpass."

"Careful. No one calls it that anymore, not since we're getting so close ourselves. It's assisted-care living."

"Bull."

"Well—yes." She smiled. "The town is much the same. There are subdivisions. One on Route 240 called Deep Valley and one on the way to Miller School. There's a brand-new grade school which cost the county a pretty penny. But pretty much Crozet is Crozet. Not beautiful. Not quaint. Just home."

"Do you need help with the reunion?"

"What a delightful question." She folded her hands together gleefully.

"That's a yes, I take it." He smiled. "Say, how does Mim look?"

"Fabulous. You know it's her fiftieth reunion this year, too, at Madeira. She endured her second face-lift. She goes to the best and truthfully she does look fabulous. Slender as ever."

"H-m-m." He dusted his fingertips to rub off the sticky icing. "Jim Sanburne... I still can't believe that. Is he good to her?"

"Now. For a long time he wasn't and the further apart they drifted the haughtier she got. She was an embittered woman and then a miracle happened. I don't know if you believe in miracles but I do. She was diagnosed with breast cancer. Larry broke the news. She had a mastectomy and reconstructive surgery. Jim stopped running after women."

"Stop drinking, too?"

"He did."

"He'd put it away in high school, I remember that. Class of '49. Good football player. I was glad I had a year after he graduated. Selfish. I wanted the attention."

"You were All-State."

"We had a good team for as small a school as we were." He paused. "I closed up the house in Kauai. I'm looking to rent a house here, or rooms. Would you know of anything?"

"I don't wish to pry but what would you be willing to pay?"

"A thousand a month for the right place."

She thought long and hard. "For how long?"

"Well, until December first at least. Our reunion is Homecoming so I might as well stay a month after that."

She smiled broadly. "I have an idea. Let me check it out first. Where are you staying now?"

"Farmington Country Club—pretty funny,

isn't it? The way I used to rail about that place being full of stupid snobs. Now I'm one of them—on a temporary basis, of course. And I heard a young fellow was murdered there—what? Two days ago?"

"Unlamented, I'm afraid. People are lining up to lay claim to the deed." She stopped. "Not very charitable of me, but the truth is no one is very upset about the demise of Charlie Ashcraft. How about if I call you tonight, or tomorrow at the latest? I may have just the place."

"Whose animals were those in the post office?"

"Oh, those are Harry's. If they aren't the smartest and cutest helpers."

"I don't remember you being that fond of animals."

She blushed. "They converted me."

He laughed. "Then they do have special powers."

13

"Use this italics pen." Chris handed Harry the fountain pen with the slanted nib.

"Let me practice first." Harry gingerly scratched the pen over scrap paper. "Kinda neat."

"I've divided up those cream-colored cards, the two-by-threes. See? Print the person's name like this." She held up a card. "*Carl Ackerman,* with the name at the top, leaving room for the title below. Got it?"

"I'll never think of stuff."

"You will, but if all the name tags are done now it will make life easier at the reunion. You'll be surprised at the ideas that will pop into your head between now and then. I bet by the time of your reunion—when is it, again?"

"End of October. Homecoming weekend."

"Right." Chris picked a card off her stack, her deep maroon nail polish making her fingers seem even longer and more tapered than they were. "That's lots of time. How about if I take the first half of the alphabet and you take the second."

"All those *M*'s and *S*'s," Harry laughed. "Thanks for having me over. The cats and dog thank you, too."

"Thanks." Mrs. Murphy sat on the floor, her eyes half-closed, swaying.

"The air conditioning is perfect." Tucker wedged next to Harry, who sat on the floor, using the coffee table as a desk.

"Right-o," Pewter agreed. She rested on the silk sofa.

Harry eyed the gray kitty. "Get off that sofa."

"Oh, I don't care."

"Silk is very expensive." Harry leaned over. "I told you to get off."

"You touch me and I'll sink a claw into this gor-

geous silk." For emphasis Pewter brandished one razor-sharp claw.

"Hussy." Harry backed off.

"She's fine. I rather like having animals about. When I bought this house I liked the fact that it's on an acre. I thought someday I might get a cat or dog."

"*Cat,*" Pewter encouraged.

"*Dog,*" Tucker countered.

"*Both,*" Mrs. Murphy compromised.

"They're funny." Chris laughed.

"That they are. Why did you come here? After the big city it must seem like the back of the beyond."

"Chicago was all I knew. I came through here two years ago on a vacation—a history tour. I just fell in love with the place. Being a stockbroker makes me pretty mobile and when an opening popped up at Harold and Marshall Securities I said, 'Why not.' I'd saved a good deal of money, which I think will tide me over as I build a new client base."

"People are cheap here. What I mean to say is, it won't be as easy to sell as it was in Chicago."

"I already know that," Chris said matter-of-factly as she inscribed names, "but I needed a shake-up. I broke up with my boyfriend. My walls were closing in on me."

A car rolled into the driveway.

"*Who goes there!?!*" Tucker sprang to the door.

"Tucker, this isn't your house."

"*Oh—yeah.*" Tucker returned to Harry as Chris opened the door, letting Bitsy Valenzuela into the cooler air.

"Hi."

"Hi, Bitsy." Harry didn't rise.

"A drink?" Chris asked.

"A Tom Collins would be heaven. I'll mix it myself." Bitsy knew the way to the bar in Chris's house, a rounded steel bar with squares cut into the polished steel harboring lights: red, green, yellow, and blue. "Harry, you drinking?"

"Coke."

"Such virtue," Chris teased her.

"That's me." Harry hated inscribing the names.

Bitsy joined them at the coffee table. She sat next to Pewter, who stared up at her and then looked away. "I'm not up to snuff," Bitsy observed.

"She can be snotty," Murphy commented.

"Flies on your tuna," Pewter grumbled, then shut her eyes.

"Where's E.R.?" Chris inquired.

"Home for a change. He's vacuuming the swimming pool. I told him I'd be back in a half hour. It's his turn to cook. He's a good cook, too. Say, if you're hungry I'll pick up two more steaks."

"No, thanks," Harry declined. "I am determined to knock out my half. I've got forty left."

Bitsy picked up a card. "Bonnie Baltier. Great name."

"Wittiest," Chris said.

"How do you know that?" Harry asked.

"Senior superlatives," Chris said. "I've studied your yearbook so much I think I know them almost as well as you do."

"This goes above and beyond losing to Susan Tucker at golf," Harry said.

"Well, I'm enjoying it. And to be honest, I'm hoping to meet some unmarried men through this. You never know." She shyly smiled.

"Take E.R.," Bitsy laughed. She loved him but she liked to complain of his foibles, one of which was the irritating habit of reading magazines backwards to forwards. "I could use a rest."

"Any husband that cooks, I'd keep," Chris told her.

"Amen," Harry said.

"Anyone seen Marcy today?" Chris asked. "I thought she might drop by this afternoon."

"I passed her on the road and waved." Bitsy swallowed half her drink. "She looked miserable. I wish she'd come out with it and say her marriage is crumbling—we all know. I think all this stress is making her sick. Her face is drawn."

"I'm sorry to hear that." Harry's eyebrows moved up in surprise.

"Another Deep Valley divorce." Bitsy drained the glass. "They barely speak to one another."

"People go through phases," Chris blandly said.

Mrs. Murphy opened her eyes. *That's a nice way to put it.*

"That's true." Bitsy got up to make herself another Tom Collins. "Chris, I owe you a bottle of Tanqueray. But how do you know what's a phase and what's a permanent part of character?" She returned to the original subject.

"You don't for a long time. By the time I figured out my boyfriend was a self-centered jerk, I'd put three years into the relationship," Chris complained.

The ice cubes tumbled into the tall frosted glass as Bitsy listened.

"What's the story on Blair Bainbridge?" Chris asked. "I can't quite get a fix on him."

"He's a model," Harry said. "Makes a ton of money. He dates Little Mim Sanburne as well as women from other places. He's kind of"—she thought for a minute—"languid."

Bitsy flopped on the couch, again disturbing Pewter, who grumbled. "He can be as languid as he wants as long as he stays that gorgeous."

"Amen, sister." Chris held up her glass, as if toasting Bitsy.

Bitsy asked Harry, "We all thought you and Fair might be getting back together."

"Did Mrs. Hogendobber tell you that?"

"No," Chris answered, "but it just seemed, uh, in the cards and Fair is very handsome."

"Fair Haristeen is the best equine vet in central Virginia. He's a good man. He was a so-so husband. If he interests you, tell him. You won't upset me."

"Harry, I wouldn't do that." Chris blushed.

"I don't care."

"*You do, too,*" Tucker disagreed.

Bitsy took a long swallow. "Harry, no woman is that diffident about her ex-husband."

"Uh." Harry changed the subject. "Market Shiflett is single. He's a nice guy."

"Doesn't look like Blair Bainbridge," Bitsy frankly stated.

"If you marry a drop-dead gorgeous man you have to accept that other women will chase him and sooner or later he'll be unfaithful. A man like Market is responsible, loyal, and true. Personally, I find those qualities very sexy. I didn't at twenty-two but I do now," Harry said.

"You've got a point there," Chris agreed.

14

There were three reasons that people attended Charlie Ashcraft's funeral. The first was to support his mother, Linda, who had never made an enemy in her life. Married young, dumped at twenty-one with a six-month-old baby, she had struggled to make ends meet. Like many an abandoned woman she spoiled her son— the only man who truly loved her—and she had bailed her offspring out of innumerable crises. Poor Linda could never see that she was part of the problem. She fervently believed she was the solution.

The second reason people came to the funeral was to see who else was there—namely, were there any teary-eyed women? Surprisingly, there were not.

The third reason people came was to make sure he was really dead.

A lone reporter from *The Daily Progress* covered the event but Channel 29 sent no cameras to mar the occasion. Then, too, the station manager had had his own brush with Charlie and enjoyed denying the egotist coverage of his last social event.

As people filed out of the simple Baptist church, Harry leaned over to Susan and whispered, "Did you notice there were hardly any flowers?"

"I did. Maybe people will give to charity."

"More than likely they'll give to an abortion clinic. That's where most of his girlfriends wound up."

Susan gasped, choking on a mint, and Harry patted her on the back. "Sorry."

Thanks to her beautiful voice, Miranda Hogendobber, a stalwart of the choir of The Church of the Holy Light, was invited to sing solo at the funeral. Linda Ashcraft asked her to sing "Faith of Our Fathers," which she did. Walking out of the back of the church, her choir robe over her arm, she caught sight of Harry and Susan.

"Unusual," Mrs. Hogendobber said under her breath.

"Uh-huh," the two friends agreed.

They walked up the hill, the church cemetery unfolding in the deep green grass before them. Ahead walked BoomBoom, Bitsy, and Chris.

"Maybe they knew Charlie better than we thought." Susan kept her voice low.

"BoomBoom's tugboats. They're missing Marcy Wiggins, though. H-m-m." Harry thought a minute. "Boom probably called in tears saying she needed support since he was her first high-school boyfriend. Amazes me how she manages to be the center of drama." She stopped as they neared the gravesite.

Linda, already at the grave, was being supported by her brother-in-law. The poor woman was totally distraught. As they gathered around the opened earth, Harry, in the back, scanned the band of mourners—if one could call them that. Apart from Linda, the mood was respectful but not grief-stricken. Meredith McLaughlin, Market Shiflett, and Bonnie Baltier were there, all from their high-school class.

Big Mim Sanburne attended, Little Mim was absent. Who was there and who was not was interesting, and Sheriff Rick Shaw and Deputy Cynthia Cooper had attended just to study the gathering.

Although they were too discreet to make notes at such a time.

"Why don't we slip away before Linda comes back through the crowd?" Rick put his hand under Cynthia's elbow, propelling the tall woman toward the church.

Harry, noticing, left Susan and Miranda to catch up to Cynthia and Rick. She said, "Sad. Not because he's dead but because nobody cares other than Linda. Can you imagine living a life where nobody truly loves you and it's your own damn fault?"

"A waste." Cynthia summed it up.

The three stopped before a recent grave festooned with flowers. The granite headstone bore the inscription *Timothy Martin, June 1, 1958 to January 29, 1997.* A racing car carved at the base of the tombstone roared from left to right. At the corners of the grave two checkered flags marked Tim's final finish line.

"I didn't know they'd done that." Rick remembered picking up what was left of Tim after he spun out on a nasty curve coming down Afton Mountain. He turned too fast on Route 6 and literally flew over the mountainside. He raced stock cars on weekends, was a good driver, but never saw the black ice that ended his life.

The flags fluttered. "It's nice that his family remembered him as he lived. He'd love this."

"They keep him covered in flowers," Cynthia remarked. "I hope someone loves me that much."

"Someone will—be patient." Rick smiled as he flicked open his small notebook with his thumb. "What do you think, Harry?"

"I'd question whoever isn't here and should have been."

He smiled again. "Smart cookie."

The crowd was dispersing from the gravesite.

"Let's forgo the reception. This is hard enough for Linda Ashcraft without two cops at the table." Cynthia headed toward her own car. They hadn't taken a squad car, and since the body was carried directly from the church to the cemetery there was no need for a police escort. Rick and Cynthia were uncommonly sensitive people.

Moving at a slow pace, Miranda, choir robe folded over her arm, and Susan came over the rise. They waved to Harry, who waited at the back church door.

Miranda exhaled, focusing on Harry. "I'd like a word with you." The two walked under the trees as Miranda encouraged Harry to take in a boarder, namely Tracy.

15

Like many doctors, Bill Wiggins, an oncologist, was accustomed to getting his way. "Stat" was his favorite word, a word meaning "immediately" in hospital lingo.

Sitting on his back deck surveying his green lawn, not one dandelion in sight, he also surveyed his wife.

"Marcy, you've lost a lot of weight."

"Summer. I can't eat in the heat." She watered the ornamental cherry trees at the edge of the lawn.

"You need to get a thorough checkup. I'll call Dinky Barlow."

Dinky Barlow was an internist at the hospital. He was unbelievably thorough.

"Honey, I'm fine."

"I'm the doctor." He tried to sound humorous.

"Probably need a B-12 shot." She smiled weakly. It would never do to tell Bill what was off was their relationship. They rarely communicated other than simple facts—like bring home milk and butter. Bill, like most doctors, worked long hours under great stress. He never quite adjusted to his patients dying, feeling in some way that it was a blot on his skills.

Marcy needed more. Bill had nothing left to give her.

Then again, he didn't look inward. As long as supper was on the table, his home kept in order and clean, he had nothing to complain about.

His silence, which Bitsy and Chris interpreted as hostility in their friend's marriage, was really exhaustion. He had little time for chatting up his wife and none for her girlfriends, whom he thought boring and superficial.

Bill flipped open his mobile phone, dialed, made an appointment for his wife, then flipped the phone so it shut off. "Next Tuesday. Eight-thirty A.M. Dinky's office."

"Thank you, honey." She hated it when he managed her like that but she said nothing, instead changing the subject. "You didn't want to go to Charlie Ashcraft's funeral?"

He swirled his chair to speak directly to

her. "Marcy, the last place I ever want to go is a funeral," he ruefully said. "Besides, he was an empty person. I've no time for people like that."

"But doesn't it upset you just a little bit that someone in your class was killed? Murdered?"

"If it were anyone but him, maybe it would." He sat up straight. "You know what gets me? Death is part of life. Americans can't accept that."

"But Charlie was so young."

"The body has its own timetable. In his case it wasn't his body, it was his mind. He brought about his own end. Why be a hypocrite and pretend I'm upset? As I said, my dear, death is a part of life."

"But you get upset when a patient dies."

"You're damned right I do. I fight for my patients. I see how much they fight. Charlie squandered his life. I wish I could give my patients those hours and years that he tossed aside." He glared at Marcy. "Why are we having this argument?"

"I didn't think it was an argument."

"Oh." Confused, he slumped back in his chair.

She continued watering, moving to the boxwoods, which were far enough away to retard conversation.

16

The 1958 John Deere tractor, affectionately known as Johnny Pop, *pop-popped* over the western hay fields.

Bushhogging was one of Harry's favorite chores. She would mow the edge of the road, all around the barn and then clear around the edges of her pastures and hay fields.

The hay needed to be cut next week. She'd arranged to rent a spider wheel tedder to fold the freshly cut hay into windrows. Then she'd go back over the flattened, sweet-smelling hay with an old twine square baler.

Hard work in the boiling sun, but Harry, born to it, thrived.

Today she chugged along in a middle gear, careful not to get too close to the strong-running creek.

The horses stayed in the barn during the day in the summers, a fan tilted into each stall to cool them and blow the flies off.

Mrs. Murphy and Pewter were hanging out at the spring house. The cool water running over the stones produced a delightful scent. The mice liked it, too.

Tucker, sprawled in the center aisle of the barn, breathed in and out—little no-see-ums rising and falling with each breath—like an insect parasol opening and closing.

Harry loved this patch of Virginia. She had great pride in her state, which boasted two ancient mountain ranges, a rich coastline fed by three great rivers, and a lushness unimaginable to a Westerner. But, then, the Westerner was freed from the myriad gossamer expectations and blood ties inherited by each Virginian. So much was expected of a Virginian that ofttimes one had to escape for a few days, weeks, or years to rejuvenate.

A poplar tree downed in an early-summer storm loomed ahead. Harry sighed. She had to cut up the big tree, then drag the sections and branches to those places in her fence line that needed repair. Poplar didn't last as long as locust, but still, it was for free, not counting her labor.

She cut off Johnny Pop and dismounted. The spotted tree bark remained home to black ants and other crawlies. Although flat on its side, roots exposed, the crown of the poplar was covered in healthy green leaves.

"Life doesn't give up easily," she said aloud, admiring the tenacity of the desperately injured tree.

She bent over the creek, cupped her hands and washed her face. Then she let the tumbling cool water run over her hands.

It suddenly occurred to her that her feelings about Charlie Ashcraft as an individual were irrelevant. The swiftness of his end sobered her. Security was a myth. Knowing that intellectually and knowing it emotionally were two different things.

She shook her hands, enjoying the tingling sensation. The sensation of death's randomness was far less pleasant.

"Given the chance, I'll fight to the end. I'll fight just like you." She patted the thick tree trunk before climbing back onto the tractor.

17

"*Smells okay.*" Tucker twitched her nose.

"*You rely on your nose too much. You have to use your other senses.*" Pewter sat impassively on the sofa, watching Tracy Raz carry a duffel bag over his shoulder.

"*Think this will work?*" Tucker, also on the sofa, asked.

"*Yep.*" Mrs. Murphy, alertly poised on the big curving sofa arm announced, "*Tracy Raz will be a godsend.*"

"*'Cause of the money? Mom's new truck payments don't leave much at the end of the month.*" Tucker, conservative about money, fretted over every penny because she saw Harry fret. A rent check of five hundred dol-

lars a month would help Harry considerably. Tucker was grateful to Mrs. Hogendobber for sitting down both Harry and
Tracy Raz to work out a fair arrangement.

*"That, too, but I think it's going to be great for
Mom to have someone around. She's lived alone
too long now and she's getting set in her ways.
Another year and it'd be—concrete."*

Pewter and Tucker laughed.

Harry led the athletically built man upstairs.
She walked down a hall, the heart pine floor
covered with an old Persian runner, deep
russet and navy blue. At the end of the hall
she opened the last door on the right to a huge
bedroom with a full bath and sitting room.
"I hope it suits. I turned on the air conditioner.
It's an old window unit and hums a lot but
the nights are so cool you won't need it.
There's always a breeze."

Tracy noticed the big four-poster rice bed.
"That's a beauty."

"Grandmother gave it to Mom as a wedding
present. Grandma Hepworth was raised in
Charleston, South Carolina."

"Prettiest city in the country." He walked
across the room, turned off the air conditioner, and threw open the window. "The
reason people are sick all the time is because
of air conditioning. The body never prop-
erly adjusts to the season."

"Dad used to say that." Harry smiled. "Oh,
here are the keys although I never lock the
house. Let's see, I'm usually up by five-thirty
so I can knock off the barn chores. If you

like to ride you can help me work the horses. It's a lot of fun."

"Rode Western. Never got the hang of an English saddle." He smiled.

"I can't promise meals..."

"Don't expect any. Anyway, Miranda told me you eat like a bird."

"Oh, if you don't shut your door at night the animals will come in. They won't be able to resist. Any magazines or papers you leave on the floor will be filed away—usually under the bed. If you take your watch off at night or a necklace of any sort put it in your bureau drawer because Mrs. Murphy can't resist jewelry. She drags anything that glitters to the sofa, where she drops it behind a cushion."

Mrs. Murphy, curiosity aroused, followed them upstairs. *"I resent that. You leave stuff all over the house. With my system everything is in one place."*

"Where we can all sit on it," Pewter, also brimming with curiosity, said.

"Those two culprits?" Tracy nodded at the two cats now posing in the doorway.

"Murphy's the tiger cat and the gray cannonball is Pewter. She used to belong to Market Shiflett but she spent so much time at the post office with my animals that he told me to just take her home. She also flicked meat out of the display case, which didn't go down well with the customers."

"They're beautiful cats."

"I knew I'd like this guy." Pewter beamed.

"He's handsome for his age." Mrs. Murphy

purred, deciding to bestow a rub on Tracy's leg. She padded over, slid across his leg, then sat down. He stroked her head.

Pewter followed suit.

"I'll leave you to get settled. You can use the kitchen, the living room. I figure if something upsets you you'll tell me and vice versa. I'm going out to finish my barn chores."

"I'll go along. There's not that much in the bag to worry about. I thought I'd do a little shopping this week."

"You don't have to help me."

"Like to be useful." He beamed.

And he was. He could toss a fifty-pound bale of hay over his shoulder as though it weighed one-tenth of that. Although not a horseman, he had enough sense to not make loud noises around them.

Tracy whistled as he worked. Harry liked hearing him. It suddenly hit her how stupid it was to retire people unless they decided to retire. The terms "twilight years" and "golden years" ought to be stricken from the language. We shove people out of work at the time when they have the most wisdom. It must be horrible to sit on the sidelines with nothing vital to do.

Simon, belly flat to the hayloft floor, peered over the side. A new human! One was bad enough.

Harry noticed him. "Patience, Simon."

Tracy glanced up. "Simon?"

"Possum in the hayloft. He's very shy. There's also a huge owl up in the cupola and a blacksnake. She comes back to hibernate each fall. Right now she's on the south side of the property. I've tracked her hunting circle. Pretty interesting."

"That was the one thing I hated about my work. Kept me in cities most of the time. I worked out in gyms but nothing keeps you as healthy as farmwork. My father farmed. You wouldn't remember him, he worked the old Black Twig apple orchard west of Crozet. Lived to be a hundred and one. The worst thing we ever did was talk Pop into selling the orchard and moving to Florida. I'll never forgive myself for that."

"He's forgiven you."

Tracy stopped a moment to wipe the sweat from his face. The temperature hovered in the low eighties even though it was seven at night. "Thanks for that."

"Possums are interesting, too." Harry tactfully returned to the subject of Simon. "They'll eat about anything. There's a bug that infects birds and if the possums eat a bird with the bug they'll shed it in their poop. If horses eat the poop they come down with EPM, an awful kind of sickness that gets them uncoordinated and weak. If you catch it in time it still takes a long time to heal. Anyway, I love my Simon. Can't kill him but I don't want my kids here to, by chance, munch some hay that Simon has—befouled. So each night I put out sweet feed and the occasional marshmallow. He's so full he doesn't roam very far and there's no room for birds."

"I can see you're the kind of person who loves animals."

"My best friends." She slid the pitchfork between the two nails on the wall. "Mr. Raz—"

"Please call me Tracy."

"Thank you. And call me Harry. I hope you don't think I'm prying but I've just got to ask you. How did Mrs. Hogendobber come by the nickname 'Cuddles'?"

As they watched the ground fog slither over the western meadow and the meadowlarks scurry to their nests, the bobwhites started to call to one another and the bats emerged from under the eaves of Harry's house. Tracy recalled his high-school days with Miranda.

"*Love bats.*" Mrs. Murphy fluffed her fur as a slight chill rolled up with the ground fog.

"*Never catch one.*" Pewter liked the way bats zigged and zagged. Got her blood up.

"*My mother caught one once,*" Murphy remembered. "*It was on its way out, though. Still, she did catch it. You know they're mice with wings, that's how I think of them.*"

"*Maybe we'd better catch the mice in the barn first.*"

Mrs. Murphy moved over to Pewter, leaning against her in the chill. "*I heard them singing in the tackroom this morning. I expect them to be saucy in the feedroom. But the tackroom. It was humiliating. Fortunately, Harry can't hear them.*"

"*An original song?*"

The tiger cat laughed. "*In those high-pitched*

115

voices everything sounds original but it was 'Dixie.'"

"*Well, at least they're Southern mice.*"

"*Pewter, that's a great comfort.*" Mrs. Murphy laughed so loudly she interrupted the humans.

"Getting a little nippy, Miss Puss?" Harry scooped her up in one arm while lifting Pewter with the other. "Pewts, light and lively for you."

A cat on each shoulder, Harry walked back to the house as Tucker trailed at Tracy's heels.

Tracy picked up where he'd left off when Murphy let out what sounded to him like a yowl. "—one of the prettiest girls in the class. Natural. Fresh."

"Was she plump?"

"Uh...full-figured. You girls are too skinny these days. Miranda sparkled. Anyway, we'd go on hay rides and trips to other high schools for football games. I played on the team. Afterwards we'd all ride back to school in our old jalopies. Fun. I think I was too young to know how much fun I was having. And World War Two ended five years before our graduation so everyone felt safe and wonderful. It was an incredible time." He chuckled as he opened the porch door for Harry. "Every chance I had I got close to Miranda and I nicknamed her 'Cuddles.'"

The kitchen door, open to catch the breeze, was shut behind them as the night air, drenched in moisture and coolness, was drawing through the house.

Harry put the cats on the kitchen counter.

"Must be a cold front coming through. The wind is picking up. This has been an unusual summer. Usually it's brutally hot, like the last few days have been."

"Nothing like a Virginia summer unless it's a Delta summer. One year in the service I was stationed in Louisiana and thought I would melt. Heat and hookworm, the history of the South."

"Cured the latter. Did I interrupt you? If I did I apologize. You were telling me about Miranda."

"In my day we were all friends. It wasn't quite as much sex stuff. I had a crush on Miranda and we did a lot of things together but as a group. I took her to the senior prom. You know, I loved her but I didn't know that either. It wasn't until years later that I figured it all out but by then I was halfway around the world, fighting in Korea. I wish you could have known Miranda as a youngster."

"I'm glad to know her now."

"More subdued now. She said you thought she was a religious nut."

"I give her a hard time. She needs someone to give her hell," Harry half-giggled. "She's more religious than I am but I don't know as she's a nut. You know, Tracy, I've known Miranda from the time I was a child but what do children know? She was bright and chirpy. George died and she took a nosedive. That's when she turned more to religion, although she was a strong church-goer before. But I've noticed this last year she's happier. It's taken her a long time."

117

"Does. Lost my wife two years ago and I'm just pulling out of it."

"I'm sorry."

"Me, too. You live with a woman for half of your life and she's the air you breathe. You don't think about it. You simply breathe."

"Poor fellow." Tucker whimpered softly.

"He's on the mend and he's sure good with chores so I hope he hangs around." Mrs. Murphy, ever practical, batted water drops as they slowly collected under the water tap.

The phone rang. Harry picked it up. Tracy noticed Mrs. Murphy and walked over to the faucet. He unscrewed the tap with his fingers, so strong was his grasp. The washer was shot. He put it back and grabbed a notepad by the phone and made a note to himself which he stuck in his pocket.

"All right. Susan, all right."

Susan, on the other end of the line, said, "Now the hysteria is, should BoomBoom use the picture with Charlie or not?"

"She should look at the proofs first."

"One of them is bound to turn out."

"Susan, what does she intend to do with the superlatives that Aurora and Ron are in? They're dead, too."

"She can't make up her mind whether to use their old photographs either."

"I'll make it up for her. Tell her we all suffered in the heat for that photograph of her and Charlie, so use it."

"You know, Harry, that's a good idea. Hang

up and call her before she emotes anymore. It *is* tiresome." Susan paused. "Go on, Harry. *You* call her."

Harry, grumbling, did just that and Boom-Boom blurted out three or four sentences of inner thoughts before Harry cut her off and told her to just use the new photo. The whole idea was to see the passage of time!

Harry finally got off the phone. "This reunion is becoming a full-time job."

"Ours is going to be real simple," Tracy said. "We'll gather in the cafeteria, swap tales, eat and dance. I don't even know if there will be decorations."

"With Miranda as the chair? She can't have changed that much in fifty years, I promise you." Harry smiled.

"That's something about one of your classmates getting shot." Tracy noticed the weather stripping on the door was ragged. "Everyone seems calm about it."

"Because everyone thinks they know the reason why. They just have to find out which husband pulled the trigger. What has upset people, though, is the mailing that went out to our classmates before Charlie was killed. 'You'll never get old!' it said."

"*Ever hear the expression, 'Expect a trap where the ground is smoothest'?*" Mrs. Murphy commented as she wiped her whiskers.

"*What made you think of that?*" Tucker, now rolled over on her back, inquired.

"*People have jumped to a conclusion. Charlie Ashcraft could have been killed for another reason.*

What if he was involved in fraud or theft or selling fake bonds?"

"That's true." Pewter, now on the table, agreed. *"No one much cares because they think it doesn't have anything to do with them."*

"Like I said, 'Expect a trap where the ground is smoothest.' "

18

The dually's motor rumbled as Harry leaned over to drop Tracy's rent check and her deposit slip in the outdoor deposit box on the side of the bank.

The truck gobbled gas, which she could ill afford, but the thrill of driving her new truck to town on her lunch hour superseded prudence.

Susan had given her expensive sheepskin seat covers, which pleased the animals as much as it pleased Harry. They lounged on the luxurious surface, the cats "kneading bread."

Harry flew through the morning's chores, then drove over to Fair's clinic at lunch.

"Hi, Ruth." She smiled at the receptionist.

"He's in the back." Ruth nodded toward the back.

Harry and the animals found him studying X-rays.

"Look." He pointed to a splint, a bone sliver detaching from a horse's cannon bone, a bone roughly equivalent to the human forearm.

"Doesn't look bad enough to operate." She'd seen lots of X-rays during their marriage.

"Hope not. It should reattach. Splints are more common than not." He switched off the light box. "Hello, kids."

The animals greeted him eagerly.

"Here, you're a peach." Harry smiled on the word *peach*. She handed him a check.

"What's this?"

"Partial payment on my old truck. Five hundred dollars a month for four months. I called Art for the real price. He told me to take anything you'd give me but I can't—really. It's not right."

"I don't want the money. That was a gift." He frowned.

"It's too big a gift. I can't take it, as much as I appreciate it."

"No strings. I owe it to you."

"No you don't." She shoved back the check that he held out to her.

"Harry, you can be a real pain in the ass."

"Who's talking?" Her voice raised.

"I'm leaving." Mrs. Murphy headed for the door, only to jump sideways as Ruth rushed in.

"Doc, Sheriff Shaw has Bill Wiggins in the squad car."

"Huh?"

Ruth, almost overwhelmed by the mass of curly gray hair atop her head, breathlessly said, "Margaret Anstein called from the station house. She's the new receptionist at the sheriff's office—or station house, that's what she calls it. She just called me to say Rick was bringing in Bill Wiggins for questioning about Charlie's murder."

"You can't get away with anything in this town." Fair carefully slid the X-rays in a big heavy white envelope.

"That Marcy is a pretty girl. Just Charlie's type." Ruth smacked her lips.

"They were all Charlie's type," Harry said.

"She wasn't at the funeral," Ruth said.

"Why should she be? She's new," Fair replied, irritated that Ruth and most of Crozet had jumped to conclusions.

"The other new people were there. A funeral is a good place to meet people," Ruth blathered.

"Unless they're dead." Pewter twitched her whiskers and followed Murphy to the door.

19

Harry no sooner walked through the back door to the post office than Miranda rushed over to her.

"There's been another one."

"Another what?"

"Mailing. Open your mail. You're always late in opening your mail."

Harry picked up her pile on the little table in the back.

"This one." Miranda pointed out a folded-over, stapled sheet.

"Who else...?"

"Susan, BoomBoom, Bill, and—"

Harry exclaimed, "What a jerk!"

Mrs. Murphy and Pewter stuck their heads over the paper that Harry held in her hands.

"What is it?" Tucker asked.

"Typed. 'Sorry, Charlie. Who's next?' and a drop of red ink like a drop of blood," the tiger answered.

Harry flipped over the page, which allowed Tucker to see it. "22905. The Barracks Road post office again. It's funny no one said anything this morning."

"Because none of your classmates came in before lunch. BoomBoom was at her therapist's and Susan spent the morning in Richmond. The only reason I know that Bill got one was that Marcy called once she got home. Guess she opens his mail. Not right to do that." Miranda believed mail was sacrosanct, the last intimate form of communication.

Harry dialed Vonda, the postmistress at Barracks Road. "Hi, Vonda, Harry. How you doin'?"

Vonda, a pretty woman but not one to babble on, said, "Fine, how are you?"

"Okay, except my classmates and I have gotten another one of these mailings from your post office. Folded over, stapled. Looks to be run off from a color Xerox."

"Bulk?"

"No. They're too smart for a bulk rate. A regular stamp and yesterday's postmark. Did anyone come to the counter with a handful?" Harry knew Vonda would remember, if she'd been behind the counter.

"No. Let me ask the others." Vonda put down the phone. She returned in a minute. "They were pushed through the mail slot. Mary says they were in the bin when she started sorting at elevenish. Second full bin of the day."

"Keep your eyes open. This is getting kind of creepy."

"I will. But it's very easy to walk in and out of here without attracting notice."

"Yeah, I know. Thanks, Vonda." Harry hung up the phone.

"Barracks Road gets more traffic in a day than we get in a week," Pewter remarked.

"Second busiest post office in the county." Mrs. Murphy knew enough to be a postmistress herself. *"Even busier than the university station."* The main post office on Seminole Trail was the busiest, of course.

"Does Rick know?" Harry asked.

"Yes. Susan called him the minute she picked up her mail." Mrs. Hogendobber paused. "Did you hear that Rick hauled in Bill Wiggins for questioning?"

"Ruth told me. I stopped by Fair's clinic."

125

"Doesn't look good, does it?" Miranda pursed her lipstick-covered lips.

"For Bill?"

"No, in general."

"I want to know why Bill?"

"Perhaps he was Charlie's doctor. It's entirely possible that Charlie had cancer. He'd never tell."

"I never thought of that." Harry looked down at Tucker, who was looking up. "That doesn't mean Bill will reveal anything. Aren't doctor-patient relationships privileged?"

"I think they are. Doesn't mean Rick won't try."

Mrs. Murphy batted at the paper. Harry dropped it on the table. "What a sick thing to do. Send out..." She didn't finish her sentence.

Mrs. Murphy and Pewter both stared at the 8½" x 11" white page.

"Looks like a warning to me," Pewter said.

"What happened back then? Back when Harry graduated," Tucker sensibly asked.

"I don't know. And more to the point, she doesn't know." Mrs. Murphy looked up at Harry. *"If something dreadful had happened and she knew about it, she'd tell the sheriff."* Mrs. Murphy sat on the paper.

"Yes. She would." Pewter shuddered.

20

Rick Shaw made drawings, flow sheets, time charts, which he color-coded, sticking them on the long cork bulletin board he installed at the station. Being a visual thinker he needed charts.

Every employee of the Farmington Country Club was questioned. Every member at the club that evening had been questioned also, which put a few noses out of joint.

He paced up and down the aisle in front of the bulletin board, eighteen feet. Although pacing was a habit he declared it burned calories. When he slid into middle age he noticed the pounds stuck to him like yellow jackets. You'd brush them off only to have them return. He'd lost fifteen pounds and was feeling better but he had another fifteen to go.

"You're wearing me out." Cynthia tapped her pencil on the side of her desk.

"Get up and walk with me." He smiled at her, his hands clasped behind his back. "This is such a straightforward murder, Coop, that we ought to be able to close the case and yet we haven't a firm suspect. Bill Wiggins is our most logical candidate but the guy has an airtight alibi. He was with a patient at Martha Jefferson Hospital."

She plopped her pencil in a Ball jar she kept on her desk for that purpose and joined him. "The fact that Charlie was shot at such a close range implies he knew who killed him."

"No, it doesn't. There's not a lot of room in the men's locker room. A stranger could have come in as though going to a locker. Charlie wouldn't have paid much attention."

"Yeah." Coop knew he was right, and it frustrated her.

"All we have is Hunter Hughes' testimony that he thought he saw a slender man come down from the landing. He heard the footsteps because he had left the counter in the golf shop and had walked outside for a smoke. He worked until nine that evening. He assumed the man was leaving the men's grill, heard the footsteps and as he turned to go back into the golf shop he saw the back of an average-sized male wearing a white linen-like jacket. This was close to the time of the murder. That's all we've got."

They both stopped in front of the detailed drawing of the country club golf shop, grill, and the men's locker room, along with a sketch of the buildings on that side of the club.

"But when we questioned the manager of the grill, he doesn't remember anyone at the bar about that time."

"Could have been a member passing through from the 19th Hole to the back stairway on the second floor, since it would be a faster route to the men's locker room."

"What if our killer came out of the pool side?" She pointed to the pool, which was behind the long brick structure containing the locker room and golf shop.

"Easy. It would have been easy to park behind the caretaker's house. The car would have been in the dark. Walking up here behind the huge boxwoods would have made it easy to escape detection." He pointed to the sketch. "For that matter the killer could have sat in his car. Who would notice back here? Whoever he is, he knows the routine and layout of the club. He knew no big party was planned that night. Then again, the schedule is published monthly, so it's easily accessible. It goes to each member plus it's posted at the front desk."

"A member." She nodded. "Knowing the layout points in that direction."

"Yeah, or an employee"—Rick folded his arms across his chest—"possible but unlikely."

"A jealous husband could have paid a professional."

"Could have."

She turned to face her boss. "But it smacks of a deeper connection. 'Up close and personal,' like they used to say during the Olympics coverage."

"Sure does. Our killer wanted to get right in Charlie's face."

21

"Not so fast!" Denny Rablan called from behind the camera. He was beginning to wonder why he was doing this, even if it was for his class reunion.

Bonnie, black curls shaking with laughter, sped on her bicycle toward a short but handsome Leo Burkey, also pedaling to pick up momentum. Bonnie and Leo screamed at one another as they approached. Chris Sharpton buried her face in her hands since she thought they'd crash.

BoomBoom, standing behind Denny, appeared immobile while Harry giggled. She knew Bonnie and Leo were thoroughly enjoying discomfiting BoomBoom, who was determined to follow through on her before-and-after idea.

The two pedaled more furiously, heading straight for one another, at the last minute averting the crash.

"That's not funny!" BoomBoom bellowed.

"Olivia, you have no sense of humor. You never did." Bonnie called BoomBoom by her given name.

Her maiden name had been Olivia Ulrich but she'd been called BoomBoom ever since puberty. Only Boom's mother called her

Olivia, a name she loathed although it was beautiful. Once she married Kelly Craycroft she happily dumped all references to Ulrich, since the Craycrofts carried more social cachet than the Ulrichs.

Eyes narrowed, BoomBoom advanced on Bonnie, who merrily pedaled away from her. "Get serious, Baltier! This is costing us. Time is money."

"God, what a rocket scientist." Leo smiled, revealing huge white teeth.

"You're a big, fat help." BoomBoom pointed a finger at him.

"I thought dear Denny was giving us his services for free." He innocently held up his hands, riding without them.

"I am. Almost," Dennis growled. "A greatly reduced rate."

"Well, Denny, my man, if you hadn't pissed away a fortune, you could do this for free, couldn't you?"

"Leo, shut up. It's over and done. I live with my mistakes and I don't throw your screwups in your face."

Leo rode in circles around the tall, thin, attractive photographer. "Maybe you're right."

"I could name your screwups. They all have feminine names."

Leo stopped the bike. He put his feet on the ground and walked the few steps to face Dennis. "So many women. So little time. Not that I'm in Charlie's league."

"Guess not. Charlie's dead."

"Did you get that asinine letter?"

"I figured you did it." Dennis smirked.

"Sure. I drove all the way from Richmond to Charlottesville to send a mailing with fake blood drops. Get real."

"I wouldn't put anything past you."

"No?" Leo's light hazel eyes widened. "Remember this: I'm not stupid. You were stupid. Sex, drugs, and rock and roll. Jesus, Denny, by the time you got off the merry-go-round you were broken. How could you do that?"

"Too loaded to care, man." Dennis's mouth clamped like a vise.

"I think you broke bad in high school."

"Leo, I don't give a damn what you think." Dennis turned his back on the shorter but more powerfully built man.

The others glanced over at the two men, then glanced away. Dennis and Leo were oil and water. Always had been.

"Shiny nose," Bitsy Valenzuela, in charge of makeup, called out.

Bonnie, ignoring BoomBoom—something she had perfected throughout high school—glided over to Bitsy.

Chris Sharpton picked up the orange cone she'd dropped when she thought the two were going to crash at high speed. Stationed at the entrance to the high-school parking lot, she put the cone upright. If anyone drove in they'd see the blaze-orange cone, see her and stop. She could direct them toward the rear. She stood there forlorn since no one drove through this early September afternoon. Many of the kids were behind the school at football practice.

"Listen, you two, we haven't got all day. Just get in position. Put the bikes down."

Finally obeying, both Bonnie and Leo approached one an-other and screeched to a halt.

"Put that bike down carefully, Leo, it's an antique," BoomBoom again commanded.

"No one is going to know if this bike is twenty years old or not. You're getting carried away with this," Leo said, but he did restrain himself from saying other, less pleasant things.

Bonnie laid her bike down, turning the wheel up just as it was in the original photograph. Leo's bike took more work. It stood on its front wheel in the original photograph as though the wreck had just happened. Harry, Susan Tucker, and a very subdued Marcy Wiggins set two blocks on either side of the front wheel. Since Leo would be sprawled on the ground his body would cover the blocks. They then braced the back side of the bicycle with a thin iron pole. As this was a balancing act, the two principals lay on the ground. The first time the shot had been taken, in 1979, the bike kept falling on Leo. The next day he was covered with bruises. Harry, Susan, and Marcy hoped they had secured the bicycle better than that but they also held their breath, hoping Nature would do likewise.

"Hurry up, Denny, this asphalt is hot!" Leo barked.

"Stay still, idiot." Denny said "idiot" under his breath. He shot the whole roll in record time.

Bonnie, thinking ahead, had taped bits of moleskin and padding on her one elbow and knee. She was on them as though she'd just hit the ground on her side. Still, the heat came through the padding.

Leo got up. "That's enough."

"We just started!" BoomBoom exploded.

The propped bicycle wobbled, falling with a metallic crash, spinning spokes throwing off sunlight.

Harry ran over, picked it up. Luckily there were no scratches.

"If that bike is broken, I'll kill you," Boom-Boom, often the butt of Leo's high-school pranks, hissed.

"Don't get your ovaries in an uproar, Boom. If the damned bicycle is scratched I'll fix it. You know, here it is twenty years later and you still haven't learned how to lighten up."

"Here it is twenty years later and you still haven't grown up," she fired back.

Chris left her cone. This was too good to miss.

Bonnie, ever the pragmatist, walked over to Denny. "Think you got it?"

"Yeah, that asphalt really is too hot to shoot this picture. The first time we did this it was later in the fall, remember?"

"October." Harry rolled the bike over to the two of them. "We voted on senior superlatives mid-October."

"What a good memory." Denny couldn't

remember what he'd eaten for supper the night before but then, given his past, a bad memory was a blessing.

"Remember when Leo made a crack to Ron Brindell in the cafeteria the day after the results were announced? Remember? Ron won Most Popular and Leo said they should shoot his picture in the locker room." Harry continued to wipe down the bike.

Leo had joined them. "Yeah."

Chris innocently asked, "Why'd you say that?"

"Ron was such a limp-wristed wimp. I said they should shoot him in the showers bent over with the naked guys behind him. He took a swing at me, that skinny little twit. I decked him and got a month of detention."

"Was he gay?" Chris wondered.

"He moved to San Francisco." Leo laughed as though that proved his point.

"That doesn't mean he was gay," Harry piped up. "I liked him."

"Yeah, you aren't a guy." Leo smoothed back his light brown hair.

"Speak no ill of the dead," Susan Tucker admonished as she picked up Bonnie's bike.

"Three of the superlatives are dead." Leo slipped his hands in his back pants pockets. "Maybe it's a bad omen." Then he imitated the *Twilight Zone* music.

"Ron and Aurora died long before now," BoomBoom, tired of Leo, said. Her alto voice carried over the parking lot. "As for Charlie, bad karma."

"He should have gone into pornographic films. Charlie Ashcraft, porn star. He would have been happier than as a stockbroker," Leo laughed.

"Funny thing is, he was a good stockbroker." Bonnie peeled off the moleskin.

"He was?" Leo was surprised.

"Prudent. He made a lot of money for people." Susan added, "Odd, how a person can be so reckless in one aspect of his life and so shrewd in another."

Marcy and Bitsy had joined them, Marcy adding to the conversation, "My husband says that men can compartmentalize better than women. There's a compartment for work, for family, for sex. It's easy for them." She'd taken to talking more fondly of Bill lately, perhaps to ward off gossip about her alleged relationship with Charlie. She was too late, of course.

Denny shrugged. "I don't know. Charlie must have had some thick walls between those compartments."

Harry took one of the bicycles, rolling it over to her red truck. She'd placed blankets on the floor of the truck bed so neither the bicycle nor the truck would get scratched. She wanted to buy a bedliner for the truck but hadn't had time to get one installed. She lifted the bike onto the dropped tailgate.

Chris came over. "Let me help."

"Okay, I'll hop in here and if you hop in on the other side we can lift it to the back. I've got ties to keep it from slipping."

"Who's taking the other bike?" Chris asked.

"Susan. It's her son's. Good thing. I'd hate to stack the bikes on one another. I think the first scratch to this truck will be a blow to my heart." She smiled. "Silly."

"Human." Chris wrapped yellow rope under the bike frame.

Bonnie and Susan walked over. "Are you going to dinner?"

"No," Harry responded.

"What about you, Chris?"

She turned to Susan. "BoomBoom told me she'd promised dinner to Bonnie and Leo since they had to drive a bit to get here. I don't want to intrude."

Susan said, "We've decided on Dutch treat. Come on. It will be fun. If for no other reason than to watch Leo torment Boom. Sure you don't want to come, Harry?"

"No, thanks. I've got chores to do." She tried to tolerate BoomBoom better these days but she'd not volunteer to spend time with her.

As she opened the door to the truck, Chris asked, "Denny asked me to dinner this Saturday. I don't know much about him. Is he an okay guy?"

Susan replied, "He's made a lot of bad decisions but, yeah, he's okay. At least he has learned from his messes."

Chris looked to Harry, who shrugged. "Go."

"He's divorced?"

"Years ago. I don't know why he married in the first place. They had nothing in common," Susan said.

"Date a lot of men, it helps refine your standards." Harry laughed. "Advice I should have taken myself."

"Thanks." Chris smiled, then walked back to Dennis, who was putting away his equipment. He smiled as she approached him.

When Harry arrived home she found that the washer in the kitchen faucet had been replaced, the weather stripping on the door was replaced, a blackboard hung next to the kitchen door, a box of colored chalk was suspended by a chain attached to the blackboard. Written in green on the blackboard was the message, "Taking Cuddles to the movies. See you in the morning. Pewter has something to show you."

"Pewts," Harry called.

A little voice answered from the living room. Harry walked in to find Pewter proudly guarding a skink that she'd dispatched. Mrs. Murphy and Tucker flanked the gray cat.

"I caught him all by myself," Pewter crowed.

"Sort of," Mrs. Murphy added.

"Pewter, what a good kitty." Harry petted her. She went outside to check the horses, finished up her chores with fading light, and went to bed, glad she wasn't forced to relive old times at dinner.

22

The phone rang at the post office at seven-thirty A.M. just as Rob Collier, the delivery man from the main post office on Seminole Trail, dropped off two bags of mail.

"Sorry I'm late. Fender bender at Hydraulic Road and Route 29." He tipped his hat as he jogged back to the truck.

Mrs. Hogendobber answered the phone as the cats dashed to the mailbags. "Crozet Post Office. Mrs. Hogendobber speaking."

"I think movies were better in our day," Tracy replied on the other end. "That movie last night was all special effects. Was there a story?"

"Not that I could decipher."

"The best part of the movie was sitting next to you."

"You flatterer." She blushed and winked at Harry.

"I'll stop by on my way to Staunton. Harry left me a note this morning thanking me for the washer and leaving me five dollars for fixing it. You tell that girl she's got to learn to let people do things for her."

"Yes, Tracy, I'll try, but a new voice might get through. See you later."

"He's still got a crush on you," Harry teased Miranda, as she untied the first mailbag to the delight of Mrs. Murphy, who wriggled through the opening.

"Isn't paper the best?" The cat slid around in the bag, which was about three-quarters full.

"Tissue paper is better but this isn't bad." Pewter squeezed into the second mailbag.

"Paper? I don't get it." The dog shook her head, retiring to the small table in the back upon which Mrs. Hogendobber had placed a fresh round loaf of black bread, a damp dish towel over the top of it. The aroma filled the post office. Freshly churned butter in a large covered glass dish sat next to it.

"Come on, Miss Puss, out of there." Harry reached in and grabbed Mrs. Murphy's tail. Not hard.

"Make me." Mrs. Murphy batted away her hand, claws sheathed.

"You're a saucy wench this morning." Harry opened the bag wider.

Mrs. Murphy peered back, eyes large in the darkened space. She burrowed deeper into the mail. *"Hee hee."* Only it sounded to human ears like "kickle, kickle."

"Murphy, cut it out. You're going to scratch the mail. Federal property. Just think. You could be the first cat convicted of tampering with the mail. Federal offense. Jail. I can see the headlines now: Catastrophe."

"Corny," the cat meowed.

"I can't get Pewter out either." Miranda bent down a bit more stiffly than Harry, but she'd been gardening on her knees for the last few days, too.

142

"*I can do it.*" Tee Tucker bounded over and bit, gently, first the large lump in one bag and then the larger lump in the other.

Two cats shot out of the bags as though shot out of cannons. They whirled on Tucker. After all, no human had jaws like that.

"*Charge!*" Mrs. Murphy ordered.

She leapt onto Tucker's back. Tucker rolled over to dispense with that but when she did, Pewter jumped on her belly. The dog loved it, of course, but this was accompanied by furious growling. A few tufts of fur floated in the air.

As Pewter clung to Tucker's white belly, Mrs. Murphy grabbed the corgi's head, literally crawling on top of her, biting her ears.

"*Uncle!*" the dog cried out.

"*You don't have an uncle.*" Mrs. Murphy laughed so hard she fell over, so now Tucker could put the cat's head in her mouth.

Pewter yelled, "*That's cheating!*"

"*No, it's not. Two against one is cheating.*" But of course the minute Tucker said this she released her grip on Mrs. Murphy, who escaped.

"*The jaws of death,*" the cat panted.

They'd all three exhausted themselves, so they fell in a heap between the mailbags.

"Crazy!" Miranda shook her head.

The front door swung open and Big Mim, wearing a flowered sundress and a straw hat, strolled in. "Don't worry." She held up her hands. "I know you haven't sorted the mail yet. Miranda, I've hired Dan Wheeler to play at your reunion. Okay?"

Miranda walked over to the divider. "He'll add so much to the event but we can't afford him. We've got the tiniest treasury."

Mim waved her hand. "I'll pay for it."

"Mim, that's very generous, especially since you graduated from Madeira."

"I might as well do something with the money. It appears I am never to have grand-children."

Mim's daughter, divorced, was childless and not at all happy about either state. Her son, living in New York, was married to an elegant African-American model but they, too, had not produced an heir.

"They'll get around to it."

"I hope before I'm dead!" came the tart response.

"We've plenty of years left. Now you just come on back here and have a piece of my fresh pumpernickel."

"Love pumpernickel." Mim whizzed through the divider.

As Miranda cut through the warm bread the glorious scent intensified. Tucker opened an eye but couldn't bring herself to move. Harry brewed a fresh pot of coffee.

"Why hasn't Tracy Raz come to see me?"

"He's just gotten here." Miranda handed Mim a napkin.

"He's been here almost a week. You tell him I'm miffed. I expect a call. Maybe we didn't go to the same school but we were all friends. After all, I was home every holiday and every summer."

"Yes, dear." Miranda had learned how to handle Mim decades ago and was amazed that the woman's daughter had never figured out the trick: agree with her even when you don't. Over time, bit by bit, present opposing points of view. Nine times out of ten, Mim would hear it. But oppose her immediately or rain on her parade and her back would go up. You'd never get anywhere. Mim's mother was the same way, as was her ancient Aunt Tally, alive and exceedingly well.

"Harry, how's your reunion coming along?"

"BoomBoom has done a good job organizing. I have to give her credit. She has some original ideas."

"That's gracious of you." Mim beamed. "Now girls, I have a bone to pick with Market Shiflett and I want your support."

Both Harry and Miranda looked at one another and then back to Big Mim. "What?" they said in unison.

"He's moved that blue dumpster parallel with the alley. Looks dreadful. I should think it upsets you, Miranda."

"Well..." She measured her words. "He has created more parking and this was the only way he could do it."

"He could go back to garbage cans." Mim pronounced judgment.

"He even tried chaining the garbage cans. That didn't work. He painted them orange and people still ran over them," Harry offered.

"I know all that," Mim replied imperiously. "Then he can set the dumpster sideways under the privet hedge and he can build a palisade around it."

"But the dumpster is picked up once a week on a huge flatbed and a clean one put down in its place. I don't see how he can build a palisade around it." However, Miranda liked the idea.

"Oh yes, he can. Put big hinges on the long end, the end facing the parking lot, such as it is"—her voice dropped—"and put rollers on the bottom. In essence it's a big gate. When the pickup truck comes all Market has to do is roll that gate back or swing it out, whichever makes the most sense. He'll have to figure that out but I know it will work. I'm going over there to speak to him right now. Could one of you come with me?"

"Uh..." Harry stalled.

"Harry, go on. I'll sort the mail. You're better suited than I am."

"I don't know if that's true." Harry wiped her hands on the napkin.

"Harry," was all Mim said.

"Okay," she replied weakly, "but before we go in there, let's look closely at the site and the dumpster. Maybe we can figure out ways to improve it even more, you know, some plantings or something."

"Excellent!"

Miranda dropped her eyes lest she laugh by connecting with Harry. If there's one thing Mim couldn't resist it was a gardening idea. Harry was shrewd enough to maneuver her into yet another beautification plan.

As it was, Mim struggled valiantly with the garden club to accept her plans for filling downtown Crozet with profusions of flowers for the spring, summer, and fall bolstered by masses of holly, pyracantha, and Scotch pine for the winter. Her master plan for the town was stunning and everyone admitted that Crozet needed help. But money could never be found in the town budget and Mim, generous though she was, felt strongly that if the plan didn't generate community support she wasn't going to cough up the funds. She'd enlisted Miranda's aid and if she could interest Harry and Harry's generation, she thought she just might pull it off.

Harry and Mim walked out the back door as Tracy walked in the front door. He'd finished his errands and returned to see Miranda.

Mrs. Murphy got up, stretched, and followed Harry out.

Tucker, exhaling loudly, did the same. Pewter, sound asleep, didn't even open an eye when Miranda picked her up, gently placing her in an empty mail cart.

The two humans and two animals stood before the blue dumpster. It was unsightly but at least it had a lid on it. Having it open would have been a lot worse.

Mim used her right hand. "Swing the dumpster around like so. He can still use it with ease but it will free up more space. The palisade on the alley side could swing out or roll back for transfer."

"If it swings out it will block traffic."

"How much traffic is on this alleyway," Mim snipped, then thought a minute. "You're right. If it rolls straight along, it will block his parking lot for a minute but the alley will be free. 'Course, the truck will be in it anyway. However, I take your point and think rollers toward us is a better idea. Did you think perhaps planter tubs on the parking lot side?"

"No. I thought since that palisade part is stable why not build three tiers and fill them with geraniums, petunias, and even ivy that could spill over."

"Now that is a good idea." Mim's eyes brightened. "It will add to the expense."

"He's got a daughter in college." Harry need say no more.

"H-m-m, I'll think of something."

"Something's not right." Tucker lifted her nose and sniffed deeply.

Mrs. Murphy, nose not as sensitive, also smelled blood. *"Let me jump up."*

"Lid's closed." Tucker barked loudly.

"Maybe we can get them to open it." Murphy soared onto the slanted lid, sliding a bit but quickly jumping over to the flat side. *"I smell blood, too. Maybe there's a beef carcass. I'll get some of it for you,"* Murphy promised her grounded friend.

"No, this isn't beef, sheep, or chicken. This is human," Tucker adamantly barked.

Mrs. Murphy thought a minute, then said, *"Together."*

The cat and dog howled in unison. The

humans looked at them as Pewter hurried out the animal door to the post office. *"What's going on?"*

"Come up here."

She leapt up next to Mrs. Murphy, sliding down harder than the slender cat. Harry caught her.

"Yell," Mrs. Murphy directed.

Pewter bellowed. She surprised Harry so much that she dropped her. The cat shook herself, then leapt up again. This time she managed to get over to the flat side. *"Uh-oh."* She smelled it, too.

All three of them hollered for all they were worth.

"What's gotten into them?" Mim put her hand on her hip, then reached over and lifted up the slanted lid. She dropped the lid with a thud reverberating throughout the alley and sending the two cats off the dumpster. She took a faltering step back. Harry reached out to catch her.

Mim's face, bone-white, frightened Harry, who at first thought the older woman might have suffered a heart attack or stroke. Mim moved her lips but nothing came out. She pointed to the dumpster lid.

"Are you all right?"

Mim nodded her head. "Yes." Then she took a deep breath and opened the lid again.

"Oh, my God!" Harry exclaimed.

23

Sitting on top of the squad car, Mrs. Murphy laconically commented, *"Could have been worse."*

The assemblage by the dumpster would have disagreed with her if they had understood what she was saying. Mim called her husband, Jim, the mayor. He rushed over. Tracy put his arm around Miranda's waist. She was upset but holding together.

As luck would have it, Marcy Wiggins and Chris Sharpton had stopped by to pick up their mail. Fair Haristeen had also come to the P.O. Marcy fainted and Chris, with Fair's help, carried her into Market's air-conditioned store. Market, rushing around the store, revived her with a spot of brandy. As soon as she was somewhat recovered he hurried back outside again.

"In my dumpster!" He wrung his hands.

Tucker, as close to the dumpster as she could get without being in the way, asked Pewter, *"What did the body look like when you first could see in?"*

Pewter peered down from the limb of the pin oak where she was reposing. She wanted a different view than Mrs. Murphy. *"Leo's mouth was open and so were his eyes. He'd stiffened up but it wasn't too bad yet. They'll have a hell of a time getting him out of there now."*

"What I meant was, can you see how he was killed?" the dog persisted.

"Right between the eyes. Like Charlie Ashcraft," Pewter informed her with some relish.

"Flies are what made the humans sick." Murphy watched intently. *"They're in the dumpster so they crawled all over him but really, it could have been worse. He's not been dead half a day."* She was matter-of-fact about these matters, but then, cats are.

Rick and Cynthia, having finished their work, had to turn to Jim Sanburne, the crowd growing by the minute behind the yellow tape. "Jim, I prefer they leave but I doubt they will so keep them back. If they break through the tape they may compromise evidence. Can you call in anyone to help you?"

Tracy stepped forward. "Sheriff, Tracy Raz, I can help."

Tracy was off in the service when Rick was young so he didn't remember him, but he knew the Raz name. "Thank you."

"I'll help, too." Fair towered over the other two men.

Tracy, accustomed to command, faced the murmuring crowd, some with handkerchiefs to their mouths. "Folks, I know this is extremely upsetting to you all but please leave. The more of us that crowd around, the more possibility that valuable evidence will be destroyed. Sheriff Shaw is doing all he can right now and he needs your help."

"Come on, gang." Fair gently shepherded his friends and neighbors back down the alleyway.

As people walked slowly they turned to see what else was happening. The last thing they saw was a big blue truck, Batten Services, come down the lane with Joe Batten emerging, his assistant and cousin, Harvey Batten, along with him. He ran the trash-removal company and he was going to take off the door to the dumpster so they could remove the body.

"You girls go back into the post office," Tracy soothingly directed, "because that's where people will gather and they'll need you to keep your heads."

"Quite right." Miranda nodded. Violent death shocked her. But she'd seen enough death in her life to accept it as inevitable, although she never could accept violence.

The cats and dog stayed at the scene of the crime. No one paid attention to them because they were careful to stay out of the way, even though Mrs. Murphy brazenly sat on top of Rick's squad car.

Joe glanced at the body, pulled a heavy wrench from his leather tool belt around his waist, and started turning a nut. "Harvey, you crippled?"

Harvey swallowed hard, walked over, and crouched down to work on the bottom bolt. He was eye-level with the loafers on the corpse but he did not look inside.

As the men worked, Diana Robb and the rescue squad crept down the alleyway, clogged with cars. The people moved away but they'd left their cars.

Diana hopped out, marched up to the opened dumpster, and peered inside. "Like Charlie. Powder burns."

"Uh-huh," Rick noncommittally grunted.

"You ready for us?" She noticed the crushed green and orange 7-Up cartons under the body.

"Yeah, you can take him." Rick leaned against the squad car to light a cigarette.

"Those things will kill you," Mrs. Murphy scolded.

He looked up at the cat looking down at him. "You don't miss a thing, do you?"

"Nope."

"Need a hand?" Tracy offered.

"We've got it, thanks." Diana smiled.

Tracy asked Rick, "If you don't need me anymore I'll be going."

"Where to?"

"The post office."

"I mean, where do you come from?" Rick inhaled.

Tracy briefly filled the sheriff in on his background. "Retired now. Came back to help with our high-school reunion."

Rick reached out to shake his hand. "Rick Shaw, sheriff."

"Deputy Cynthia Cooper." She shook Tracy's hand also, as did Fair.

"I'm renting rooms at Harry's farm. If you need me I'll be there." He opened the back door to the post office, slipping inside.

Fair, face white with upset, hands in jeans pockets, said, "Quite an ending for someone as fastidious as Leo Burkey. To be dumped with garbage."

"Harry made a similar comment," Rick noted.

Market bustled back again. "Sheriff, I hope you don't think I did this. I couldn't stand Leo, but I wouldn't kill him. Besides, he lived far enough away he didn't work on my mood." Market's voice was tremulous, his hands were shaking.

"Market." Rick paused. "Why didn't you like him?"

"Smart-ass. In high school—well, always."

"Yes, he was," Fair confirmed.

"As bad as Charlie Ashcraft?" Cynthia watched as Joe and Harvey lifted the blue metal door off its hinges, leaning it up against the side of the dumpster.

"*What's worse, reaching in the garbage or picking up the body?*" Pewter giggled.

Tucker whirled around, hearing before the rest of them. "*What's worse is here comes Channel 29.*"

Diana, now seeing the van with the dish on top, as she was looking down the alleyway, urged, "Come on, let's get him out of here and in a body bag before they jump out with the damned cameras."

Too late. Even before the van pulled over the cameraman was running toward them.

"Stand back!" Rick barked, holding up his hand.

A brief argument followed but the cameraman and on-air reporter did stay twenty yards back as Diana, with three assistants, lifted out the body. Since rigor was taking over, getting him into a body bag required effort.

"Why don't they break his arms and legs?" Pewter sensibly suggested.

"They'd pass out. Humans are touchy about their dead." Mrs. Murphy noticed the outline of his wallet in his back pocket. It would appear robbery wasn't the motive.

Market returned to the question Cynthia had posed before they were interrupted by the television crew. "No, Leo wasn't as bad as Charlie Ashcraft. Charlie was in a class by himself. Leo wanted us to think he was a ladies' man but he was more bark than bite. He had a smart mouth, that's all. Hurt a lot of feelings. Or I should say he hurt mine. And he was handsome, I couldn't compete with him for the girls. Not too many of us could." He looked up at Fair. "Like you, the class ahead. You always got the girls."

"Hope I didn't have a smart mouth." Fair still watched fixedly as they struggled with the body.

"You were a good guy. Still are," Market said. He leaned against the car with Rick, as he couldn't stop shaking. "I don't know what's wrong with me. I feel dizzy."

"The shock of it." Rick patted Market on the back. "No one expects to come to work in the morning and find a dead body in the garbage."

"If I'd kept those old garbage cans it wouldn't have happened," Market moaned. "That will teach me to leave well enough alone."

"Until they scattered all over the alleyway again," Fair reminded him. "You did the right thing. Someone took advantage of it, that's all."

"*Someone who doesn't much care about how they dispose of bodies. Two men, same age, same high-school class, shot between the eyes and left for the world to see. There's a message here.*" Mrs. Murphy walked over the back window, careful not to smear paw prints on it. "*Like those stupid mailings. I think the message will get more clear in time.*"

"*Both senior superlatives, too.*" Pewter backed down the tree to join her friend. "*That's odd.*"

"*Mom's a senior superlative.*" Tucker barked so loud she distracted one of the rescue-squad men and he tripped, then righted himself.

"*We know,*" the cats said. Then Murphy continued, "*But so far the murdered are handsome men, well-off. Don't panic yet.*"

"*I'm not panicking,*" the dog grumbled, "*only observing.*"

"*They say that when someone dies their features relax.*" Pewter walked toward the post office, her friends walking with her. "*But Leo Burkey looked surprised, like a bear had jumped out at him, like something totally out of the blue had shocked him.*"

"*We didn't see Charlie but it's a sure bet he was surprised, too.*" Tucker pushed through the animal door into the post office.

Mrs. Murphy sat in front of the door, irritating Tucker who stuck her head back through to see where the cats were. *"There's human intelligence to this. That's the trick, you see. Killers often start from an irrational premise and then are completely rational and logical when they act."*

24

Glad to be home after an extremely upsetting day, Harry wearily pushed open the screened porch door. It didn't squeak. She noted the hinges had been oiled. She heard pounding behind the barn.

Mrs. Hogendobber had given her freshly baked corn bread in a square pan which the older woman had thoughtfully covered with tinfoil. Harry placed the pan inside the refrigerator.

"Look!" Pewter trilled.

Mrs. Murphy, whiskers swept forward, bounded up to Pewter in front of the refrigerator. Tucker ran over, too, her claws hitting the heart pine floorboards with clicks.

"Wow, this is a first," Tucker exclaimed.

Harry grinned. "Hasn't been this full since Mom was alive."

Milk, half-and-half, bottled water, and

Dortmunder beer filled the beverage shelf. Chicken and steak, wrapped in cellophane, rested on another shelf. Fresh lettuce, collard greens, pattypan squash, and perfectly round cherry tomatoes spilled over the vegetable compartment. On the bottom shelf, neatly placed side by side, gleamed red cans of real Coca-Cola.

Stacked next to the refrigerator were a variety of cat and dog canned foods with a few small gourmet packs on top.

"A cornucopia of delight." Pewter flopped on her side, rolling over then rolling back in the other direction.

"He must be rich to buy so much food at once." Tucker admired the canned food, too.

"It is amazing." Murphy purred, too, excited by the sight of all those goodies.

Harry closed the door, turned to wash her hands in the sink, and noticed her yearbook and a 1950 yearbook resting on the table side by side. She opened the 1950 yearbook and saw Tracy's name in youthful script in the upper right-hand page. Strips of paper marked her yearbook. She flipped open to each one. Tracy had marked all the photographs in which Charlie Ashcraft and Leo Burkey appeared.

She closed the book and walked outside toward the sound of the pounding.

Tracy, shirt off, replaced worn fence boards with good, pressure-treated oak boards, piled neatly in one paddock.

"Tracy, you must be a good fairy or whatever the male version is." She smiled.

He pushed back his cowboy hat. "Oak lasts longer."

"Please give me the bill for the wood and the groceries. Otherwise, I'll feel like I'm taking advantage of you."

"I love for women to take advantage of me." He laughed. "Besides, you don't know how good it feels to be doing something. Bet the post office was wild today, wasn't it?"

She knew he'd changed the subject because he didn't want to hear anything more about repayment. "Yes."

"Damn fool thing. I read through your yearbook. I hope you don't mind."

"No."

"Dead bodies don't bother me. Got used to that in Korea. But wanton killing, that bothers me."

"Me, too. Can't make rhyme or reason of this."

"Patience." He lifted another board, she grabbed the far end to help.

"What's that expression, 'Grant me patience, Lord, but hurry.' I recall Mom saying that a lot." She stepped to the side, nearly stepping on Tucker, who jumped sideways. "Sorry, Tucker."

"Cutest dog."

"*Thank you.*" Tucker cocked her head at Tracy.

"Being all over the map, I couldn't keep a dog. Li had one. Well, I guess it was mine, too, but since I was on the road so much it was really hers. Beautiful German shepherd. Smart, too. I knew as long as Bruno was with her, she was safe. You know, two weeks after Li died, Bruno closed his eyes and died, too. Granted he was old by then but I believe his heart was broken." Tracy's eyes clouded over.

"I couldn't live without Mom." Tucker put her head on her paws.

The cats listened to this with some interest but neither one would admit to such excessive devotion. The truth was, if anything ever happened to Harry, Mrs. Murphy would be devastated and Pewter...well, Pewter would be discomfited.

Harry stooped down to pat Tucker's head, since she was whining. "When I was little Mom and Dad had a German shepherd named King. Wonderful dog. He lived to be twenty-one. Back then we had cattle, polled Herefords and some horned Herefords, too, and Dad used King to bring in the cattle. Mom always had a corgi—those dogs herd as efficiently as shepherds. Someday I'd like to get another shepherd but only when I'm certain a puppy won't upset Tucker and the kitties. They might be jealous."

"A puppy! I'll scratch its eyes out," Pewter hissed.

"No, you won't. You'll hop up on the table or chairs. You like babies as much as I do." Murphy laughed at the gray blowhard.

"No, I don't and I don't recall you liking puppies or kittens that much. I recall you telling those two kittens of Blair Bainbridge's ghost stories that scared the wits out of them."

Murphy giggled. *"They grew up into big healthy girls. Of course, we hardly see them since they spend half their life at the grooming parlor."*

Harry lifted another board. She and Tracy were getting into a rhythm. "Corgis are amazing dogs. Very brave and intelligent. Tee Tucker's a Pembroke—no tail. The Cardigans have tails and to my eye look a little longer than the Pembrokes. Pound for pound, a corgi is a lot of dog." She bragged a touch on the breed, a common trait among corgi owners.

"I noticed when I came out back this morning—back of Market's, I mean—that Pewter was in a tree. She could see everything. Mrs. Murphy sat on the squad car. She, too, could see everything, as well as hear the squad radio calls. And Tucker sat just off to the side of the dumpster door. Her nose was straight in the air so she smelled everything. Miranda said it was the animals that called attention to the dumpster."

"I did." Tucker puffed out her white chest.

"True, you have the best nose. I'd bet you against a bloodhound." Mrs. Murphy praised the dog.

"Don't get carried away," Pewter dryly said to the tiger.

"Chatty, aren't they?" Tracy pounded in nails.

"You sure notice everything."

"That's my training. I noticed something else, too. When they pulled the body out of the dumpster there was a stain across the seat of

161

his pants, noticeable, like a crease. The killer sat him on the edge of the dumpster before pushing him back into it. As Leo was a big man and as the crease was pronounced, he sat there for a minute or two at the least before the killer could maneuver the body into the dumpster and close the lid. That's what I surmise. Can't prove a thing, of course. And I asked Miranda if she heard a car back there but her bedroom is away from the alley side of the house. She said she heard nothing. I would assume, also, that the killer was smart enough to turn off his headlights and that Leo Burkey's car will turn up somewhere."

Harry stepped aside as he nailed in the last of the boards. He'd also brought out the fence stain so he could stain them right away. She counted twenty-seven boards that he'd replaced.

"I'll get another brush." She walked to the toolshed where she kept brushes of every shape and size, all of them cleaned and hung, brush side down, on nails. Harry never threw out a paintbrush in her life. By the time she returned he'd already painted one panel.

"It's not going to look right with some freshly painted and the others faded so I'm going to do the whole thing. Now you don't have to work with me. After all, this was my idea, not yours."

"I'd like to work with you. I'm so accustomed to doing the chores alone."

"When was the last time you stained these fences?"

"Eight years ago."

He studied the faded boards and posts. "That's good, Harry. Usually this stuff fades out after two or three years. I pulled five gallons out of the big drum you've got there. I'm impressed with your practicality. Had the drum on its side on two wrought-iron supports, drove a faucet in the front just like a cask of wine. You know your stuff, kid. What is this, by the way?"

"Fence coat black. You can only buy it in one place in the U.S., Lexington Paint and Supply in Lexington, Kentucky. They ship it out in fifty-five-gallon drums. I've tried everything. This is the only stuff that lasts."

"Smart girl." He whistled as he painted, carefully, as he did everything. He was a tidy and organized man. "Is there a connecting link between the two victims?"

"Huh?"

"Leo and Charlie."

"Well, they graduated in 1980 from Crozet High School. They were both handsome. That's about it. They weren't friends. I don't think they saw one another after high school."

"Nothing else? Did they play football together or golf or did they ever date sisters or the same woman? Were they involved in financial dealings together?"

Harry was beginning to appreciate Tracy's ability to construct patterns, to look for the foundation under the building. "No. Charlie wasn't much of an athlete. He thought he was but he wasn't. Leo was much better. He played football and basketball in high school and then he played football in college, too."

163

"Where'd he go?"

"Uh, Wake Forest."

"What about Charlie?"

"He went up north. Charlie was always smart in a business way. He went to the University of Pennsylvania. Charlie had a lot of clients. He was an independent stockbroker. I don't know if Leo was one or not, though I doubt he was."

"Anything else?"

"They were both senior superlatives. I can't see that as much of a connection, though. Not for murder, anyway."

"I saw you had two superlatives."

"I know you were Most Athletic."

"Yep. We have that in common." He smiled at her. "Keep a notebook handy. Has to be little so you can stick it in a pocket. When ideas occur, write them down. No matter how silly. You'd be surprised at what you know that you don't know."

"*Interesting.*" Murphy got up and headed for the barn.

"*Where are you going?*" Pewter enjoyed eavesdropping.

"*Tackroom. I am determined to destroy those mice.*" She flicked her tail when she said that.

Tucker laughed. Murphy stopped, fixing the corgi with a stare, a special look employed by Southern women known as "the freeze." Then she walked off.

"*We'll find the killer or killers before she gets one thieving mouse.*" Tucker laughed loudly.

That quick, Murphy turned, leapt over a star-

164

tled Pewter, bounded in four great strides to the corgi. She flung herself upon the unsuspecting dog, rolling her over. Tucker bumped into the big paint bucket. A bit slopped out, splattering her white stomach.

"Murphy!" Harry yelled at her.

Murphy growled, spit, swatted the dog as she righted herself, then tore toward the barn, an outraged Tucker right after her. Just as Tucker closed the gap, Murphy, the picture of grace, leapt up, and the dog ran right under her. The cat twisted in midair, landed on the earth for one bound, was airborne again as she jumped onto the bumper of the red dually, then hurtled over the side into the bed. She rubbed salt into the wound by hanging over the side of the truck bed as the dog panted underneath.

"Cat got your tongue?"

"Murphy," Tucker said between pants, *"I'll get you for that."*

"Ha ha." Murphy jumped onto the dome of the cab.

The truck, parked in front of the barn entrance, gleamed in the rich late-afternoon light.

Harry laid her paintbrush on the side of the can. "Don't you dare put paw prints on my new truck." She advanced on the tiger, who glared insolently at her, then chased her tail on the cab hood to leave as many paw prints as possible.

Just as Harry reached the door to open it so she could step inside and gain some height to grab the little stinker, Murphy gathered herself together, hunched down, and then jumped way, way up. She just made it into the open hayloft, digging up the side with her back claws as she hung on with her front paws. Her jet stream rocked the light fixture, which looked like a big Chinaman's hat poised over the hayloft opening.

She looked down at her audience. *"I am the Number One Animal. Don't you forget it."* Then she sauntered into the hayloft.

Tracy laughed so hard he doubled over. "That's quite a cat you've got there, Harry."

"Heatstroke," Tucker grumbled furiously.

"More like the big head," Pewter replied.

"I still say she won't catch one lousy mouse."

"Tucker, if I were you, I wouldn't say it any too loudly. Who knows what she'll do next?" Pewter advised.

25

"—everybody."

"That's very edifying." Rick leaned toward BoomBoom sitting opposite him in her living room. "But I'd like to hear the names from your lips."

"Well, Leo Burkey of course, Bonnie Baltier,

Denny Rablan, Chris Sharpton, Bitsy Valenzuela, Harry, Marcy Wiggins, who mostly
stood around, and Susan."

"Then what?"

She shifted in her seat, irritated at his pick-
iness. "Have you interviewed everyone else?"

He counted names on his notepad. "No."

"Are you going to tell me who's left?"

"No. Now, BoomBoom, get on with it.
What did you do, and so forth."

"We were reshooting the senior superlative
which was Wittiest with Bonnie Baltier and
Leo Burkey for the reunion. After we finished, everyone went to the Outback to eat.
Marcy called her husband, Bill, who met her
after work. They're making a point of spending
time together. And Bitsy called her husband,
E.R., to invite him. He took a pass, said he was
tired. Funny, he was such a quiet guy in high
school. To think he'd go out and start a cellular phone company. He has no class spirit,
unfortunately. Neither does Bill."

"No tension at dinner?"

"No, because Harry went home. She doesn't
like me," BoomBoom flatly stated. "And I have
tried very hard to make amends. It's silly to
carry around emotions, negative emotions."

"I wouldn't know." He reached in his pocket
for the red Dunhill pack and offered her a cigarette. "Mind?"

"No. Those are expensive."

"And good. I tried to wean myself off
smoking by buying generic brands. Awful
stuff."

"I have some herbal remedies if you decide to stop again."

"I'll let you know."

"Anyway, nothing much happened. We all ate, told tales, bored Marcy and Chris and Bitsy, but they were gracious about it. Denny flirted with Chris. She didn't seem to mind. Then we went home."

"Did Leo linger with anyone in the parking lot? Talk to a waitress?"

She put her finger to her chin. "He cornered Bitsy for a minute as we left but well, you'd have to ask her. I think they were discussing mutual friends and whether E.R. could give Leo a deal on a cell phone."

"Uh-huh."

"Do you have any leads? I mean surely you've noticed the two victims were killed right after their senior superlative reshoot. That's what bothers me. That and those offensive, cheap mailings!"

"Yes, we have leads." He exhaled, then continued his questioning. "Did anyone wear L.L. Bean duck boots that night?"

"What?"

"You know, the boots that made L.L. Bean famous. We call them duck boots but I guess today that means the short rubber shoe. Short, tall, did anyone wear them?"

"No. That's an odd question."

"Did anyone wear heels? Not spike heels, but say about two inches."

"Do you think I spend my time cruising people's feet?" She laughed.

"I know you are a woman of fashion. I expect you take in everything, BoomBoom."

"Let's see." She studied a spot at the left-hand corner of the ceiling. "Baltier wore white espadrilles. Susan wore navy blue flats, Pappagallo. Susan loves Pappagallo. Bitsy wore a low heel, Marcy wore sandals, Chris wore a slingback with a bit of heel. Harry wore sneakers, as you would suspect, since it's summer."

"Why?"

"Harry wears sneakers in the summer, Bean boots in the rain, or riding boots. Oh yes, and her favorite pair of cowboy boots. That's the repertoire."

"Did she wear her Bean boots?"

"No, I just said, she wore sneakers."

He dropped his eyes to his notes. "So you did."

"How big are the footprints?" BoomBoom asked.

He crossed his arms over his chest, uncrossed them, picked up his cigarette out of the ashtray, taking another drag. "BoomBoom, you don't ask me questions. I ask you."

"I hate to think of Leo like that." Her eyes brimmed suddenly with tears, but then it was well known BoomBoom could cry at a telephone commercial. "He was such fun. He—" She shrugged, unable to continue.

Rick waited a moment. "He was an old friend."

"Yes," came the quiet reply.

"Did you know he was divorcing his wife?"

169

"Yes." She opened her hands, palms upward. "He told us at the Outback. I think he was upset, although Leo always made a joke about everything."

"Will you go to the funeral?"

"Of course I'll go."

"It's in Richmond, isn't it?"

"Yes. St. Thomas. The most fashionable church in Richmond."

"Leo from a good family?" He dropped the verb.

"Yes, but he married higher on the social ladder. His wife is a Smith. The Smiths."

"And I don't suppose they've named any of their daughters Pocahontas."

"Uh..." The corners of her mouth turned upward. "No."

"I expected you to be more upset." He ground his cigarette into the ashtray until tiny brown strands of tobacco popped out of the butt. "You're the emotional type."

"I guess I'm in denial. First Charlie. Now Leo. It's not real yet."

"Did they ever date the same girl?"

"In high school?"

"Any time that you can recall."

"No. Not even from grade school."

"Can you think of anyone who hated Leo?"

"No. His wit could rip like a blade sometimes. But a true enemy? No. And I don't think his wife hated him either. After all, divorce is such a pedestrian tragedy."

"That's poetic."

"Is it?" She batted her long eyelashes at Rick,

not a conventionally handsome man but a very masculine one.

He smiled back. "If you think of anything, give me a call." He stood up to leave and she rose with him.

"Sheriff, do you think Charlie and Leo were killed by the same person or persons?"

"I don't know, and I'm not paid by your tax dollars to jump to conclusions."

She showed him the door and bid him good day.

Later that same day he compared notes with Cynthia Cooper. Between the two of them they had buttonholed everyone who'd been at the shoot that day. Better to catch people as soon after an incident as possible. Rick was a strong believer in that.

They'd found Leo's car still in the parking lot at the Outback. None of the restaurant staff remembered seeing him get into another car, but they had been inside working. The small gathering of friends didn't remember him getting into another car either.

They sat in his office drawing up a flow chart for Leo. Each person's story confirmed what every other person said. There were no glaring omissions, no obvious contradictions.

"Boss, he could have picked someone up after the dinner and gone to wherever they went in their car. Charlottesville is a college town. There's a semblance of night life." Not for her. She fell between the college students and the married, which put her in the minority.

"Could have."

"You think he knew the killer just as Charlie probably did, don't you?"

"If he didn't know the killer I'm convinced the killer is innocuous in some fashion. A nonthreatening person or functionary, you know, like a teacher." He stopped. "Someone you wouldn't look at twice in terms of physical fear. Leo could have been killed by a woman for that matter."

"She'd have to be fairly strong to hoist him into the dumpster," Cynthia said.

"Yes, but it could be done. The man Hunter Hughes saw go into the locker room at Farmington was thin. Average height, but as it was from a distance the man could have been shorter. Doesn't mean it's our killer, and it doesn't mean the same person killed both men. But it's odd."

"That it is."

"Have you talked to Charlie's ex-wives?"

Cynthia cracked her knuckles. "Yes. Finally reached Tiffany, wife number four—don't you love it—'Tiffany,' in Hawaii. Said she'd heard he was shot and she was sorry she hadn't done it herself. When I asked for suspects she said apart from herself, the person who hated him most when she was married to him was Larry Johnson."

"Larry Johnson? That doesn't make any sense." Rick ran his hand over his balding head. "Or maybe it does."

"Abortions. Does Larry perform abortions?"

"He's a general practitioner, so no, he doesn't. But he knows where the bodies are buried, as they say." He noted the clock on the wall, five-thirty in the afternoon. "The best time to talk to Larry is in the morning. Maybe we should both make this visit. Oh, did you talk to Mim yet?"

"Yes, she's fine as long as she knows things before anyone else does."

"I asked BoomBoom about shoes. She remembered everybody's shoes. Another thing: for BoomBoom she was remarkably self-possessed. No vapors. No lace hankies to the eyes and thence to the bosom. Another oddity."

"What do you think of Tracy Raz?" Cynthia asked.

"A trained observer and a damned sharp one at that."

"Ran a check on him. Legit. Korea. A solid Army career, Major when he mustered out and into the CIA."

"If he hadn't pointed out those prints in front of the dumpster before more people walked around I might have missed them. He said nothing. He motioned with his eyes and then turned to push the gawkers back. He's a pro." He slapped his hand on his thigh. "You know what I'm going to do?" She shook her head and he continued. "Take the wife to the movies."

"Good for you." She wished she had someone in her life. She'd go out with a guy but eventually her schedule and work would turn him off. "I'll see you at Larry's office. Seven."

"Yep."

He stopped at the door. "Two footprints next to each other at the dumpster isn't much to go on. The Bean footprint is a man's, size eight and a half or nine. The heel footprint, well, we couldn't tell, since the toe would have been on a rock."

"Could have been a man and woman, side by side, heaving in Leo," Coop said. "He was a short, but stocky man. But then, some of the trash in there was heavier than cartons."

"Some memories are heavier than others, too." He opened the door. "I don't think it's coincidence that Charlie's death came now. And now Leo." He shrugged. "Gotta go."

26

Fair measured Poptart around the girth. He'd dropped by to see how Harry was doing after the shock. He glanced at last week's figures on the chart hanging outside each horse's stall.

Poptart quietly stood in the center aisle. The horse, a big girl, half-closed her eyes.

Mrs. Murphy, sitting on the tack trunk, asked, *"Don't you ever get hungry for meat?"*

"No."

"Not even an eensy piece?"

"Do you get hungry for timothy or for grain?" Poptart's large brown eyes focused on the tiger, now standing on her hind legs to touch noses with the large creature.

"No. You're right. I can't expect you to like what I like and vice versa."

"We like lots of the same things. Just not foods."

"You'll be surprised at how much less grain you'll need to feed her."

"I like my grain," Poptart protested.

"She's an easy keeper." Harry patted the gray neck. "I give her half a scoop, a couple of flakes of hay, plus she's got all that grass to eat."

Fair also patted Poptart on the neck, then led her out to the pasture behind the barn, where she kicked up her heels and joined Gin Fizz and Tomahawk, who had been measured before she had.

"How come you didn't tell me about Tracy Raz?"

"Fair, he just started renting here."

"Seems a good man."

"Miranda likes him. I've noticed she doesn't quote the Scriptures around him as much as she does around us."

Fair laughed as he leaned over the fence. Poptart bucked, twisted, and bucked some more.

They walked back to the house. The evening had begun to cool down. Tracy was calling on

Big Mim. They sat in the kitchen together along with Murphy, Pewter, and Tucker.

"Sure you're okay?" He reached for her hand.

"Yes." She squeezed his offered hand. "It shocked the hell out of me. Both Mim and I about fell over."

"I would have about passed out myself."

"A dead body is bad enough but the"—she paused—"incongruity of it...that's what shocked me."

"It looks like this reunion might be, uh... eventful."

"Well, that's just it." She grew suddenly animated. "I don't remember anything from high school. I mean I don't remember some awful thing that would provoke revenge. Especially senior year, the big one."

"Yeah. I can't remember anything either. But maybe something did happen in your senior year. You know how sometimes things are vague or you're on the edges of it? Obviously, I was a freshman in college. All I remember from that year is missing you."

"I wrote you a letter a day. I can't believe I was that disciplined." She laughed.

"Maybe you loved me," he softly suggested.

"I did. Oh, Fair, those were wonderful and awful times. You feel everything for the first time. You have no perspective."

"You had some perspective by the time we married. I mean, you dated other men."

She patted his hand, removed hers, then

noticed the animals, motionless, had been watching them. "Voyeurs."

"Interested parties." Murphy smiled.

"If this is going to get mushy I'm leaving," Pewter warned.

"Bull. You're as nosy as we are." Tucker giggled.

"I feel like we're the entertainment tonight." Fair spoke to the animals.

"You are," Pewter responded.

"They're my family," Harry said.

"So am I. Like it or not." Fair leaned forward in his chair.

"Can you remember how you felt back then? The wild rush of emotion? The sense of being your own person?"

"I remember. People grow in lots of different ways. Sometimes they stop. I think Charlie stopped. Never got beyond high school. Leo got beyond it but his defenses stayed the same: shoot from the hip. Susan has matured." He thought for a moment. "I think I have, too."

"Have I?"

"Yes, but you won't trust anyone again."

"I trust Mrs. H. I trust Susan."

"I should have said men. You won't trust men."

"I trust Market."

"Harry, you know what I mean. You won't trust men as romantic partners. You won't let a man into your life."

"I guess." Her voice sounded resigned.

"You know, I dropped by tonight to see

177

how you were—check the horses, too. I don't know if it's your reunion or because I'm getting close to forty...the murders or that this late summer has been uncommonly beautiful, but whatever it is—I love you. I have always loved you, even when I was acting a fool. And I think you love me. Love me the old way. Down deep."

She stared into his clear light eyes. Memories. Their first kiss. Dancing on the football field to the car radio. Driving to colonial Williamsburg in Fair's old 1961 Chevy truck. Laughing. And finally, loving.

"Maybe I do."

"Equivocal?"

"I do."

He leaned across the table and kissed her.

"It would be more romantic if they'd wash one another's heads," Pewter advised.

"They're not cats," Mrs. Murphy said.

"Nobody's perfect." Tucker burst out laughing.

27

At seven in the morning a haze softened the outline of trees, buildings, bridges. Rick Shaw and Cynthia Cooper, in separate vehicles, pulled into the paved driveway to the doctors' offices. Johnson & McIntire, a brass plaque, was discreetly placed next to the dark blue door.

The white clapboard building looked like the house it once was. Back in the early fifties, Larry Johnson bought it and the house next door, where he continued to live.

Larry, slightly stooped now, his hair a rich silver, opened the door himself when the officers of the law knocked.

"Come in, come in." He smiled genially. "If you all are up as early as I am, it must be important. The murders, I suppose."

"Yes." Rick closed the door behind him as they followed Larry into his office covered with a lifetime of service awards and his medical diploma.

"Can I get you all some coffee?"

"No, no, thank you. We're already tanked." Deputy Cooper fished her notebook from her back pocket.

"Larry." Rick called the doctor by his first name as did most people. "You knew Charlie Ashcraft and Leo Burkey."

"I delivered them. In those days you did everything. G.P. meant just that."

"You saw them grow up?" Rick stated as much as he asked.

"I did."

"And you would therefore have an assessment of their characters?"

"I think so, yes." Larry leaned back in his chair. "Are you asking for same?"

"Yes. I took the long way around." Rick laughed at himself.

"Charlie was a brilliant boy. Truly brilliant. He covered it up as any good Southern gentleman would do, of course. His success in the stock market didn't surprise me as it did others. He was upright in his business dealings. Even as a child he was interested in business, and honest. As you know, his downfall was women. He was like most men who were spoiled and coddled by a mother. They go through the rest of their life expecting this treatment and what amazes me is there is always a large pool of women willing to be used. But if you separated Charlie from the woman thing, he was a decent man."

"What about Leo?" Coop asked.

"Strong. Even as a child, quite physically strong. A pleasing boy. You had to like him. Another good-looking kid, not as dramatically handsome as Charlie but good-looking. I saw little of him after he left for college and then moved to Richmond."

"Did these two have anything in common that you could see?"

"No."

"What about medically? Was there anything they both suffered from? Depression or something?"

"No. Not as far as I know. After all, I stopped being Leo's doctor after high school. Both boys had the usual round of strep throat, flu, chicken pox. But nothing out of the ordinary."

"Could either man have infected sex partners with venereal diseases?" Rick was zeroing in on the area he sensed would be most fruitful.

Larry put his hands behind his head, leaning back. He glanced at the ceiling, then back at the two before him. "As you know, the relationship with a patient is confidential."

"We know, but both patients are dead and I hope and pray these murders are at an end. But Larry, what if? I've got to find out everything I can. Everything."

Larry's voice dropped as he brought his hands back on his desk. "Rick, the two men don't have anything in common medically. Again, I haven't seen Leo Burkey as a patient since he graduated from college, which had to be, well, 1984 or 1985, I guess."

Cynthia checked her notes. "Right. 1984."

"So there are no illegitimate children from high-school days? No follies?"

"Not for Leo. Again, not under my care. Charlie, as you would imagine, was quite a different matter."

"Yes," Rick said. "Tiffany said you'd know everything."

"She did, did she?" Larry shook his head. "Life is too short to be so unforgiving. Of all Charlie's ex-wives and ex-flames she's the one who hates the most. It will destroy her in the end."

"Could you be more specific?" Cynthia tried to hide her impatience.

"He fathered a child after graduating from high school. The child was put up for adoption. The rumor always was that he fathered the child in high school but it was during his college days. That was the beginning of a

181

career of sexual irresponsibility that rivals that of any rock star. He refused to use any form of birth control. He believed if a woman went to bed with him that was her responsibility. He used to say, 'If she's dumb enough to want the baby, she should have it.' That sort of thing. He slept with so many people he contracted genital herpes, which he happily passed along. I treated him for gonorrhea eight times in his lifetime. Curiously, he never contracted syphilis."

"What about AIDS?"

Larry leveled his gaze. "Yes. At the time of his death he was HIV-positive but showing no signs. He had resources and could afford every new drug that came down the pike, plus, apart from the sexual risks he took, he kept himself in good shape."

"He could have infected others?" Cynthia was scribbling as fast as she could.

"Could and did."

"Will you give us their names?" Rick knew he wouldn't.

"I can't do that."

"Any of them married?"

"Yes."

"Brother." Rick sighed.

"The husband doesn't know and I suppose he won't know until he discovers he's infected or his wife shows symptoms. People can be HIV-positive for years and not know it. This virus mutates, it alters its protein shell. In a strange fashion it's an intelligent virus. Every day we learn more but it's not enough."

"Charlie slept with woman A. Did she become positive immediately?"

"I don't honestly know. Yes, I can't give you a hard and fast answer. We do know of cases where an uninfected person has repeated contact with an infected person, sexually, and does not contract the disease. There's a famous case of two female cousins, African-American, who are prostitutes. They have been repeatedly exposed to AIDS, yet remain immune. The other oddity is that different people show clinical signs of infection at different times. A fifteen-year-old boy may show signs quite soon after becoming positive whereas a thirty-five-year-old man might not show any for years. It's puzzling, infuriating, and ultimately—terrifying."

Rick and Cynthia sat silent.

Cynthia finally spoke. "Does the woman know she's HIV-positive?"

"Yes. One is in denial. I see that quite often when a person learns they have a disease for which there is no cure. Flat denial." He folded his arms across his chest, glanced at the ceiling. "The other woman died last year. There were two. There may be more but I've only treated two. I'm not the only doctor in town."

"I see." Rick clasped and unclasped his hands.

"People are capable of great evil—even nice people. Life has taught me that. Korea opened my eyes and then general practice did the rest." He paused. "Having said that,

183

I think I'm a good judge of character. The woman still alive would not kill Charlie Ashcraft. I really believe that. I don't think Leo Burkey is even in the picture on this one."

"Would Charlie Ashcraft ever sleep with men?" Cynthia surprised both men by asking what to her was obvious: Charlie and Leo could have been lovers.

A considered moment followed. Larry cleared his throat. "Under the right circumstances, yes. Charlie was driven—and I mean *driven*—by sex. He was irrational and irrationality is always dangerous. We tend to laugh off sexual dysfunction in men, especially if it's of the aggressive variety, satyriasis."

"Beg pardon?"

"The male version of nymphomania," Larry answered Cynthia.

"Oh."

"We laugh and tell jokes about what a stud he is but in fact he's sick. In Charlie's case he was sick in body as well as in mind."

"Did Tiffany know about the AIDS?" Rick inquired.

"He was not infected when they were divorced, which was three years ago. Charlie became HIV-positive shortly thereafter and displayed no signs of the disease. In other words, he was HIV-positive but he had not yet developed full-blown AIDS. I don't know if Tiffany knew about it. She would, of course, know about the genital herpes and she no doubt suspected there were unclaimed children along the way."

"More than the one?" Cynthia was surprised, although on second thought she wondered why.

"Yes—but only one lives here. The others were out of town."

"My God, did he provide for them or anything?" Like most women, Cooper had a strong maternal streak and couldn't understand how some men could be so callous concerning their offspring.

"As far as I know he didn't do squat." Larry rose from his chair and sat on the edge of his desk before them. "We're professionals. You and I see things most people do not see and don't want to see. We aren't supposed to be emotional. Well, I fail because there were times when I could have killed Charlie myself— and yet, I liked the guy." He held up his hands.

"Larry, the mother might have strong motivation to kill Charlie."

"Not now. The child is in the late teens and in no danger from infection. Charlie became HIV-positive seventeen years after the child's birth. As for the other women, why kill him now? Furthermore, Rick, the murders of Charlie and Leo appear to be by the same person. Yes?"

"Yes."

"The connection is the answer and I don't have it." He cleared his throat. "When do you get the autopsy report on Leo?"

"Not until next week. Everyone is on vacation. The coroner's office is shorthanded."

"Would you like me to call in and ask for special blood work?"

"Yes, thank you. If they both were HIV-positive that would be a beginning."

"I'll call them right now. We can talk to them together." He glanced at the clock on his desk. "Someone will be there by now."

The rest of the day Cynthia Cooper thought about the young person in Crozet. She hoped the person would have Charlie's looks and his brilliance but not his grotesque irresponsibility. Then she thought how she looked at people every day but didn't really see them. They were all accustomed to one another. If there was a resemblance to Charlie, she'd missed it.

28

The slight drone of a bumblebee, growing stronger by the moment, irritated Mrs. Murphy to the point where she opened one glittering green eye. The marvel of insect engineering zoomed closer. She batted at it with a paw but the large black and yellow creature zigged out of the way.

"*Losing your touch,*" Tucker laconically commented.

"*Bull. I'm lying on my side. If I'd been sitting*

up that bomber wouldn't have had a chance. 'Course, if I'd been sitting up she wouldn't have come near me."

"Yeah, yeah," Tucker, also on her side under a hydrangea bush, said.

Mrs. Murphy sat up. "Where's Pewter?"

"In the post office. Leave the air conditioning? Ha!"

The sweltering heat intensified. Mrs. Murphy and Tucker had left the post office to scrounge around Miranda's garden in the late morning. It didn't seem so hot then but they couldn't find anything of interest despite a soft, lingering chipmunk scent, so they fell asleep.

BoomBoom's elegant BMW rumbled down the alleyway. She parked behind the post office, getting out of the driver's side as Marcy Wiggins and Chris Sharpton emerged from the passenger and rear doors.

Chris glanced over at the dumpster and shuddered.

"Guess I shouldn't have parked here." BoomBoom's hand flew to her mouth. "I didn't think of it. I haven't processed all this emotionally. I mean, I still have such unresolved—"

"Let's go inside." Chris cut her off before BoomBoom's lament could gather steam.

Marcy kept staring at the dumpster. "I heard he was covered in maggots."

"No." Chris shook her head. "Stop this."

Marcy began shaking.

Tucker and Mrs. Murphy crept to the edge of Miranda's yard to listen more closely.

"Marcy, are you going to be sick?" Boom-Boom moved toward her to help.

"No, no, but I can't take this. People talking behind our backs. Talking about Bill killing Charlie. Talking about me and Charlie. This is a vicious little town!" She burst into tears. "I wish we'd never moved here. Why did I let Bill talk me into this? He wanted to come home. He said he'd be head of oncology faster in Charlottesville than in some huge city."

BoomBoom put her arm around the frail woman. "Things will get better."

Chris put her arm around her from the opposite side. "People gossip in big cities, too."

"But you can get away from them. Here, you're"—she gulped for air—"trapped. And I'm not working on your high-school reunion anymore! I'm sorry but it's too dangerous."

"Marcy, that's okay," BoomBoom soothingly said. "But this awful stuff doesn't have anything to do with our reunion. It's some bizarre coincidence. Come on, let's get you in the air conditioning. Harry will let you sit in the back while you, uh, regain your composure."

Marcy allowed herself to be led into the post office.

"*Gossip.*" Tucker shook her head. "*People would be much improved if their tongues were cut out of their heads.*"

"*Maybe.*" Mrs. Murphy yawned.

"*If I say red, you say black. If I say apples you say oranges. You're contrary.*"

Mrs. Murphy smiled. "*Sometimes I am, I guess. It's the feline in me.*"

"*Bum excuse.*"

"*Gossip is ugly stuff said about people behind their backs. But people, being a herd animal, need to be in touch. They need to talk about one another. There's good talk and bad talk but think about it, Tucker, the worst thing that can happen to a human being is not to be talked about,*" Murphy expounded.

"*Never thought of that,*" Tucker replied.

"*Follow me.*"

The dog padded after the cat, the small pieces of gravel hot in the sun. They stopped in front of the dumpster. The yellow cordoning tape had been removed.

"*Nothing left.*"

"*I'm not so sure. Let's look where they put the plaster casts. See, there's little bits of plaster left in the indentations.*"

"*I see that,*" the dog crabbily said as she stared at the chain-link heel mark from the Bean boot and the high-heel mark not far from it.

"*Left foot and right.*"

"*Could be anybody's and these marks may have nothing to do with Leo's demise but if Rick Shaw took plaster casts we ought to pay some atten-tion to them. They're close together.*"

"*Like two people, you mean. One holding him on the left side and one on the right. That's why the heel mark is deep on this right side.*"

"*It's a possibility.*"

"*So that means there are two people in on this.*"

"*That, too, is a possibility.*" She lifted her head, sniffing the air. "*Rain coming.*"

Tucker sniffed. *"Tonight."*

"The bullet into Leo's forehead was fired at close range. And the humans are saying that means he knew who killed him. But who else, I mean, what manner of stranger, would a man allow close to him?"

"A child."

"Or a woman."

"Ah, the two marks. A woman. She kills him and her male partner helps dispose of the body."

"I don't know, but I'm leaning that way."

"It could have been Marcy and Bill Wiggins."

"Could have been Laurel and Hardy, too."

"There you go again. Smartmouth." The dog headed toward the animal door of the post office.

The cat came alongside, brushing against her friend. *"You're right. I'm awful."* She walked a few steps, then stopped. *"What bothers me is that we're missing something and I won't feel reassured until we know it. I don't like that Mom knew these two as well as she did."*

"She wasn't romantically involved with either of them."

"For which we should be grateful."

"And no women have been killed."

"Grateful for that, too."

Tucker blinked, then sneezed. *"Lily pollen."*

"It's on your coat, too."

"Don't want Miranda to know I was in her lilies."

"Roll in the dirt."

"Then I'll get yelled at."

"Better to be yelled at for that than for creeping through the lily beds."

190

"You're right." Tucker rolled over.

When they slipped through the animal door no one noticed them, since everyone was ministering to Marcy Wiggins.

Tucker crawled under a mail cart. Mrs. Murphy hopped into it, landing on a recumbent Pewter, who jumped up, spitting and hissing.

"Pewts, Pewts, I'm sorry," Murphy laughed.

Pewter, not yet in a forgiving frame of mind, lashed out, cuffing Mrs. Murphy on the cheek.

Mrs. Murphy returned the favor and soon the mail cart was rolling, thanks to their violence. Tucker's rear end stuck out behind the cart.

"Hey, you two!" Harry clapped her hands over the mail cart, which diverted the cats' attention. Then her eye fell on a dirty corgi behind. "What have you done?"

"Nothing," came the meek reply.

"Fleas," Mrs. Hogendobber declared. "Rolling in the dirt because of fleas."

"Guess it means a bath and flea powder when we get home." Harry sighed.

"Thanks, Murphy," Tucker growled.

"How was I to know?" she said, then whispered to Pewter what had happened. Pewter giggled.

"It's like having children," Chris laughed.

"Marcy, feeling better?" Mrs. Hogendobber offered her more iced tea.

"Yes, thank you." She nodded, then turned to Harry. "I told BoomBoom and Chris I'm not working on your reunion anymore. Who knows what will happen next?"

"I understand." Harry didn't believe in trying to convince people to do what they didn't want to do.

"And I'll thank you all to stop talking about me."

"We aren't talking about you." Harry wrinkled her brow, puzzled.

"Everyone is. You think I don't know." She stood up and whirled on BoomBoom. "And don't tell me I need to drink chamomile tea or some other dipshit herbal remedy! You all think I'm having marital problems. You think I slept with Charlie Ashcraft and—"

"Marcy, you need to go home." Chris grabbed her friend under the elbow, pushing her out the back door as Marcy continued to babble.

"Paranoid," BoomBoom flatly said.

"That's a pretty harsh judgment," Harry countered.

"Call it what you like then."

"Well, BoomBoom, try to see it from her point of view. She doesn't have the advantage of being one of us," Harry said.

"*Right now I'd say that was not such an advantage,*" Pewter called out from the mail cart.

"Boom, you seem out of sorts today." Miranda hoped to calm the waters.

"I am." She glared at Harry. "Cynthia Cooper called on me this morning before I left for golf and do you know what she asked me? If I had had any illegitimate children with

Charlie Ashcraft or if I had any sexually transmitted diseases!"

"How come you're yelling at me?"

"Because you baited her into it."

"Boom, I don't know anything about such... matters."

"Well, you obviously think my life is one big promiscuous party!"

"Girls." Miranda held up her hands. "I do wish you two would make some kind of peace."

"Peace? She nips at me like a Jack Russell. Sex. Always sex. Right, Harry?"

"Wrong." Harry's face darkened as the animals watched, fascinated. "I haven't said a word to Cynthia, and why would I even think about venereal disease? God, BoomBoom."

"Then who did?"

Miranda looked heavenward. "Please, dear Lord, don't send anyone into the P.O. for a while." She returned to the battling pair. "Time out. Now you two sit down, be civil, and discuss this or I am throwing you both out. Do you hear me?"

"Yes, ma'am," they both said, startled at Miranda's vehemence.

"Sit down." She pointed to the table. They sat. "Now, questions such as BoomBoom is asking do not come out of the blue. Instead of accusing Harry, why don't you both think back. Think back as far as you have to go."

They sat mute.

Harry fingered the grain on the old table. "Remember in our junior year, people whispered that Charlie got someone pregnant."

BoomBoom thought about it. "Yes, but no one left school."

"If the baby was due at the end of the summer she might not have had to leave," Miranda said. "Some women show less than others."

"There's always gym class. If someone was packing on the pounds, we'd know," Harry said.

"Did anyone get an excuse from gym class?"

"Lord, I don't know. That was twenty years ago."

"Perhaps it wasn't someone at your high school. There's St. Elizabeth's, or it may have been someone already out of school," Miranda offered.

"That's true. Cynthia must be getting desperate, running down ancient rumors." BoomBoom folded her arms across her ample chest.

"Charlie's death could have old roots."

"Twenty years is a long time to get even," BoomBoom said.

"Depends on how angry you are," Mrs. Murphy said. *"Someone hurt badly enough might live their entire life waiting for revenge."*

"What do you want in there?" Harry called out to the cats in the mail cart.

"Nothing. We're trying to help," Murphy replied.

"There were rumors about Charlie right up to the present." BoomBoom softened somewhat. "I'd heard that he'd gotten AIDS. Heard that at the club. He'd slept with some society queen in Washington, no surprise, but I heard she died a year ago. The papers hushed it up. Said she had heart failure."

"Did you tell Coop?"

"Yes. And I also told her that anyone infected with the AIDS virus by him could be mad enough to kill."

"A mother wishing to protect a child might also have plenty of motivation," Miranda added. "But it's a dreadful thing to do. I would think the child would find out who her father was, sooner or later."

"Her?" Harry looked quizzically at Miranda.

"Him."

"Do you know something we don't?" Boom-Boom's voice grew stronger.

"No, I don't. But remember your Bible. Numbers. Chapter thirty-two, Verse twenty-three. 'Be sure your sin will find you out.'"

Chris popped her head back in the door. "BoomBoom, if you need more time, I'll run Marcy home. She's having a hard time."

BoomBoom rose. "I'll be right there." She paused before Miranda. "Do you think it's a sin to have a child out of wedlock?"

"No. I think it's inadvisable but not a sin. To me the sin is in not caring for the child."

BoomBoom silently opened the door and left.

"Miranda, you surprise me."

"You thought I'd say the woman should be stoned?" The older woman smiled ruefully. "Harry, I've lived long enough to know I can't sit in judgment of anyone. So many young women out there want to be loved and don't know the difference between sex and love."

"Then what sin were you referring to when you quoted Numbers?"

"Oh." She dropped her head for a moment. "The sin of cruelty. The sin of bruising another's heart, of abandoning someone to pain that you have caused. The sin of careless-ness and callousness and self-centeredness. I don't know what Charlie's sins were, I mean, other than gossip. And I certainly don't know what Leo's sins were, but someone out there feels he or she has suffered enough."

29

"You're sure you want to do this?"

Mrs. Hogendobber tossed her head. "Absolutely. I used to be on the lacrosse team." She paused. "Granted that was some time ago but my athletic abilities haven't completely eroded."

Tracy placed two skateboards on the macadam surface. The parking lot at the back of the grade school was empty. Nobody dri-ving by would see them, which was just how Miranda wanted it.

"H-m-m." He gingerly put one sneakered foot on the board to test the rollers.

Knee guards, elbow guards, and helmets made the two senior citizens look like creatures from outer space, or perhaps older space.

"Before I hop on, how do I stop?"

"Make a sharp turn in either direction and as you slow, tip the nose forward. At least, I think that's what you do."

"M-m-m." She breathed in. "Here goes." She put her right foot on the back of the board, her left foot on the front. Nothing happened.

Tracy, now aboard himself, coached, "Push off with your right foot."

She reached down and shoved off with more force than she had intended. "Whoa!"

Mrs. H. rolled along the level parking lot, her arms outstretched to balance her, laughing and hollering like a third-grader.

Tracy pulled alongside. "Not bad for our first time out!"

"Harry is going to die when I fly past her in the hallway."

"Cuddles, you won't be able to wait until the reunion. You'll surprise her before then." He started to wobble and hopped off.

"I thought you said turn sharply." Which she did.

"Didn't take my own advice." He bent over to pick up the skateboard. "I'll do it right this time." He hopped back on, pushed off, then practiced a stop. "I get it. Twist from the waist."

Miranda, watching him, tried it. She lurched to the side but didn't lose her balance. "Stopping is harder than moving on."

"Is in skiing, too."

"I don't know how young people go down

banks, circle around in concrete pipes." She recalled footage she'd seen on television.

"We don't have to do that." He laughed as he rolled along even faster.

She picked up the skateboard, examined the brightly colored rollers, put it back on the macadam, and got on again. "You know, I don't do enough things like this. Oh!" She picked up speed.

"You're busy every minute. That's what Harry says." He executed another stop, better this time.

"Sedentary stuff. I need to get out more. Maybe then I'll lose a little weight. I don't know how you managed to keep your figure. I guess for men we don't say figure."

"Thank you, ma'am, but you look good to me."

"I don't believe you, but I love to hear it." She stopped. "I'm quite out of breath."

"Walk. You don't have to jog. Walking will do the trick. And if you really want to lose weight cut out the fats and sugars."

"Oh dear." She grimaced.

"It's either that or exercise for three hours a day. I work out for an hour in the gym, always have. Now that I'm doing farmwork, I'm getting double workouts."

She twisted her lower body and did a turnabout, didn't have enough speed and slipped off but caught herself, merely falling forward with three big steps. "Say, that's hard."

He tried it. "It is."

"How do you like Harry? They say you

never really know someone until you live with them."

"I like her fine. She's paying off her ex-husband for the old truck, you know. Hard-headed, isn't she? He just redeposits the check in her account and then they fight about it."

"Has a fear of obligation. Whole family was like that. But she especially doesn't want to be beholden to him. He dropped by and told me he'd had a talk with Harry. He says he's going to aggressively win her back."

"Faint heart ne'er won fair lady." He crouched low to pick up speed. "This is fun, you know?"

"Yes, it is. Hate the helmet, though."

"They are weenie but your head is precious—Precious." He called her "Precious," then stood up, slowed down, and hopped off while the skateboard kept going. "Those babies are well balanced."

"And so are you."

They both laughed as Miranda cut sharply to the right and neatly stepped off.

A siren far away pierced the late-afternoon quiet.

"Heading east," Miranda observed.

Within a few moments another siren attracted their attention. A squad car roared down from Whitehall, past the grade school, into town. Then it, too, headed left.

"Good heavens, what could it be this time?" Miranda wondered.

Harry, tape measure around Tomahawk, heard the phone ring in the tackroom. She ignored it, then gave in.

"Hello."

"Marcy Wiggins has shot herself." Susan Tucker's voice had none of its customary lilt.

"What?"

"Shot herself in the temple with a .38. Bitsy Valenzuela found her when she stopped by to pick up a picnic hamper she'd lent Marcy."

"When?"

"About an hour ago. Maybe longer. Bill Wiggins called Ned asking for legal representation in case it isn't a suicide. Bill was the first person Rick questioned, too. That's all I know."

"Is she dead?"

"Yes."

"That poor woman." Harry put her hand to her temple. "She was definitely strange at the post office yesterday. Chris and Boom-Boom took her home. She said everyone was talking about her and she couldn't stand it. Stuff like that. I should have paid more attention. Did she leave a note?"

"I don't know. Ned left the instant he hung

up the phone. I believe this has something to do with Charlie."

"Yeah," Harry weakly replied. "What a September this has turned out to be."

31

Marcy's autopsy report revealed she had been HIV-positive. This, of course, was kept confidential. Leo Burkey's autopsy revealed him to be robustly healthy.

But the real shocker was when ballistics tests proved the gun that Marcy used to kill herself was the same one used to kill Charlie and Leo.

People assumed Marcy had been having an affair with Charlie. He tired of her. She snapped. Others said Bill killed Charlie but there was no evidence to link Bill to her demise. Rick and Cooper had been thorough on that count. She couldn't live with her guilt for betraying her husband. No one could figure out why she wanted to do in Leo but the scientific fact remained: it was her gun.

She did leave a suicide note which simply said, "I can't stand it anymore. Forgive me. Marcy."

The rest of September passed with no more murders. People breathed a sigh of relief.

The plans for the reunion remained in full swing. Dennis Rablan dated Chris Sharpton, which set tongues wagging. Some people thought she was wasting her time. Others thought he was dating her in hopes of getting her to wisely invest what little he had left. A few thought they made a cute couple. Dennis was happy again. Market asked her out once but she gracefully declined, saying she was focusing on Dennis. Blair Bainbridge dated Little Mim under the glare of a silently disapproving Big Mim. Everyone remarked how well they danced together but not in front of Big Mim, of course. The speculation on Blair and Little Mim was even hotter than the gossip concerning Dennis and Chris.

Harry went to the movies every Wednesday night with Fair, Tracy, and Miranda. However, she was in no hurry to get closer to her ex, but she did draw closer to Tracy—closer than she could have imagined. Theirs was a father-daughter sort of relationship. He, wisely, never asked about her romantic status with Fair, figuring sooner or later she would discuss it.

Once the sirocco of gossip died down, Crozet returned to normal. Mim bossed everyone about—but she was gaining more support for her gardening project. BoomBoom obsessed about the reunion. Harry was doing a great job on publicity. Susan had the caterers lined up. One for breakfast and lunch, a different one for dinner only because two of the participants ran catering businesses.

The horses gained weight on the alfalfa

cubes. Harry had to cut back on the amount she was feeding them.

Pewter actually lost some weight during the September heat wave. Everyone commented on how good she looked.

Tucker endured a flea bath once a week.

Mrs. Murphy refused to accept that Marcy Wiggins had killed two men. No one paid any attention to her, so she finally shut up. Murphy kept repeating that she *"wasn't the type."* It was Leo Burkey's murder that kept Murphy on alert.

She crouched in the tackroom just to the side of a mouse hole on this beautiful early-October day. Pewter walked in, as did Tucker.

"Hear anything?" Pewter inquired.

"They're singing again."

Tucker cocked her head. *" 'The Old Gray Mare'—where do they get these old songs?"*

"Beats me." Mrs. Murphy, disgusted, shook her head. *"I'll figure that out just about the time I figure out the murders."*

"Oh, Murph, don't start that again. It's over and done." Tucker put her head flat on the tackroom floor as she tried to peer into the mouse hole.

"All right, but I'm telling you, something is coming out of left field. Just wait."

Pewter, opinionated, said, *"Why would a murderer jeopardize himself after getting off scot-free? I mean, if it wasn't Marcy, why would that person kill again?"*

"Because the job isn't finished."

Tucker gave up on seeing the mice. *"Murphy, you always say that murders are committed over love or money. Marcy had the love angle."*

203

"*No one was robbed. Nix the money,*" Pewter chipped in.

"*Remember the humans thought there might be an insurance payoff, but Leo left no insurance and Marcy's policy was quite small. No trust funds either,*" Tucker said.

"'*...she ain't what she used to be, ain't what she used to be...*'" The mice boomed out the chorus.

"*I hate them.*" Mrs. Murphy's striped tail lashed back and forth.

"*Let's go outside. Then we don't have to listen,*" Pewter sensibly suggested, and the three animals trotted to the roses at the back of the house.

"*Great year for roses.*" Pewter sniffed the huge blooms.

"*Silly refrain, 'ain't what she used to be many long years ago,*'" Murphy sang the chorus. Much as she scorned the song, she couldn't get it out of her head.

32

Crozet's citizens walked with a snap in their step. They were two days from a big weekend.

Crozet High would play Western Albemarle for Homecoming. The class of 1950 was having its fiftieth reunion and the class of 1980 was celebrating its twentieth.

The Apple Harvest Festival would follow that, filling up the following week.

Fall had arrived with its spectacular display of color and perfect sixty-degree days, followed by nights of light frost.

Everyone was in a good mood.

Harry sorted the mail. She liked the sound the paper made when she slipped envelopes into the metal post office boxes. She tossed her own mail over her shoulder. It scattered all over the floor.

Miranda glanced at the old railroad clock hanging on the wall. "Another fifteen minutes and Big Mim will be at the door." She pointed to Harry's mail on the floor. "Better get that up."

"*Not yet!*" Pewter meowed as she skidded onto the papers.

Mrs. Murphy followed.

"*Copycat,*" Tucker smirked.

"*If this were a dead chicken you'd be rolling in it.*" Murphy bit into a brown manila envelope.

"*Of course.*" Tucker put her nose to the floor so her eyes would be even with Murphy, now on a maniacal destruction mission.

"*Dead chickens!*" Pewter pushed a white envelope with a cellophane window deeper into the small pile of increasingly tattered paper.

Harry knelt down. Two pairs of eyes, pupils huge, stared back at her. "Crazy cats."

"*Sorry human,*" Pewter replied.

"*You can't say that.*" Tucker defended Harry.

"All humans are sorry. Doesn't mean I don't love her. Oh, this sounds divine." Pewter sank her fangs into the clear address panel and it crackled.

"Tucker, you take life too seriously." Murphy had stretched to her full width over the mail.

"Enough." Harry started pulling papers from underneath the cats, who would smack down on the moving paper with their paws. "Let go."

"No," Pewter sassed.

"She's a strong little booger." Harry finally pulled out a triple-folded piece of paper, stapled shut. Four claw rips shredded the top part. The staple popped off as she pulled on a small piece of paper attached to it.

Harry opened what was left. A small black ball, no message, was in the middle of the page. She checked the postmark: 22901, the main post office in Charlottesville. "Looks like another one."

"Oh, no." Miranda hurried over. "Well, I don't know."

"I'll check the other boxes."

Her classmates each had a letter, too.

Miranda was already dialing Rick Shaw.

Big Mim knocked at the front door. Harry unlocked it, letting her in at eight A.M. on the dot.

"Good morning, Harry."

Miranda hung up. "Morning, Mim."

"Look." Harry showed Big Mim the mailing.

"Not very original, is he?" Mim sniffed, as she held the torn paper in her gloved hands.

"No." Harry sighed. "But each murder occurred after each mailing."

"Call Rick?"

"Just did," Miranda said.

"Whoever this is seems determined to spoil your reunion." Mim tapped the countertop.

"He already has, in a way. We won't be talking about what we've learned in twenty years or remembering the dumb things we did in high school. We'll be talking about the murders." Harry was angry.

" 'Enter by the narrow gate; for the gate is wide and the way is easy, that leads to destruction, and those who enter it are many.' " Miranda quoted Matthew. Chapter seven, Verse thirteen. "I don't know why that just popped into my head."

33

Streamers dangled from clumps of shiny metallic balloons, hanging like bunches of grapes. Mrs. Murphy and Pewter raced around the gym, leaping upwards to bat the strings. Tucker sat under a ladder watching the reunion crew frantically hanging the blown-up photo posters of the senior superlatives.

A light frost covered the ground with a silvery glaze. The gym, large and unheated for decorating, proved chilly. Fortunately, it would be heated in the morning.

Harry and Chris had set up three long tables by the entrance. These they covered with white tablecloths. Sitting on the tablecloths were beautifully marked stand-up cards for each letter of the alphabet. In neat piles in front of the alphabet cards were the identification badges for each returning class member. Each badge, on the upper left-hand side, carried a small photograph of the individual from high-school days. This had proved costly, causing another row between Harry and BoomBoom, but even Boom admitted, once she saw the badges, that it was effective. Some people change so much that the high-school photograph would be the only way to recognize them.

Susan brought sandwiches. Always organized, she had arranged the food for the two-day celebration but she'd even thought of the hard work the night before. They only had Friday night in which to prepare, since Crozet High was in use throughout the week.

BoomBoom surprised everyone by having the photo frames built weeks before. Every balsa-wood frame was numbered, as were the low baskets in the shape of a running horse, the centerpieces on the table.

T-shirts were rolled and wrapped with blue and gold raffia. Disposable cameras, one for each participant, were also in the baskets, along with items from local merchants. Art

Bushey threw in Ford key chains. Blue Ridge Graphics gave a deep discount on the T-shirts. The baseball caps, on the other hand, were on sale to raise money to pay for cost over-runs. The T-shirts were meant to be money raisers but Bob Shoaf, who'd made a bundle in pro football, contributed the money for them so no one would be left out in case they hadn't enough money for mementos.

Harry's job was over. She'd stepped up publicity with each succeeding week. She'd done radio spots, appeared on Channel 29 Nightly News—along with BoomBoom, who never could resist a camera. She'd created clever newspaper ads using the mascot and pictures from 1980.

Local bed-and-breakfasts, as well as one hotel chain, offered discounts for returning members of the class of 1980 as well as the class of 1950.

Out of one hundred and thirty-two sur-viving classmates, seventy-four had sent in their deposits, as well as complaints about the strange mailings.

For Mrs. Hogendobber the return rate was one hundred percent. A fiftieth high-school reunion was too special to miss.

"Looks good." Harry admired the entrance tables. "It's simple. There's nothing to knock over. No centerpiece. They can pick up their badges and go."

"Now, where's the pile of badges for people you couldn't think of, I mean, you couldn't think of anything to say. You'll have to think fast," Chris said.

"They're here in this paper bag on my seat." Harry nervously pointed to the bag. "But I don't know if I'll be able to think of anything."

"Well, since I have no preconceived notions, I'll pop over from time to time and whisper in your ear—things like 'He looks like a warthog!'" She smiled. "Got your dress?"

"Yes. Miranda and Susan hauled me to town. Only have to wear it to the dance. I'm not wearing it the rest of the time."

A whoop from the hallway diverted their attention.

"Harry! You owe me ten dollars," Miranda's voice rang out.

Harry, along with the animals, hurried out into the long, polished hallway to behold Miranda on a skateboard, Tracy just behind her.

"I don't believe it!"

"Ten dollars." Miranda triumphantly held out her hand.

"Did I say ten dollars?" She grinned, then fished in her pocket. She'd forgotten the bet but vaguely remembered a crack about Miranda not being able to skateboard.

"She can do wheelies," Pewter remarked.

"Frightening, isn't it?" Tucker guffawed. *"That's a lot of lady to hit the ground."*

As though she understood the corgi, Miranda pushed off with her right foot and headed directly for the dog, who had the presence of mind to jump out of the way.

Mrs. Murphy said, *"She's lost a lot of weight, Tucker. There's not so much lady to hit the ground. But still..."*

210

"Sweetest ten dollars I ever made." Miranda held up the green bill after stopping.

Tracy stepped off his skateboard to put his arm around Miranda. "This girl practiced. She can even go down hills now."

"Mrs. H., you're something else." Harry laughed.

"Never underestimate the power of a woman." Miranda again waved the ten dollars in the air as Susan, BoomBoom, and Chris entered the hallway to see what was going on.

"*Hee hee.*" Mrs. Murphy, eyes gleaming, hopped on Miranda's skateboard, rolling a few yards down the hallway.

"Human. That cat is human," Chris marveled.

"*Don't flatter yourself.*" Mrs. Murphy got off, made a circle at a trot, then hopped on again, picking up a little speed.

Miranda finally took the skateboard from her, putting it behind the door of the cafeteria. Murphy would have pushed it out to play some more but Harry scooped her up to take her home. She was tired, even though the name-tag display hadn't been that trying. It was the anticipation that was exhausting her, that and a tiny ripple of dread.

34

Heart racing, Harry threw another log on the fire in the bedroom fireplace. She crawled into bed, finding the sheets cold. Then she crawled out, grabbed a sweatshirt, pulled it over her head, and slid back under the covers. Keeping an old house warm was a struggle, especially for Harry, who watched her pennies.

"Will you settle down?" Pewter grumbled from the other pillow.

The dry cherry log slowly caught fire, releasing a lovely scent throughout the room.

Harry tilted the nightstand light toward her, picked up her clipboard and reviewed tomorrow's agenda. Mrs. Murphy, cuddled on her left side, observed. Tucker was stretched out in front of the hearth, head on her paws.

"Okay. The tables are already set alongside the gym for breakfast. Susan's having the food delivered at seven-thirty. Bonnie Baltier said she'd be here in time to help me man the check-in table. She understands she has to write something, anything on the name cards with names only on them. The band will set up tonight when we go home to change. Amazing how many amps those electric guitars and stuff suck up. And I suppose we'll all hold BoomBoom's hand, who's really supposed to be in charge, but by now is Miss Basketcase Crozet High." She parked her pencil behind her right ear. "My second superlative photo didn't turn out so badly. I think it's better than BoomBoom's."

"*Me, too,*" Tucker called up to her.

"*Just don't draw a mustache on BoomBoom's, Mom—or at least wait until the end of the reunion.*"

"Mrs. Murphy, maybe I'll put a blue and gold bow on you for the festivities."

"*Won't she be fetching,*" Pewter meowed.

"*Don't be catty,*" Murphy rejoined.

"*Ha, ha,*" Tucker dryly commented.

"You guys are a regular gossip club tonight." Harry scanned her clipboard, then put it on the nightstand. She put her right hand over her heart. "My heart is thumping away. I don't know why I'm so nervous. I wasn't nervous at our fifteenth reunion." She stroked Murphy's silken head. "People know I'm divorced. Oh, I'm not really nervous about that. They can just hang if they don't like it. I'm hardly the only person in our class who's suffered romantic ups and downs. Don't know. Of course, how many divorced people are dating their exes? Guess it's seeing everybody at the same time. Overload."

"*Sure, Mom,*" Mrs. Murphy purred, closing her eyes.

She snatched her clipboard again. "Fair said he'd be there as a gofer. Everyone will be glad to see him. Half the girls in my class had a crush on him. I think he wants to be there—in case." She again spoke to Mrs. Murphy since Pewter had curled up in a ball, her back to Harry. "Say, can you believe Miranda on that skateboard? Or you, Murphy."

"I can do anything."

"Oh, please." Tucker rolled on her side. *"Why don't you two go to sleep. Tomorrow's going to be a long, long day."*

As if in response, Harry replaced the clipboard and turned out the light.

35

Screams echoed up and down Crozet High School's green halls as classmates from 1980 and 1950 greeted one another. Southern women feel a greeting is not sufficiently friendly if not accompanied by screams, shouts, flurries of kisses, and one big hug. The men tone down the shouts but grasp hands firmly, pat one another on the back, punch one another on the arm, and if really overcome, whisper, "Sumbitch."

Harry, up at five-thirty, as was Tracy, finished her chores in record time, arriving at the school by seven. Tracy picked up Miranda so he arrived at seven-fifteen. Everything was actually organized so Harry sat next to Bonnie

Baltier checking people in. Dennis Rablan, three cameras hanging around his neck, took photographs of everyone. Chris assisted him with long, smoldering looks as she handed him film.

Tucker sat under Harry's legs while Mrs. Murphy defiantly sat on the table. Pewter ditched all of them, heading toward the cafeteria for Miranda's reunion. The food would be better.

The class of 1950 arranged tables in a circle so everyone could chat and see one another. Pewter zoomed into the cafeteria, which was decorated with blue and gold stallions built like carousel horses and fixed to the support beams. Miranda had said that Tracy was working on something special but no one realized it would be this special. The beams themselves were wrapped with wide blue and gold metallic ribbons. The room was festooned with bunting. The cafeteria actually looked better than the gym with its huge photographs, then and now, and blue and gold streamers dangling from huge balloon clusters.

Best, to Pewter's way of thinking, was the breakfast room itself. Miranda had sewn blue and gold tablecloths. On each table was a low, pretty, fall floral bouquet.

Pewter noticed Miranda's and Tracy's skateboards resting behind the door. She also noticed that this reunion, forty-two strong, was quieter. There were more tears, more genuine affection. One member, a thin man with a neatly trimmed beard, sat in a wheelchair. A few others needed assistance due to the vicissitudes of injury or illness. Apart from that, Pewter thought that most of the class of 1950 looked impressive, younger than their years, with Miranda glowing. She'd lost twenty-five pounds since the beginning of September and Pewter had never realized how pretty Miranda really was. She wore a tartan wrap-around skirt, a sparkling white blouse, and her usual sensible shoes. She also smiled every time she glanced at Tracy. He smiled at her a lot, too.

"Pewter Motor Scooter!" Miranda hailed her as the gray cat dashed into the room. "Welcome to the class of 1950."

"What a darling cat. A Confederate cat." A tiny lady in green clapped her hands together as the gray cat sauntered into the room.

"We work together," Miranda laughed, telling people about Pewter's mail-sorting abilities while feeding her sausage tidbits.

"I am so-o-o happy to be here," Pewter honestly said.

About ten minutes later Harry ducked her head into the room. "Hi, everybody. Aha, I thought I'd find you here."

"I like it here!"

"Folks, this is Doug Minor's girl—remember Doug and Grace Minor? Grace was a Hepworth, you know."

Martha Jones, quite tall, held out her hand. "I know your mother very well. We were at

Sweet Briar together. You greatly resemble Grace."

"Thank you, Miss Jones. People do tell me that."

"Your mother was the boldest rider. She took every fence at Sweet Briar, got bored, jumped out of the college grounds, and I believe she jumped every fence on every farm on the north side of Lynchburg."

People laughed.

Miranda said, "Mary Minor is a wonderful rider."

"Thanks, Mrs. H., but I'm not as good as Mom. She was in Mim's class."

"Where is Mimsy?" the thin man in the wheelchair bellowed.

"I'm here. You always were impatient, Carl Winters, and I can see that little has changed that." Mim swept in dressed in a buttery, burnt-sienna suede shirt and skirt. "You know, I wish I had graduated from Crozet High. Madeira wasn't half as much fun, but then, all-girls schools never are."

"You're really one of us, anyway." A plump lady kissed Mim on the cheek.

"I'll take my thief back to the gym," Harry said while the others talked.

"She can stay. She'll come back anyway. It's fine."

"*Please, Mom.*" Pewter's chartreuse eyes glistened with sincerity.

"Well...okay," Harry lowered her voice, leaning toward Miranda. "Your decorations

217

are better." She raised her voice again. "Tracy, the carousel horses are spectacular!"

She left them smiling, talking, eating Miranda's famous orange sticky buns.

She ran into Bitsy Valenzuela and Chris Sharpton dragging an enormous coffee urn down the hall.

"Guys?"

"BoomBoom called me on the car phone and told me she was panicked. There wasn't enough coffee so we dashed over to Fred Tinsley's, which got Denny's nose out of joint since Chris was assisting him. I had to promise Fred six months free on his car phone to get this damn thing. E.R. will kill me," Bitsy moaned. "Is he here yet?"

"Yes, he brought miniature flashlights shaped like cell phones."

"That's my E.R. for you: ever the marketer."

"Would you like me to take a turn here? That looks heavy," Harry offered.

"Why don't you run in and get someone strong—like a man—to do this. That's what men are for." Bitsy gave up and slowly set down her side of the urn, as did Chris.

"Are we still allowed to say stuff like that?" Chris giggled.

"Yeah, among us girls we can say anything. We just can't say it publicly." Bitsy laughed, "Nor would I admit to E.R. that I need him. But I do need him."

Harry dashed into the gym, returning with Bob Shoaf, Most Athletic, who had played for seven years with the New York Giants as cornerback. Apart from having a great body, Bob wasn't hard to look at. He was, however, blissfully married, or so the newspapers always reported.

"Girls, you go on. I'll do this." He hoisted the urn up to his chest. "You two should look familiar to me but I'm afraid I can't place you."

"They helped us all summer and fall, Bob, but these two lovely damsels aren't from our class. Bitsy Valenzuela—Mrs. E. R. Valenzuela—and Chris Sharpton, a friend."

"Forgive me if I don't shake hands." He carried the urn into the gym, where BoomBoom greeted him as though he had brought back the Golden Fleece from Colchis.

Bitsy and Chris stopped inside the door. "It's odd."

"What?" Bitsy turned to Chris. "What's odd?"

"Seeing these people after staring at their yearbook pictures. It's like a photograph come to life."

"Not always for the best." Mrs. Murphy lifted her long eyebrows. The class of 1980 had been on earth long enough for the telltale spider veins in the face to show for those who drank too much. The former druggies might look a bit healthier but brain cells had fried. A poignant vacancy in the eyes signaled them. A lot of the men were losing their hair. Others wore the inner tube of early middle age, not that any of them would admit that middle age had started. Nature thought otherwise. Bad

219

dye jobs marred a few of the women but by and large the women looked better than the men, testimony to the cultural pressure for women to fuss over themselves.

Bonnie absentmindedly stroked Mrs. Murphy as she double-checked her list. Everyone had checked in except for Meredith McLaughlin, who wouldn't arrive until lunch. Harry rejoined her while Chris joined Dennis, wreathed in smiles now that she was back.

"Done." Bonnie put down her felt-tip pen.

"You're a fast thinker. I should have remembered that." Harry smiled. "When you came up with 'Secret Life, Televangelist' for Dennis Rablan, I could have died. That was perfect. Even he liked it!"

"Had to do something. What do you put down for the Best All-Round who has..." She shrugged.

"Zipped through a trust fund and unzipped too many times," Harry laughed.

"And then there's you. Most Likely to Succeed and Most Athletic, running the post office at Crozet," Bonnie said.

"I guess everyone thinks I'm a failure."

"Not you, Mom, you're too special." Tucker reached up, putting her head in Harry's lap.

"No." Bonnie shook her head. "But if there were a category for underachiever, you'd have won. You were, and I guess still are, one of the smartest people in our class. What happened?"

Harry, dreading this conversation, which would be repeated in direct or subtle form over the next day and a half, breathed deeply. "I made a conscious choice to put my inner life ahead of my outer life. I don't know how else to say it."

"You can do both, you know," remarked Baltier, successful herself in the material world. She ran an insurance company specializing in equine clients.

"Bonnie, I was an Art History major. What were my choices? I could work for a big auction house or a small gallery or I could teach at the college level, which meant I would have had to go on and get my Ph.D. I never wanted to do that and besides I married my first year out of college. I thought things were great and they were—for a while."

"I'm rude." Baltier pushed back a forelock. "I hate to see waste. Your brain seems wasted to me."

"If you measure it by material terms, it is."

"The problem with measuring it in any other way is that you can't."

"I think it's time we join the others. I'm hungry."

"You pissed at me?"

"No. If BoomBoom had asked me I'd be pissed." Harry then nodded in the direction of an attractive woman on the move up, one face-lift to her credit, holding court by the pyramid of Krispy Kreme doughnuts. "Or her."

Deborah Kingsmill, voted Most Intellectual, truly thought she was superior to others because she was book-smart and because she'd escaped her parents. And that's exactly where her intelligence ended. She'd never learned that people with "less" intelligence possessed other gifts.

Deborah and Zeke Lehr, the male Most Intellectual, were pictured together reading a big book in Alderman Library. Zeke owned a printing business in Roanoke. He'd done well, had three kids and kept himself in good shape. He was pouring himself a second cup of coffee while listening to BoomBoom discuss the sufferings of organizing the reunion.

"Hey, thanks for your work." Rex Harnett, already smelling like booze, kissed Harry on the cheek.

"You know, it turned out to be fun," Harry admitted to the broad, square-built fellow, who had been voted Most School Spirit and would easily have qualified for Most School Spirits.

"Fair coming?"

"He is but he's probably on call this morning. He'll get here as soon as he can. He's as much a part of our class as his."

"You two getting back together?"

"Not you, too!" Harry mocked despair.

"I have personal reasons. You see, if you aren't interested in the blond god then I'd like to ask you out."

"Rex?" Harry was surprised and mildly revolted.

Tucker, on the floor, was even more surprised. *"He's to the point. Gotta give him credit for that."*

"I thought you were married."

"Divorced two years ago. Worst hell I've ever been through."

"Rex, I'm flattered by your attention"—she eased out of his request—"but we aren't the right mix."

He smiled. "Harry, you can say no nicer than any woman I know." He glanced across the room. "The redhead and the blonde look familiar but I can't place them."

"Bitsy Valenzuela, E.R.'s wife."

"The other woman?"

"Chris Sharpton. She moved here from Chicago and she and Bitsy helped us organize."

"Market looks the same. Less hair," Rex said. "Boom's the same."

"She's beautiful. She's surrounded by men," Harry flatly stated.

Bonnie Baltier, having grabbed a doughnut, joined them, as did Susan Tucker.

"Isn't this something?" Susan beamed.

"We've all got to go down the hall and congratulate the class of 1950," Harry suggested. "After breakfast. You can't believe how they've decorated the cafeteria."

"We can see ourselves thirty years from now." Rex smiled.

Bonnie was staring at the huge superlative photos. "You know who I miss? Aurora Hughes. What a good soul."

"I suppose with each reunion we'll miss a few more," Rex bluntly said.

"What a happy thought, you twit." Bonnie shook her head.

"Hell, Baltier, people die. For some, Charlie could have died even earlier."

Susan asked, "Remember the rumor that Charlie had an illegitimate child in our junior year?"

Rex shrugged. "Yeah."

Harry said, "Guys talk. You say things to each other you wouldn't say to us. Any ideas on who the mother was—or is, I should say?"

"No," Rex replied. "He dated a lot of girls. Raylene Ramsey was wild about him but she didn't leave school and she didn't gain weight. Wasn't her."

"Yeah, we thought the same thing," Susan said.

Bonnie dabbed the sugar crumbs from the corners of her mouth. "It doesn't matter. Let's concentrate on the good times."

"I'm for that. When's the bar open?" Rex held up his coffee cup.

"Six o'clock."

"I could be dead by then." He laughed as Bitsy, Chris, Bob, and Dennis joined their group. He slipped a flask from his pocket, taking a long swig.

"If you keep drinking the way you do, that's a possibility." Baltier let him have it.

"S-s-s-s." Rex made a burning sound, putting his finger on her skin.

36

By nine-thirty the whole group, including Fair, were called to attention by BoomBoom.

"Ladies and gentlemen, may I have your attention."

She didn't immediately get it.

Bob Shoaf cupped his hands to his lips. "Shut up, gang!"

The chatter frittered away, and all eyes turned toward BoomBoom, standing on a table. Modestly dressed by her standards, in a blue cashmere turtleneck, not too tight, a lovely deep-mustard skirt, and medium-height heels, she presented an imposing figure. She exuded an allure that baffled Harry, who saw BoomBoom as a silly goose. Harry wrote it off to the awesome physical asset that had given Olivia Ulrich her nickname. This was a mistake.

Women like Harry had a lot to learn from women like BoomBoom, who prey on male insecurities and unspoken dreams. Harry expected everyone, including men, to be rational, to know where lay their self-interest and to act on that self-interest. No wonder Mary Minor Haristeen was often surprised by people.

"Welcome, class of 1980." BoomBoom

held out her hands as if in benediction. As the assemblage roared she turned her palms toward them for quiet. "All of us who worked on this reunion are thrilled that all of you have returned home. Mike Alvarez and Mignon, his wife, flew all the way from Los Angeles to be with us, winning Most Distance Traveled." Again the group roared approval.

As BoomBoom spoke the homilies reserved for such occasions, Harry, standing at the back with Mrs. Murphy and Tucker, surveyed her class. They were a spoiled generation.

Unlike Miranda's generation, who emerged from the tail end of World War II only to be dragged through Korea, Harry's generation knew the brief spasm of Desert Storm. Luckily they had missed Vietnam, which forever scarred its generation.

Everyone expected and owned one or two vehicles, one or more televisions, one or more computers, one or more telephones including mobile phones. They had dishwashers, washers and dryers, workout equipment, stereo systems, and most had enough money left over for personal pleasures: golf, riding horses, fly-fishing in Montana, a week or two's vacation in Florida or Hawaii during the worst of winter. They expected to send their children to college and they were beginning, vaguely, to wonder if there'd be any money left when their retirement occurred.

Most of them were white, about ten percent were black. She could discern no difference in expectations although there were the obvious differences in opportunities but even that had improved since Miranda's time. Walter Trevelyn, her Most Likely to Succeed partner, a café-au-lait-colored African-American, did just that. He was the youngest president of a bank in Richmond specializing in commercial loans, a bank poised to reap the rewards of the growth Richmond had experienced and expected to experience into the twenty-first century.

About half the class was working class, a gap in style as much as money, but those members also had one or more vehicles, televisions, and the like.

The sufferings her generation endured were self-inflicted, setting apart the specters of gender and race. She wondered what would happen if they ever really hit hard times: a great natural catastrophe, a war, a debilitating Depression.

Susan slid up next to her. "You can't be that interested in what BoomBoom is saying."

Harry whispered back, "Just wondering what our generation will do if the proverbial shit hits the proverbial fan."

"What every other generation of Americans has done: we'll get through it."

Harry smiled a halfway funny smile. "You know, Susan, you're absolutely right. I think too much."

"I can recall occasions where you didn't think at all," the tiger cat laconically added to the conversation.

Tucker, bored with the speeches, wandered to the food tables to eat up the crumbs on the floor.

"Harry!" BoomBoom called out.

Harry, like a kid caught napping in school, sheepishly blinked. "What?"

"The senior superlatives are asked to come forward."

"Oh, BoomBoom, everyone knows what I looked like then and now. You all go ahead."

Susan, her hand in the middle of Harry's back, propelled her toward the two big photographs as she peeled off to stand in front of her superlative, Best All-Round. Under the old photo the caption read Susan Diack. Under the new one, Susan Tucker. She glanced up at her high-school photograph. She and Dennis Rablan sat on a split-rail fence, wearing hunting attire, a fox curled up in her lap. Unlike Harry, she had changed physically. She was ten pounds heavier, although not plump. It was rather that solidness that comes to many in the middle thirties. Her hair was cut in the latest fashion. As a kid she had worn one long plait down her back. Dennis had grown another four inches.

Harry first stood at the Most Athletic, sharing a joke with Bob Shoaf, whom she liked despite his silly swagger. Then she dashed over to Most Likely to Succeed with Walter Trevelyn, who gave her a kiss on the cheek.

Everyone laughed as the superlatives laughed at their own young selves.

Then BoomBoom walked from her superlative, Best Looking, to Most Talented. "Folks, let's remember Aurora Hughes. Hank, what do you remember most about Aurora?" She turned to Hank Bittner, the Most Talented.

"Her kindness. She had a way of making you feel important." He smiled, remembering the girl dead almost twenty years.

Hank, talented though he was as a youth, had prudently chosen not to keep on with his rock band. Instead he moved to New York, began work in a music company, and had risen to become a powerful maker and breaker of rock groups.

Next BoomBoom walked to Most Popular. Meredith McLaughlin, late because of a prior commitment, had just skidded under her photographs. She glanced up at herself, young and old, and twice her former size to boot.

"Was that really me?" She hooted.

"Yes!" The group laughed with her.

"Meredith, what do you remember most about Ron Brindell?"

"The time he decided to wear a burnoose to class because we were studying the Middle East. Do you all remember that?" Many nodded in assent. "And old Mr. DiCrenscio pitched a fit and threw him out of class. Ron marched to Mr. Thomson, our principal, and said it was living history and he'd protest to the newspaper. Funniest thing I ever saw, Mr. Thomson trying to pacify both Ron and Mr. DiCrenscio."

"Thank you, Meredith."

She then walked over to Wittiest, where Bonnie Baltier muttered something under her breath, although by the time the tall woman reached her she was all smiles.

"What do you remember about Leo Burkey?" BoomBoom asked.

"His smart mouth. He got mad at Howie Maslow once and told him he could use his nose for a can opener."

People tittered. Howie Maslow, class president of 1978, had a nose like a hawk's beak. In fairness to Leo, the power had gone to Howie's head.

Then BoomBoom walked back to her own superlative and looked up at Charlie in 1980 and 2000. "He was always gorgeous. He was highly intelligent and fun. He had a terrific sense of fun. As to his weakness, well, who among us shall cast the first stone?"

A dead silence followed this until Hank Bittner called out, "I'll cast the first stone. He made my life miserable. Stole every girlfriend I ever had."

Everyone erupted at once. BoomBoom paled, waving her hands for people to quiet.

Finally, Fair, the tallest among them, bellowed, "Enough, guys, enough."

"Shut up, Fair, you're '79," Dennis Rablan hollered.

"Doesn't matter. Speak no ill of the dead." Market Shiflett defended his friend, Fair.

"Dead? Did they drive a stake through his heart? I'm sorry I missed the funeral," Bob Shoaf sputtered, and it was an amusing sight seeing a former cornerback and probably a man eventually to be inducted into the Hall of Fame, sputter.

"I'd like to find whoever shot him and give the guy a bottle of champagne," Hank called out.

The women silently observed the commotion among the men and without realizing it they gravitated together in the center of the room.

"This is going to ruin our reunion." Boom-Boom wrung her hands.

"No, it won't. Let them get it out of their systems." Bitsy Valenzuela comforted Boom.

"People don't hold back here, do they?" Chris's eyes never left the arguing men.

Harry picked up Mrs. Murphy, who reached up at her to pat her face. "Boy, I haven't seen Market Shiflett this mad in years."

Market stood toe-to-toe with Bob Shoaf, shaking his fist in Bob's face. Rex Harnett stepped in, said something the ladies couldn't hear, and Market pasted him right in the nose. Dennis, like the paparazzo he longed to be, got the picture.

BoomBoom implored Harry, "Do something."

Harry, furious that BoomBoom expected her to solve the problem while she stood on the sidelines, stalked off, but as she did an idea occurred to her.

She walked to the corner of the room where Mike Alvarez had set up the dance tapes he'd made for the reunion. A huge tape deck, professional quality, loaded and ready to go, gave her the answer. She flipped the switch and Michael Jackson's "Off the Wall" blared out.

She coasted back to the women. "Okay, everyone grab a man and start dancing. If this doesn't work we'll go down the hall and visit the class of 1950. Maybe we'll learn something."

BoomBoom glided up to Bob Shoaf. Harry, with a shudder, took Rex Harnett. Chris paired off with Market Shiflett to his delight, Bitsy wavered then chose Mike Alvarez. Susan took Hank Bittner. Once all the men were accounted for, the place calmed down, except that Fair Haristeen strode up, tapping Rex on the shoulder.

"No," Rex replied.

"A tap on the shoulder means the same thing everywhere in the world, Rex."

"Lady's choice. I don't have to surrender this lovely woman even though you so foolishly did."

Fair, usually an even-tempered man but possibly overheated from the men's debacle, yanked Rex away from Harry.

Rex, fearing the bigger man, slunk to the sidelines, bitching and moaning with each step. Hank Bittner laughed at Rex as he passed him. In the great tradition of downward hostility, Rex hissed, "Faggot."

Shoaf, with his lightning-fast reflexes, tackled Rex as Fair grabbed Hank. The two combatants were hustled by their keepers outside the gym, Rex screaming at the top of his lungs. Tracy Raz, hearing the commotion, left his own reunion to assist Fair with Hank.

Although the music played the dancers stopped for a moment.

Chris was appalled. "Is that guy a Neanderthal or what?"

Harry said, "Neanderthal."

"What's he talking about?" Susan asked Dennis. "Calling Hank a faggot."

Dennis, lips white, replied, "I don't know."

37

Chris Sharpton headed for the door as Bitsy grabbed E.R. by the wrist, pulling him along to go outside.

BoomBoom hurried to them. "Don't let this bother you. It's just part of a reunion, confronting and resolving old issues."

"Hey, my reunion wasn't like this," Chris replied. "Then again, it's good theater. Bad manners but good theater."

E.R. stared. "BoomBoom, I don't believe old issues ever get resolved. It's all bullshit."

"Don't get started, E.R.," Bitsy said again, pulling her husband along. "I have to get my purse out of the car."

Chris watched them go down the hall, then followed.

Mrs. Murphy sauntered past BoomBoom. *"Ta ta."*

Harry, who hadn't heard E.R. tell Boom what he thought in plain English, followed her cat. Tucker had already zipped down the hall after Fair.

Harry walked down the hall to the far end, away from the parking lot, and pushed open the front doors. Fair and Hank stood under a flaming yellow and orange oak tree. Tucker sat at Fair's feet.

"Don't say it."

"I'm not saying anything." Harry tightly smiled as Hank shoved his hands in his pockets, his face red.

"Are you sufficiently calmed down?" She spoke to her old high-school friend.

"I suppose." He smiled. "It's funny. I live in New York City. I come back and it's like I never left."

Mrs. Murphy breathed in the October air for the day was deliciously warm, the temperature in the middle sixties. Tucker, far more interested than she was in these emotional moments, stayed glued to Fair. The tiger cat hitched her tail up with a twitch and a jerk.

"I'm going to walk around a little bit."

"I'm staying here," Tucker announced.

"Okay." Mrs. Murphy walked toward the back of the school. As she passed the parking lot she noticed Bitsy and E.R. heatedly talking at their car. Chris, carrying a large box of

reunion T-shirts, pushed open the school doors with her back. They'd already sold out one box of T-shirts. Chris was resigned to being a gofer. She ignored Bitsy and E.R.

"You can stay, I am going!" Bitsy, hands on hips, faced her husband.

"Ah, honey, come on. It will get better."

Pewter circled the building from the other end. At the sight of the tiger cat, Pewter broke into a lope.

"You won't believe it." Her white whiskers swept forward in anticipation of her news. *"Rex Harnett is back there carrying on like sin. I mean, he needs to have his mouth inspected by the sanitation department."*

"Because of Hank?"

Pewter puffed out her chest. *"Hank, Charlie, Dennis, you name it. He's, uh, voluble."* She opened her right front paw, unleashed her claws, then folded them in again. *"Mostly it's babble about how he couldn't make the football team and was elected Most School Spirit as a sop. Get a life! He did say that he knows who Charlie got pregnant."*

"Well?"

"Nothing. He needed to sound important. I don't think he knows squat. Tracy Raz got disgusted and went back to his reunion. His parting words were 'Grow up.'"

"I'm not sure what really started the fight but I do know that Rex Harnett may be a drunk but that doesn't mean he's totally stupid. Maybe he does know something."

"Rex is hollering that he's no homosexual."

Pewter loved the dirt. *"Bob Shoaf told him to shut up. If Rex were homosexual, homosexuals would be grossed out. Pretty funny, really."*

"I thought you were in the cafeteria with the golden oldies." Mrs. Murphy turned in a circle, then sat down.

"I ran out with Tracy. The hall amplifies noise." Pewter paused for effect, returning to the scene outside with Rex: *"Then, and I tell you I about fell over, Rex started crying saying that no one ever liked him. He did not deny being a drunk, however. Are they all nuts or what? I thought reunions were supposed to be happy. Miranda's is. Anyway, Rex stormed off to the men's room. I think Bob walked around to the other side of the school to find Fair and Hank."*

"The hormone level is a lot lower at Miranda's." The tiger smiled. *"They're just animals, you know. That's what so sad. They spend their lifetime denying it but they're just animals. I can't see that we act any worse when our mating hormones are kicking in than they do."*

"Paddy proves that," Pewter slyly said, making an oblique reference to Mrs. Murphy's great love, a black tom with white feet and a white chest, a most handsome cat but a cad.

"If you think you're going to provoke me, you aren't. I'm going back inside. Who knows, maybe someone else will blow up or reveal a secret from the past."

Pewter had hoped for a rise out of Murphy. *"Me, too."*

They bounced onto the steps of the side door. The old, two-story building had a front door with pilasters, a back door into the gym, and two side doors which were simple double doors.

One side door was propped open. They walked down the main hall toward the gym.

Susan Tucker, Deborah Kingsmill, and Bonnie Baltier barely noticed the cats as they walked by them.

"—ruin the whole reunion."

"They'll get over it," Susan replied.

"I wish everyone would stop speculating about who Charlie got pregnant. I fully expect everyone to sit down with their yearbooks and scrutinize every female in the book from all three classes. That's not why we're here and anyway, nothing anyone can do about it."

"Baltier, people love a mystery," Susan said.

"No one even knows if it's true," Deborah Kingsmill sensibly replied. "Because he was so handsome people make up stories. If it isn't true they want it to be true. It's like those tabloid stories you read about superstars drinking lizard blood."

The women laughed.

"*What's so strange about drinking lizard blood?*" Pewter asked.

"*Pewter.*" Mrs. Murphy reached out and swatted Pewter's tail.

As the cats laughed and the three women headed back to the gym, Harry came into the hall from the front door.

Before the cats could run to her and Tucker, a shout from the men's locker room diverted their attention. Dennis Rablan threw open the door, stepped outside, leaned against the wall and slid down. He hit the floor with a thump. He scrambled up on his hands and knees, tried to clear his head and stood upright.

As Susan, Bonnie, and Deborah ran to him from one direction, Harry and Tucker ran from the other.

"Call an ambulance," Dennis croaked.

38

"Don't go in there." Dennis barred the way as Harry and Susan moved toward the men's locker-room door.

"They'll never notice us. " Mrs. Murphy slipped in since the door was easy to push open. Pewter and Tucker followed.

They ran into the open square where the urinals were placed. Three toilet stalls were at a right angle to the urinals. A toilet stall door slowly swung open, not far.

"There. " Pewter froze.

Rex Harnett's feet stuck out under the stall door.

"I'll check it out. " Tucker dashed under the adjoining stall, then squeezed under the opening between the two stalls.

Mrs. Murphy, unable to contain her famous curiosity, slipped under from the other stall since Rex was in the middle one.

"*He's dog meat,*" Mrs. Murphy blurted out, then glanced at Tucker. "*Sorry.*"

"*You'd better be.*"

"*What is it? What is it?*" Pewter meowed. Being a trifle squeamish, she remained outside.

Face distorted, turning purple, Rex's eyes bulged out of his head; the tight rope around his neck caused the unpleasant discoloration. His hands were tied behind his back, calf-roping style, quick, fast, and not expected to hold long. Between his eyes a neat hole bore evidence to a shot at close range with a small-caliber gun. No blood oozed from the entry point but blood did trickle out of his ears.

"*Fast work.*" Murphy drew closer to the body. "*What does your nose tell you?*"

"*What is it!*" Pewter screeched.

"*Shot between the eyes. And trussed up, sort of, scaredy cat.*"

"*I'm not scared. I'm sensitive,*" Pewter responded to Murphy, a tough cat under any circumstances.

Although the odor of excrement and urine masked other smells as Rex's muscles had completely relaxed in death, Tucker sniffed the ankles, got on her hind legs and sniffed the inside of the wrists, since his arms were turned palm outward.

"*No fear smell. This is a fresh kill. Maybe he's been dead fifteen minutes. Maybe not even*

240

that, Murphy. So if he had been terrified, I'd know. That scent lingers, especially in human armpits. " She reached higher. *"No. Either he never registered what hit him, or he didn't believe it. Like Charlie Ashcraft. "*

"And Leo Burkey. " The sleek cat emerged from under the stall to face a cross Pewter.

"I am not a scaredy cat. "

"Shut up, Pewter. " Murphy smacked her on the side of the face. *"Just shut up. You know what this means. It means the murders* are *about this reunion. And it means that Marcy Wiggins didn't kill Charlie. She may have been killed because she got too close. We can't discount her death as suicide. "*

"What are we going to do?" Tucker, upset and wanting to get Harry out of the school, whimpered.

"I wish I knew. " Murphy ran her paw over her whiskers, nervously.

"We know one thing. " Pewter moved toward the door. *"Whoever this is, is fast, cold-blooded, and wastes no opportunities. "*

"We know something else. " Tee Tucker softly padded up next to the gray cat. *"The murderer wants the attention. Most murderers want to hide. This one wants everyone to know he's here. "*

"That's what scares me. " Murphy solemnly pushed open the door as the humans from both reunions piled into the highly polished hallway.

39

Harry could hear the wheels of the gurney clicking over the polished hall as Diana Robb carted away Rex Harnett's body. Her stomach flopped over, a ripple of fear flushed her face. She took a deep breath.

"Damnedest thing I ever saw," Market Shiflett said under his breath.

Harry and Market walked into a classroom only to find Miranda, Tracy, and others there from the other reunion. The two cats and dog quietly filed in. Mrs. Murphy sat in the window ledge in the back, Pewter sat on Harry's desk, and Tucker watched from just inside the doorway.

Within moments, BoomBoom entered. "After all our hard work. Twenty years ruined."

"Really ruined for Rex," Harry said, but with no edge to her voice.

"Well...yes," BoomBoom said after a delay.

Susan ducked into the room. "Most people are filing back into the gym. Cynthia Cooper is herding us in there. I guess we'll be questioned en masse."

"Lot of good that will do." BoomBoom ran her forefinger through her long hair. "The murderer isn't going to confess. After all, any of the men could have killed Rex." Because she didn't protest that the murder had nothing to do with the reunion, meant she'd accepted the fact that it was connected.

"So every man is a suspect?" Harry's voice rose in disbelief.

"Girls, this won't get you anywhere." Miranda's lovely voice shut them up. "Whatever is going on presents a danger to everyone, but we can't let the killer erode the trust we've built over the years. The way to solve these heinous crimes is to draw closer together, not farther apart."

"You're right," Susan said.

"What if one of us were to see the killer? How long do you think we'd live?" BoomBoom trembled.

"*Not long,*" Pewter answered.

"Let's not give way to fear," Market advised. "Hard not to, I know."

"Maybe the person who did it got away. That's why Cynthia and Rick want us in the gym, to count heads." BoomBoom allowed herself a moment of wishful thinking.

Tracy leaned toward her. "Whoever did this is *in* the gym."

"Come on then, let's get it over with." Harry marched out of the classroom.

"*Come on.*" Mrs. Murphy tagged behind as Pewter and Tucker followed, too.

"If there's a killer in there, I'm not going." BoomBoom's voice rose.

"You're safer in there than you are out here." Miranda put her hand under Boom-Boom's elbow, propelling her out of the classroom.

243

40

"Class of 1950 over here." Sheriff Shaw indicated the left side of the gym. "Class of 1980 to the right. Who has the rosters?"

"I do." Miranda stepped forward with her attendance list.

Rick took it from her hand. "Coop, go down the list with Miranda. Meet each person and check them off."

"Right, boss."

"Okay, what about 1980?"

"I've got it." Bonnie Baltier walked back to the table, picked up the Xeroxed sheets, and walked back, handing them to the sheriff.

"You stay with me. I want you to check off each name and show me who the person is. Use a colored pen. You've already got them checked off in black."

"Anyone got a colored pen?" Baltier called out.

"I do." Bitsy stepped forward, handing Bonnie a red pen. "E.R. is a member of this class and he was with me in the parking lot at the time of the murder," she told the sheriff.

E.R. called out, "Bitsy, don't bother the sheriff."

Chris Sharpton moved up alongside Rick. "It's not *my* reunion."

"Well, it is for now. Sit down." He pointed to the check-in table. "I'll get to you last and then you can go home. I assume you want to go home."

"Yes," she nodded slowly.

"All right." Rick walked with Bonnie. "One-two-three."

As they worked their way down the line, Harry observed how differently people deal with authority. Some classmates answered directly. Others exhibited attitude, not at all helpful under the circumstances. The doctors in the room felt it necessary to behave like authority figures themselves. A few people were intimidated. Others were clearly frightened.

As they neared the end of the list, Hank Bittner asked to go to the bathroom.

"You'll have to wait until I'm through with this. Another five minutes. We're almost at the end."

Bob Shoaf called out, "Don't forget Fair Haristeen."

"I sent an officer out to find him." Rick's voice remained even. He felt as if he were a teacher with a room full of misbehaving children. In a way, he was.

"We're also missing Dennis Rablan." Bonnie scanned the familiar yet older faces. "Hey, anyone seen Dennis?"

"The last I saw, he'd come out of the bathroom," Harry spoke up, and a few others corroborated her statement.

"Did he walk down the hall? Go outside for a breath of fresh air?" Rick tapped his fingers against his thigh. He held on to his temper but he was greatly disturbed. Dennis might be the witness he needed—or the killer. However, there was a lot of commotion. People don't expect murder at their high-school reunion. And they don't think to keep track of one another.

"Tucker, you stick with Mom. Pewter and I will scout around for Dennis," Mrs. Murphy ordered the corgi.

Pewter was out the door before Mrs. Murphy finished her sentence.

Since the class of 1950 consisted of forty-six people, Cynthia had finished the name check and was taking down whatever information the attendees might have. Nothing useful emerged since all of them, including Tracy Raz, were gathered in the cafeteria for the welcoming ceremonies.

"Boss"—Cynthia crossed over to Rick—"we can let them go. At least, let them go back to the cafeteria."

"Yeah, okay."

Cynthia dismissed the class.

Martha Jones of the 1950 class said to a squatty fellow, bald as a cue ball, "I'm not at all sure I want to go back to the cafeteria."

"There's safety in numbers," he replied. "This is their problem, not ours."

As the last member of the class of 1950 filed out, Cynthia joined Rick.

"Let's divide them into groups of ten." He lowered his voice. "I don't think I can hold them here all day. The best we can do is—"

Hank Bittner interrupted him. "Sheriff, the five minutes is over."

"Go on." Rick waved him off. "Everyone else stay here."

Fair Haristeen passed Hank as he made for the men's room, stopped in front of the one cordoned off, then turned heading in the other direction, toward another bathroom.

As Rick questioned Fair, who sat next to Bitsy, E.R., and Chris, Mrs. Murphy and Pewter prowled the hallway, sticking their heads in every classroom.

"Nothing here. If someone were dead and stuffed in a closet we could smell him," Pewter remarked. *"Fresh blood carries."*

"You know we have ten times the scent receptors in our nostrils than humans do," Murphy casually said. *"And they say that hunting hounds have twenty million receptors. More even than Tee Tucker."*

"I'd keep that to myself. You know how proud Tucker is of her scenting abilities." The tiger peeked into the cafeteria, where the class of 1950 was again getting settled, disquieted though they were. *"Pewter, let's go upstairs."*

The cats turned around and walked to the stairway to the second floor. There was one stairwell at the end of the building but they walked up the main one, the wide one, which was in the middle of the hall. The risers bore thousands of scuff marks; the treads, beaten down also, bore testimony to the ceaseless pounding of teenaged feet. Although the school sanded and finished the stairs once a year the wood had become thin, concave in spots, the black rubber of sneakers leaving the most obvious marks on the worn surface.

The cats reached the second floor. A chair rail ran along the green walls; small bits had broken off and were painted over. The floor was as worn as the stair treads.

Mrs. Murphy turned into the first classroom, hopped on the windowsill, and looked down.

Pewter jumped up to join her. As she looked down she saw a bluejay dart from a majestic blue spruce. *"Hate those birds."*

"They don't like you either."

"What are we looking for?" Pewter sneezed. *"Dust,"* she said.

"Dennis Rablan. First order of business. Second order of business is to memorize the school. We can see a lot from here."

"Wonder if Dennis is dead?"

"I don't know." Mrs. Murphy put her paws on the wall, gently sliding down. *"He was an average-sized man. There aren't too many places a killer can stuff a fellow like that. Closets. Freezers. Let's check out each room, go down the back stairway, and then we can check out the cars. I don't remember what kind of car Denny drove, do you?"*

"No. Wasn't a car. It was one of those minivans."

They inspected each classroom, each bathroom, then trotted down the back stairs. They jumped on the hood of each car in the parking lot but no bodies were slumped over on the front seat.

"Don't jump on Mom's hood. She gets testy about paw prints." Pewter giggled.

A sheriff's department car pulled into the parking lot. Sitting in the front seat next to the officer was Dennis Rablan. The cats watched as the officer parked, got out, and Dennis, handcuffed, swung his feet out, touching the ground.

"Please take these off," Dennis pleaded. "I'm not a killer. Don't make me walk into the reunion like this."

"You left your reunion in a hurry, buddy, you can walk right back in wearing these bracelets. Eighty miles an hour in front of the Con-Agra Building. If you aren't guilty then you're running scared."

The cats followed behind the humans, who didn't notice them. As the officer, a young man of perhaps twenty-five, propelled Dennis into the gym, people turned. Their expressions ranged from disbelief to mild shock.

"I didn't do it!" Dennis shouted before anyone could say anything.

"Sheriff, I searched his van and found a hunting knife and a rope. No gun."

"Let me see the rope." Sheriff Shaw left for a moment as Dennis stood in the middle of the room.

He quickly returned, wearing thin rubber gloves, rope in hand. "Rablan, what's this?"

"I don't know. I didn't have a rope in my van this morning."

"Well, you sure have one in your van now."

"I didn't do it. I thought Rex Harnett was

a worthless excuse for a man. I did. A useless parasite." He turned toward his classmates. "I can't remember him ever doing anything for anybody but himself."

"Maybe so but he didn't deserve to die for it." Hank Bittner, back from the bathroom, spoke calmly.

"*Tucker,*" Mrs. Murphy softly called, "*sniff the rope.*"

The beautiful corgi walked over to the sheriff, her claws clicking on the gym floor. She lifted her nose before Rick noticed. "*Talcum powder.*"

When the sheriff looked down at the dog looking up, he paused as if to say something but didn't. He stared at Harry instead, who whistled for Tucker. She instantly obeyed.

"I didn't do it." Dennis set his jaw.

BoomBoom folded her arms across her chest. "Sheriff, he's not the type."

"Then who is?" the sheriff snapped back. "I have seen little old ladies commit fraud, fifteen-year-old kids blow away their parents, and ministers debauch their flocks. You tell me, who is?"

"If none of you are going to stand up for me, I'll tell everything I know about our senior year," Dennis taunted the others.

"You bastard!" Bittner lunged forward, reaching Dennis be-fore Cynthia could catch him. With one crunching uppercut he knocked Dennis off his feet.

Rick grabbed Hank's right arm as the young officer pinned the other one.

"He's a liar. He doesn't know anything about anybody," Hank snarled.

Bob Shoaf confirmed Hank's opinion. "Right, Rablan, make up stories to save your own ass."

Dennis, helped to his feet by Cynthia, sneered. "I'll tell what I want to when I want to and I'll extract maximum revenge. It was never my idea. I just happened to be there."

"Be where?" Rick asked.

"In the showers."

"Let me get this straight." Rick motioned for Jason, the young officer, to unlock the handcuffs. "You're talking about today? Or 1980?"

"He's scared out of his wits," Pewter whispered.

Dennis looked around the room and his bravado seemed to fade. "I don't remember anything. But someone planted that rope in my van."

"Fool's blabbing about the rope before it's tested." Market Shiflett was disgusted with Dennis.

"Can I go home?" Chris sighed.

"No," Rick curtly answered.

Harry, next to Fair, said, "What did happen my senior year?"

Susan, on her other side, whispered, "Those that know are rapidly disappearing."

"Yeah, all part of the in-group clique." Harry felt dreadful, half-queasy over the deaths and the lingering presence of intended evil.

"All men," Susan again whispered.

"So far," Fair said. He was worried for all of them.

41

"Now what's the story." Rick folded his hands on the wooden desk with the slanted top, and leaned forward.

Cynthia remained in the gym checking everyone's hands for residue from firing the gun. She also checked their purses and pockets for surgical gloves. As lunchtime approached Rick decided the class of 1980 could enjoy their lunch as planned. Susan, in charge of the food, was rearranging tables with help. It would be a somber group that ate barbecue.

Rick meanwhile commandeered a classroom down the hall. Then he intended to interview the senior superlatives since they were the ones dying off, the men, anyway.

Market was number one on the list.

"I heard it second—no, thirdhand." Market coughed behind his hand. "I didn't think about it—even then—because Charlie was always bragging about himself. But..."

"Just tell me what you heard," Rick patiently asked.

"You know about senior superlatives?"

"Yes."

"I heard that on the day the class of 1980 elected theirs, which would have been mid-October, I think, there was the usual round of excitement and disappointment, depending on whether you were elected or not. But what I heard was that Charlie Ashcraft, Leo Burkey, Bob Shoaf, Dennis Rablan, and Rex Harnett pinned down Ron Brindell and raped him." Market grimaced. "They said if that faggot was going to be elected Most Popular they'd make sure he was popular. Or words to that effect. But Ron never reported them and he seemed on friendly terms with those guys. Just another one of those high-school rumors, like Charlie getting a girl pregnant."

Rick sighed. "Adolescent boys are terrified of sex and their own relation to it. Their answer to anything they don't understand is violence."

"I don't remember feeling all that violent," Market replied. "But I can't believe Ron would stay friendly with them after something like that."

"Depends on what he thought he had to do to survive. It's hard for many men to understand what it's like to be the victim of sexual violence," Rick said.

"I never thought of that." Market wondered what else he never thought of by virtue of being a man, a straight man.

"We worship violence in this country. Turn on your television. Go to the movies. I can tell you it makes my job a lot harder. Anyway, who told you this?" Rick returned to his questions.

"I wish I could remember. As I said, I dismissed the story and I never heard any more about it. I don't think the rumor made the rounds or it would have lasted longer. Damn, I wish I could remember who told me."

"Too bad."

"Maybe Ron wasn't a homosexual. Maybe he was just effeminate." Market thought a moment. "Must be hell to be a gay kid in high school."

"Anything else?"

"No. Well, Ron Brindell killed himself. His parents died shortly after that. From grief. He was their only son, you know. All that misery. I can't imagine killing myself."

"Self-hate." Rick offered Market a cigarette, which he refused. "All manner of things derail people: greed, lust, obsessions, sex, revenge, and self-hate. Then again I sometimes wonder if some people aren't born sorrowful." He inhaled. "Market, we've known each other for a long time. I don't mind telling you that we're sitting on a time bomb."

"Because everyone's gathered together?"

"Yes."

"But two murders took place before the reunion."

"That they did—with Marcy Wiggins' .38."

"Guess it was too good to be true." Market stopped. "I don't mean good that Marcy killed herself, but her gun...we all let our guard down."

Rick nodded in agreement. "Our first thought was a crime of passion. Bill had discovered the affair with Charlie, shot her, and made it look like suicide, taking the precaution to have her write a confession in her own hand. But Dr. Wiggins happened to be at the Fredericksburg Hospital that day. She could have been murdered by someone else but I don't think so. All indications were suicide."

"But her gun—"

Rick interrupted. "I know. I have a thousand theories and not one useful fact but I am willing to bet you a hundred dollars of my hard-earned pay that our murderer is sitting in the gymnasium right now. For whatever reason, this twentieth reunion has triggered him."

"Jeez, I just want to get out of here."

Rick frowned. "A normal response. I'm not sure I can let you all go. Not just yet, anyway."

As Market left the room, Rick thought about bringing in Dennis next. However, having Dennis in the gym would disquiet the others. Maybe he'd get more information from them if they stayed agitated. He decided to call Hank Bittner next.

Market walked back into the gym. Cynthia kept everyone on a short leash. No one could rush up to Market. He sat down at the end of the table, his grim visage further upsetting the others. Market was usually so cheerful.

Walter Trevelyn asked Cynthia, "Are we trapped in the gym or what?"

"Once Rick finishes his interviews, he'll make a decision." She kept checking hands.

"I think we should forget the reunion,"

Linda Osterhoudt, who'd looked so forward to this reunion, suggested. "How can we go on? At least, I can't go on."

BoomBoom put down her barbecue sandwich. "If we cancel our reunion then the murderer wins. He's spoiled everything."

"I'd rather have him win than me be dead," came the sharp retort from Market.

Others spoke in agreement.

Mike Alvarez dissented. "I came all the way from Los Angeles. If we stick together what can he do?"

"I have something to say about that." Mike's attractive wife spoke up. "We came all the way from L.A. and it would be perfect if we could live to go all the way back—soon."

He declined to reply.

"We could market this," Bonnie quipped. "You know, like those mystery party games? We'll create one, Murder at the Reunion. If you get a lemon, make lemonade."

"Baltier, how insensitive," BoomBoom chided.

Hank Bittner returned, telling Bob Shoaf to go out. Bob glared at Dennis, who glared right back. Then Bob turned on his heel and left to join Rick Shaw.

Chris sat, avoiding eye contact with Dennis. Market moved and sat on the other side of Chris, as if to reassure her.

Rick returned with Bob Shoaf, who didn't seem as upset as Market had been on his return to the group. Rick still wasn't ready to pull Dennis out of the room.

BoomBoom started to cry. "All my hard work..."

"Oh for Christ's sake." Harry smashed her plastic fork down so hard it broke. "This isn't about you."

"I know that but I wanted it to be so great. It's your hard work, too, and Susan's and Mike's and Dennis's. I bet he didn't get any pictures either."

"Yes, I did. Up until the murder."

"How long will it take you to develop them?" Cynthia inquired.

"If I take the film to my studio I can be back in an hour."

"You're not going to let him go?" Hank Bittner was incredulous.

"There's not enough evidence to book him," Cynthia answered.

"He left the scene of the crime!" Hank exploded.

"I didn't do it."

The room erupted again as Rick shouted for quiet. "We've got your names and addresses. We've got the hotels where you're staying. We'll get in touch with you if we need to. I have no desire to make this more uncomfortable than it has to be."

"Are you going to book Dennis?" Hank insisted.

"No, I'm not, but I'm going back with him to his studio," Rick stated.

Dennis bit his lip until it bled, realized what he had done and wiped his mouth with a napkin.

As Rick and Dennis left, Cynthia remained. BoomBoom stood up, then sat down abruptly as Susan pulled her down. They whispered for a moment.

Mrs. Murphy followed Dennis and Rick out to the squad car.

"You don't believe me, do you?" Dennis demanded.

"Look, Dennis"—Rick put his hand on the man's shoulder—"I know you're scared. I don't know why you're scared and I wish you'd tell me. Think a moment. You have to live in this county. Whatever it is that frightens you can't be as bad as ending up dead."

"I didn't do it." Dennis stubbornly stopped, planting his feet wide. "I did not rape Ron Brindell."

Rick paused a minute as this was an unexpected response. "I believe you. Why are you so frightened? That was twenty years ago. I believe it happened. I believe *you*. Why did you run away today? The only thing I can figure is you ran away from the others who were in on it. Or you think you're next."

He mumbled, "I don't know. It's crazy. People don't come back from the dead."

"No, they don't, but there's someone in that gym who loved Ron Brindell. A girlfriend who wants retribution for his suffering. Another man perhaps. He could have had a lover. None of you knew. The man's come back for his revenge after all these years. He could be married and have children. How would you know? We called Ron's cousin in Lawrence,

258

Kansas, to see if she had any ideas. She said they were never close. She lost contact with him after high school. Right now, Dennis, you're my only hope."

Dennis hung his head as Mrs. Murphy scampered back to tell Pewter and Tucker. "I don't know anything."

The cat could hear the shouting from the gym and she wasn't halfway down the hall. She loped to the open double doors to behold all the humans on their feet, everyone shouting and screaming. BoomBoom was the only person seated and she was in tears.

Tucker ran over to greet Mrs. Murphy. Pewter, wide-eyed, remained on the table. The commotion mesmerized her. She wasn't even stealing ham and barbecue off plates.

The only people not fighting were Harry, Susan, Fair, Bitsy, and Chris. Even E.R. was yelling at people.

"I thought we were a good class." Susan mournfully observed the outbreak of bad manners and pent-up emotion.

"Maybe we should go down to Miranda's reunion," Harry said.

"And ruin it?" Fair bent over and brushed the front of his twill pants. "I say we all go home. No one in their right mind would stay for the dance tonight."

"Jesus, guys, what am I going to do with all the food that's been ordered? It's too late to cancel it. Someone's got to eat it."

"I never thought of that." Harry briskly walked back to the center of the melee. "Shut up!" No response. She stood on the table and yelled at the top of her lungs. "Shut up!"

One by one her classmates quieted, turning their faces to a woman they'd never had reason to doubt.

BoomBoom continued sobbing.

"Boom." Susan reached her, patting her on the back. "Wipe your eyes. Come on. We've got to make the best of it."

With all eyes on her, Harry took a deep breath, for she wasn't fond of public speaking. "We'll solve nothing by turning on one another. If anything, this is a time when we need one another's best efforts. As you know, the sheriff has released us. Before we scatter to the four corners of the globe, what are we to do with all the food Susan has ordered and you've paid for? Remember, we have the supper in the cafeteria tonight before the dance. We can't cancel it. We've paid for it. What do you want to do?"

"Let the class of 1950 have it," Hank said.

"They've organized their own dinner," Susan informed him.

"Can't we send it to the Salvation Army?" Deborah Kingsmill asked.

"I'll call them to find out." Susan left for her car. She'd left the cell phone inside it.

"We could eat our supper and go. It seems obscene to have a dance under these circumstances," Linda Osterhoudt said. "And it seems obscene to waste all that food if the Salvation Army won't take it."

Others murmured agreement.

"Shall we vote on it?" Harry asked.

"Wait until Susan comes back," Bonnie Baltier suggested.

"Even if we vote on it, it doesn't mean the majority rules." Market shook his head. "You can't make people come and eat."

"Well, we can count heads. And we can divide up what's left among those who choose to come back for supper." Harry turned as Susan reentered the room. "What'd they say?"

"Thanks for our generosity but they've only got six men in the shelter right now."

"Okay then, how many are willing to come back for supper in the cafeteria? No dance."

Feet shuffled, then a few hands were timidly raised. A few more moments and more hands shot up.

Fair and Harry counted.

"BoomBoom, surely you're coming." Susan handed her another tissue.

"I am," she weakly replied.

"You're coming, Cynthia?" Harry smiled as the deputy raised her hand.

"Wouldn't miss it for the world."

"Thirty."

"Thirty-one." Fair finished his count.

"How'd I miss one?" Harry wondered.

"You didn't. You just forgot to count yourself," he said.

"Okay then. We'll see you all tonight for supper, six o'clock in the cafeteria. Bring coolers and stuff so you can carry food back home." She put her hand on the edge of the table, swinging down, her feet touching the floor lightly.

"Graceful—for a human," Mrs. Murphy noted.

"Where's Chris?" Susan didn't see her.

"The minute Rick said we were free to go she shot out of here. Just about the time everyone started yelling at everyone else," Harry said.

"Can't blame her. She'll probably never talk to us again." Susan sighed.

"It wasn't your fault." Fair smiled at Susan.

"In a way it was. I roped Chris into this because of a bet we made on a golf game this summer. Of course, she was really hoping to meet a man and she found Dennis. Right now, I doubt she's too happy about that, too."

"I didn't say one thing about all that extra food." Pewter waited for praise to follow.

"Miracle. I've lived to see a miracle." Mrs. Murphy gaily sped out of the gym.

Cynthia sat in her squad car in the parking lot. The school, even with the heat on, was a bit chilly. The car heater warmed her. She'd found no residue on anyone's hands or clothing. The killer probably wore plastic gloves. She'd had every garbage can at school checked. While she held everyone in the gym, Jason went through the dumpster. Nothing—but disposing of a thin pair of gloves would have been easy.

42

As Harry drove away from Crozet High School she glanced in her rearview mirror at the brick building. The four white pillars on the front lent what really was a simple structure a distinguished air. Stained glass over the double-door main entrance bore the initials CHS in blue against a yellow background.

Situated on a slight rise, the school overlooked a sweeping valley to the east, a view now partially obscured by the brand-new, expensive grade school on the opposite side of the state road. The mountains, to the west, provided a backdrop.

Like most high-school students, when she attended Crozet High she took it for granted. She never thought about architecture, the lovely setting, the nearness to the village of Crozet. She thought about her friends, the football games, her grades.

A memory floated into her mind, a soft breeze from an earlier time. She had been wearing a beautiful fuchsia sweater and Fair wore a deep turquoise one. They hadn't intended to color coordinate but the effect, when they stood together, was startling.

She remembered that junior year, hurrying from her classroom during break, hoping to catch sight of Fair as he moved on to his next class. When she'd see him her heart would skip a beat like in some corny song lyric. She didn't know exactly what she was feeling or why she was feeling it, only that the sensation was disquieting yet simultaneously pleasurable. She thought she was the only person in the world to feel like this. People didn't much talk about emotions at Crozet High or if they did, she'd missed it. Then, too, an extravagant display of emotion was for people who lived elsewhere—not Virginia. Young though they all were, they had learned that vital lesson. And today most of them had forgotten it, good manners worn out by fear, police questioning, and suspicion of one another.

Harry burst into tears.

"Mom, what's the matter?" Mrs. Murphy put her paws on Harry's shoulder to lick the right side of her face.

"Don't worry, we'll protect you." Tucker's soft brown eyes seemed even kinder than usual.

"Yeah, scratch that murderer's eyes out!" Pewter puffed up.

"Damn, I never have Kleenex in the truck." She sniffled. "I don't know what's the matter with me. Nostalgia." She petted Murphy, then reached over her to pat the other two as she turned right toward home. "Why is it that when I look back, it seems better? I was so innocent, which is another word for stupid." She sniffed again but the tears continued to roll. "I fell in love with my high-school boyfriend and married him. I actually thought we'd live happily ever after. I never thought about—well—the things that happen. I never even thought about paying the bills. I supposed I would live on air." She pulled over to the side of the road, put on her flashers, and reached under the seat, pulling out a rag she used to clean the windshield. She wiped her eyes and blew her nose. "Smells like oil. I must have used this to check my oil. That's dumb—putting it back in the cab." She closed her eyes. A headache fast approached from the direction of lost youth.

"*We love you,*" Tucker said for all of them.

"I love you guys," she replied, then bawled anew, feeling, like so many people, that the only true love comes from one's pets. "I love Fair, but is it real? Or is it just the memories from before? This is one hell of a reunion."

Mrs. Murphy tried the sensible approach. "*Time will tell. If you two can be together, you'll know it if you just go slow. About your reunion, how could anyone not feel terrible?*"

"*Some nutcase,*" Pewter said. "*Someone who is now feeling very powerful.*"

Tucker nuzzled up to Harry. "*Mom, it's the reunion. It's stirred up feelings, good and evil.*"

She blew her nose again, popped the truck in gear, and headed toward home. "I guess when I was in high school I thought trouble happened to other people, not to me. I had a wrong number." She ruefully laughed. "But you know, kids, that love is so pure when you're young. It never comes again. Maybe you fall in love again and maybe it's a wiser and better love but it's never that pure, uncomplicated love."

"Humans worry too much about time," Pewter observed. *"Suppose they can't help it. There's clocks and watches and deadlines like April fifteenth. It'd make me a raving lunatic."*

"Hasn't helped them any." Tucker nudged close to Harry and stared out the window as the familiar small houses and larger farms ticked by.

Mrs. Murphy sat on the back of the seat. She had an even higher view.

"I look around at everyone at the reunion and wonder what's happened to them. How'd we get here so fast? With a murderer in our midst. Our class? I read somewhere and I can't remember where, 'Time conquers time'— maybe it's true. Maybe I'll reach a time when I let it all go. Or when I'm renewed with a spiritual or even physical second wind."

"Mom, you've missed the turn!" Tucker acted like a backseat driver.

"She's clearing her head. Whenever she needs an inner vacation she cruises around. Cruising around in the dually is a statement." Mrs. Murphy didn't mind; she appreciated the plush upholstery covered with sheepskin. *"She had to show up at her reunion in this new truck. Funny, isn't it? The desire to shine."*

The warm autumn light turned the red of cow barns even deeper, the fire of the maples even brighter.

Harry loved the seasons but had never applied

them, an obvious but potent metaphor, to her own life. "Know what's really funny? No one ever believes they'll get old. There must be a point where you accept it, like Mrs. Hogendobber." She thought a moment. "But then Mim hasn't truly accepted it. And she's the same age as Miranda." Her conversation picked up. The ride was invigorating her. "Here's what I don't get. First, someone is killing off men in the class of '80. Someone is actually carrying out a plan of revenge. I've been mad enough to kill people but I didn't. What trips someone over the edge? And then I think about death. Death is something out there, some shadow being, a feared acquaintance. He snatches you in a car wreck or through cancer. By design or by chance. But he's oddly impersonal. That's what gets me about this stuff. It's brutally personal."

43

Harry had no sooner walked through the kitchen door than the phone rang.

"Hello," Fair said. "I'm at the clinic but I can be there in fifteen minutes."

"I'm fine. I'll meet you at school for supper. Don't worry." She hung up the phone and it rang again.

"Hey," Susan said. "I dropped off two English boxwoods for Chris. I feel guilty. She's not coming to the dinner tonight, obviously. She was funny, though. She said if we survived our reunion she'd love to play golf next weekend. Oh, she's through with Dennis, too. Said she's shocked at the way he behaved. That's what really upset her."

"Well—good for her. Did you think of anything for Bitsy? It's really E.R.'s responsibility to thank her for her work but, well, I liked working with her."

"The full treatment at Vendome." Susan mentioned the most exclusive beauty parlor in town, where one could have a haircut, massage, waxing, manicure, pedicure, and complete makeover, emerging rejuvenated.

"That's a good idea. We'll get BoomBoom to cough up the money. Those two worked as hard on our reunion as we did."

"I paid for the boxwoods. It was my bet. If Boom won't pay for Vendome, I'll do it. It's only right."

"I'll split it with you."

"No, you won't. You put away that money you're getting on rent."

"I guess Tracy will leave after his reunion. He hasn't said anything. I'll tell you, though, his rent money has made my life easier."

"You're the truck queen of Crozet." Susan laughed, since she knew the rent money went to pay for the truck.

"Susan, are you scared?"

"About the dinner?" They'd known one

another since in-fancy so elaborate explanations weren't needed, nor were transitions between subjects.

"Yeah."

"No. I'll have Ned with me. Also, I don't think we're involved except as bystanders."

"There won't be that many people there. I wonder if the killer will attend? And I wonder if we're doing the right thing. We haven't even had time to process Rex's murder. I feel like we're being whittled away."

"Are you scared?" Susan asked.

"Yes. I'm not afraid I'll get bumped off. I'm afraid of what I'll feel."

"Blindsided." Susan referred to the manner in which emotions flatten a person.

"You, too?"

A long pause followed. "Yes. I joked about who was that young person in the Best All-Round photograph but I meant it. And then I look at Danny and Brooks." She referred to her son and daughter. "And I realize they're feeling all the same emotions and confusions we did but in a different time. I'm beginning to believe that the human story is the same story over and over again, only the sets change."

"A in History," Harry laughed.

Susan thought back on her A's in History and just about everything else. "The difference is that I understand it now—before, I just knew it."

"Can you understand the murders?"

"No. I don't even know what to call the way I feel. Intense...disturbed? No, I don't understand it and I don't remember anything that horrible from high school. I mean, nothing out of the ordinary like two people hating one another so much it lasts for twenty years. But we're in the dark. Even Market seems to know something we don't, and Dennis—good Lord."

"Think Denny Rablan will show his face?"

"He doesn't dare."

44

Denny sat there as big as life and twice as smug. No one wanted to sit next to him. Finally Harry did, only because Susan had put out the exact number of chairs based on the head count. The sheer quantity of food overwhelmed the tables: spicy chicken wings, corn bread, perfectly roasted beef with a thin pepper crust, moist Virginia ham cooked to perfection, biscuits, shrimp remoulade, a mustard-based sauce for the beef, sweet potatoes candied and shining orange. Three different kinds of salad satisfied those who didn't wish such heavy foods. The women sat down, claiming they'd stick to the salads. That lasted five minutes.

The desserts, reposing on a distant table,

beckoned after the main course. Carrot cake, tiny, high-impact brownies, fruit compote, luxurious cheeses from Denmark, England, and France rested among heaps of pale green grapes. If that wasn't enough, a thin, dense fruitcake with hard sauce filled out the menu.

The bar was open, which somewhat raised the conversation level.

The thirty-one people who came to the dinner ate themselves into a stupor. Mike Alvarez did not return. His wife had put her foot down but he left the tapes for everyone to enjoy, if "enjoy" was the right word. During dinner BoomBoom played the slow tapes. "Digestion tapes," she called them.

Mrs. Murphy, Pewter, and Tucker ate from paper plates on the floor under the table. Since there was so much food, Harry didn't think anyone would begrudge her animals.

Fair sat on the other side of Harry, her left side. Hank Bittner refused to sit next to Dennis even though he came in late and seats were taken. Bonnie Baltier switched seats with Hank so she sat on the other side of Dennis.

"Anything turn up in the lab?" Bonnie asked Dennis as her fork cut into the steaming sweet potato.

"No. Rick Shaw took the pictures and left. He said he had suspects but they always say that. I just said, 'Yeah, the whole class.'"

"Is there a digital time frame on the photographs?"

Dennis answered Harry. "No. I'm using a

Nikon that's thirty years old. Never found a camera I liked better."

"Oh." Harry returned to her dinner.

Miranda and Tracy ducked their heads in the open doors. Susan waved them in. Harry hadn't seen them.

"Miranda, you look stunning." Fair stood up to compliment her.

"Sit down, sit down. I'll spoil your dinner." She blushed.

"She's the belle of the ball." Tracy beamed. "Doesn't that emerald green dress set off her hair and her eyes?"

"Yes," they agreed.

"Mrs. Hogendobber, come down to the studio in that outfit. I'll take a picture—for free. I should have my camera with me but I forgot it."

"You've," Miranda paused, "been dis-combobulated."

"Mrs. Hogendobber, you should be a diplomat," Hank Bittner laughed. "And you do look lovely. If the women look as good as you do when we have our fiftieth reunion, I'll be a happy man."

"You men will turn my head." She blushed some more as Tracy winked at the men.

"Come on, beautiful. I don't trust these guys." Tracy gently put his hand in the small of her back, guiding her out of the room.

Susan, on her way for second helpings, swooped past Harry. "Are they getting serious or what? She really does look fabulous. That treadmill has worked wonders."

"Tracy has worked wonders." Fair smiled. "It's a magic that never fails." He turned to Harry and whispered, "You'll always be magic to me, Sweetheart."

Harry blushed and mumbled, "Thanks."

BoomBoom raised her glass. "Here's to the class of 1980!"

The group hesitated, then raised their glasses. "Hear. Hear."

"What's left of us." Dennis held up his glass for a second toast.

"Rablan, shut up." Bittner stood and held up his glass. "To the organizers for their hard work and their heart when things didn't turn out quite as they—or any of us—expected."

Everyone cheered.

"I don't remember Hank being so eloquent," Fair remarked.

"He learned somewhere along the way." Bonnie leaned over Dennis. "Brightwood Records wouldn't promote an unpolished stone. I'd kill to have his stock options."

"You'd have to," Dennis laughed.

"You haven't exactly made a fortune. In fact, you lost one," Bonnie replied.

"You're right." He shut up.

The cats and Tucker decided to walk under the tables. This was a stroll, not a search for crumbs. They'd eaten too much.

Hee hee." Pewter nudged Mrs. Murphy as she watched a lady, heels off, run her foot over a man's calf. He wore charcoal pants.

Mrs. Murphy popped her head from under the tablecloth. "*BoomBoom.*"

Pewter ducked out on the other side. *"Bob Shoaf."*

"Figures," Murphy said as she walked back under the tablecloth.

"He's married, isn't he?" Tucker could have told them it was BoomBoom since Tucker paid a lot of attention to shoes and smells.

"Yes. He left the Mrs. at home, though," Pewter said.

Bored with their stroll, the animals emerged by the food tables.

"I could probably eat one more piece of beef." Tucker gazed upward.

"Don't. You've stuffed yourself. If you eat too much you'll get sick on the way home," Mrs. Murphy counseled.

Their conversation didn't finish because an explosion from Bonnie Baltier sent them back to that table.

"What are you talking about?" She slammed her hand on the table, making the plates jump.

"I thought you knew." Dennis blinked.

Hank leaned over Bonnie. "None of the women knew, you asshole!"

Bonnie stood up, walked around Dennis to Harry. "Did you know about a gang rape on the day senior superlatives were voted?"

"No." Harry gasped as did Susan.

"Is it true?" Bonnie, very upset, turned on Dennis. "It must be true. Why would anyone make something like that up!"

Bob Shoaf stopped playing footsies with BoomBoom. His eyes narrowed, he pushed back his seat as he strode over to Dennis, towering above him. "Rablan, there's something wrong with you. I'd call you a worm but that would insult worms." He bent over, menacing, as Fair rose from his seat just in case. "I don't know why you're making up this story about Ron Brindell getting raped in the showers but I do know that you were the person who found Rex Harnett dead and no one else was in the men's room. Do you think we're that stupid!"

Dennis, shaking with rage, stood up, facing off with Bob. "I'm not making it up. I wish I'd done something at the time. I felt guilty then and I feel guilty now."

Bob reached for Dennis's neck but Fair grabbed Bob's arms. Bob Shoaf had been a great pro football player but Fair Haristeen was a six-foot-four working equine vet. He was strong and he had one advantage: his knees still worked.

"You aren't going to listen to him! He's guilty and the sheriff is waiting for him to make a mistake," Bob exploded.

"Why would I kill Charlie Ashcraft and Leo Burkey?" Dennis became oddly calm.

"You tell me," Shoaf taunted. "It's like your story about knowing who Charlie Ashcraft knocked up. You don't know anything. You say these things to make yourself important. You don't know shit."

"I do. You know I do."

By now Hank Bittner was on his feet. Everyone else was watching.

"Then who's the mother?" Bob stepped back, already dismissing Dennis.

"Olivia Ulrich," Dennis loudly said.

"I am not!" BoomBoom flew out of her chair. "You liar. I am not."

"Come on, Boom. You loved his ass," Dennis mocked.

Susan, now at Harry's side, said, "I don't recall Dennis being this snide."

"Me neither. Something's sure brought it out of him."

"Fear," Mrs. Murphy said.

"If he was afraid he should have stayed home." Pewter moved farther away from the humans in case another fight broke out.

"Maybe he's safer here than at home," Tucker sagely noted. *"He has no family. All alone. The killer might not want to slit his throat but there are a few people here who wouldn't mind. If I were Dennis, I'd rent a motel room for a couple of nights."*

"Or maybe he has to be here," Murphy shrewdly said.

BoomBoom, shaking, pointed her finger in Dennis's face. "Because I'd never go to bed with you—this is your revenge. You waited twenty years for this. My God, you're pathetic."

"But you did have an illegitimate child."

"I did not and you can't prove it."

"You know, I take class pictures for the schools in town. And I recall a beautiful girl who graduated three years ago who had your coloring but Charlie's looks. Western Albemarle. You gave that girl up for adoption."

"Never! I would never do that." Boom-Boom was so furious she couldn't move. She had never before felt a paralyzing rage.

"Boom, don't try to pull the wool over our eyes. You don't care about the consequences. You never did. You steal people's husbands." Dennis looked at Harry when he said that. "You dump inconvenient children. Why, if Kelly Craycroft had known about the girl he'd have never married you. You wanted his money."

"I married Kelly Craycroft after I graduated from college. Do you think I was thinking about marrying money in high school? You're out of your mind."

"Think it's true?" Pewter asked Murphy.

"I don't know."

"And furthermore, I didn't steal anybody's husband. They aren't wallets. You can't just pick them up, you know." She put her hands on her hips. "As for the rest of you, I know what you think. The hell with you. I do as I please. Ladies, virtue is greatly overrated!"

Harry whistled. "At long last, the real BoomBoom!"

BoomBoom stalked out of the room with Bob Shoaf following after her, reaching to slow her down.

Hank Bittner sat back down, calling over his shoulder, "Dennis, Rex may be physically dead, but buddy, you're dead socially."

Everyone started talking at once.

Mrs. Murphy watched Dennis sit down next to Hank. She hurried over to hear the conversation since there was so much noise.

"You're an even bigger coward than I am, Bittner. I just figured it out. Sheriff Shaw said something to me today. He said if these murders are revenge for Ron Brindell's rape then someone who loved Ron has to be committing them. He said what if Ron had a lover, another high-school boy that no one knew about. The boy stood back and didn't stop the rape. He didn't want anyone to know he was gay. He never lifted a finger to help Ron. And no one ever suspected. That was you."

Hank deliberately put down his fork, turned to Dennis, and said softly, "Dennis, if I were gay I would like to think I would have the courage to be what I am. I would like to think I would have fought for Ron. But I'm not gay. It wasn't me and I don't know what's wrong with you—unless that coward is *you*."

45

Sheriff Shaw had taken the precaution of having Dennis Rablan tailed to the reunion dinner. He also had a plainclothes officer watching Dennis's house in Bentivar, a subdivision up Route 29.

He'd pinned another flow chart to the long bulletin board in the hallway. The interior of the school was neatly drawn. Exits and entrances were outlined in red, as was each window.

Cynthia Cooper was to have attended the dinner but Rick changed his mind: he thought her presence might inhibit people. Little could have inhibited that group, though, and Coop hoped Harry and Susan would save the leftovers. She beseeched them to bring a lot of Ziploc bags and containers.

"You think the killer will crack?"

"It's his or her big night, isn't it? Whoever it is has waited twenty years."

"Are you expecting someone to be blown up in the parking lot?"

He shot her a sharp glance. "I wouldn't put it past our perp."

"I think he's enjoying the chaos—and the fear in the eyes of whoever is left on his list. I think he's sitting in that gym loving every second of it."

"Wish we knew more about Brindell. His parents have passed away. His cousin was no help and snotty, to boot. There's got to be somebody who can tell us who his boyfriend was— or girlfriend. One of the girls could have loved him even if he was gay. People don't have much control over love. Mim Sanburne is proof of that." He smiled because the Queen of Crozet had married beneath her, although everyone conceded that Jim Sanburne, in his youth, was one sexy man.

"This is what bothers me." Cynthia, suddenly intense, stubbed out her lit cigarette. "The killer knows we know this is the big weekend. He knows we're expecting another incident at the dinner or right after since they canceled the dance. He knows," she repeated for emphasis. "Is he going to risk it? He knocked off two this summer. He's killed this morning. He might just wait, enjoy the panic, then strike when it suits him. Whoever he or she is—this lover or best friend—he's fooled us."

"You don't buy that it's Dennis Rablan. He had access to everyone. Not much in the way of alibis but then we've both seen ironclad alibis suddenly get produced in the courtroom, along with the expensive lawyer." The sheriff rubbed his chin, opened his drawer, pulling out a cordless electric razor.

"Boss, do that in the car. Let's go over there."

"Jason's in the parking lot."

"Like a neon sign."

"What are we, then?"

"I don't know but I think we ought to—" The phone rang, interrupting her.

"Sheriff Shaw," Rick answered as the operator put the call through. "Well, stay with him." He hung the phone up. "Jason says Dennis Rablan ran out of the high school, fired up his van, and is pulling out of the parking lot."

"Jason can stay with Dennis. Let's go to Crozet High."

"I hope so."

46

"Jesus, what a mess." Harry watched as the reunion dinner fell apart. "We might as well clean up and go home."

"Yeah." Susan, also dejected, picked up the plates, depositing them in huge trash bags. "One good thing, they ate more than I thought they would. We'll have a lot to take home but at least people enjoyed the food."

Fair stayed behind, as did Hank Bittner, Bonnie Baltier, Market Shiflett, and Linda Osterhoudt. Within an hour and a half the place looked as though they'd never been in it. The huge senior superlative photographs easily came down. Market rolled them up, placing them in large tubes.

"You might as well throw those out," Fair told him.

"Maybe our thirtieth reunion will be better. Anyway, there's plenty of space in the attic of the store. Who knows, huh?"

Mrs. Murphy, Pewter, and Tucker, tired from the rich food and the human fuss, sat down under the raised basketball backboard.

"Guess that's it." Harry put her hands on her hips, surveying the polished gym floor. "Too bad we couldn't have had the dance. Alvarez made serious tapes. He was always good at that kind of stuff."

"His wife sure tells him what to do," Hank Bittner laughed. "I thought he might sneak back to the dinner."

"She probably dragged him to Monticello. That's what all the out-of-towners want to see." Susan pressed her hand to the small of her back. All the bending over and lifting had made her ache a little. "I hate to see our reunion end this way."

"Yeah," the others agreed.

Harry asked Hank, "Do you believe the story about Bob, Rex, Charlie, and Leo attacking Ron?"

"Yes," Hank replied.

"Was Dennis there?" Harry continued her inquiry.

"I think he was. I think he stood by the door to watch out for Coach. I can't prove any of it but I believe it."

"How did you hear about it?" Fair asked.

"Ron told me," Hank said, looking truly sorrowful.

"Why didn't you go to the principal or Coach or somebody?" Harry blurted out. She didn't want to sound accusatory but she did.

"Because Ron said he would deny what happened. He didn't want anyone to know. He especially didn't want Deborah Kingsmill to know. He was taking her to the Christmas dance. He thought she'd break the date if she knew." Hank paused. "And if he'd told, who knows what they would have done to him. There was a kind of wisdom to his silence."

"If she really cared about him, she'd go anyway," Susan said.

"Not Deborah." Hank half-smiled. "She didn't care about anybody—which made the guys want her. And remember, she was a cheerleader and all that crap. Even then, her ambition made her cold. Ron felt like he was, I don't know, moving up, I guess, having a date with her."

"Did you know he was gay?" Harry wondered.

"Kinda." Hank shrugged. "What do you know at that age? I'm not sure even Ron knew. I do know that Leo, Charlie, Bob, and Rex spent the rest of the year teasing him but they weren't violent again."

"Maybe Dennis was his boyfriend?" Fair stooped over to pick up a carton loaded with food. He was going to start carrying food and drinks out to his truck, Harry's truck, and Susan's car.

"He's got two kids and one ex-wife," Susan said.

"That doesn't mean he's not gay." Hank also bent over to pick up a carton. "Hell, I've been married and divorced three times—to the same woman. That doesn't mean I'm nuts."

"Hank, I've been meaning to ask you about that." Fair smiled as the men walked out of the gym.

"I'm going home. Thanks for the food, Susan." Bonnie kissed Susan on the cheek.

"Drive safely." Susan kissed her back. "That ninety miles can get truly boring."

"Back to Washington." Linda Osterhoudt did her round of kisses. "Call me when you come up. The opera this year is worth the trip."

"We will," Susan and Harry said. "Hey, why don't you let the guys carry that out for you?"

"I'm not taking that much home." She lifted her small carton and left.

Market came back in for more tubes. Subdued, he waved and left.

Harry and Susan sighed simultaneously.

"It's a bitch," Harry exhaled.

"Yeah. I understand revenge. But why wreck the reunion for everyone else?"

"Guess your mind warps after a while. Hey, Boom let us all have it, didn't she? And you know, she's right. It's her body. A husband isn't a purse. You can't snatch him unless he wants to be snatched. I give her credit for fighting back."

"You're mellow."

Harry clapped her hands together for the animals. "Sick of it. Not mellow. I'm sick of being angry at her, angry at him, angry at me. Done is done. Took me a long enough time to get there, though. In a strange way this reunion has helped me."

"I'd like to know how?" Susan asked, genuinely interested.

"I've had ample proof of what carrying around anger, hate, and the desire for revenge can do to somebody—whoever that somebody is. So he's winning. Winning what? His life is reduced to this one issue, a very great pain, a terrible wound and it would seem an equally terrible act of cowardice. But life moves on. Our killer didn't. In my own little way, I don't want to be like that." She smiled as the three animals trotted toward her. "I've seen enough embittered women not to want to become one."

Susan hugged Harry fiercely. "I love you."

"I love you, too. I couldn't ask for a better friend."

The two women stood there with tears in their eyes.

"Maybe it wasn't such a bad reunion after all." Susan wiped away her tears and Harry's, too. "Shall we?"

They bent over to pick up two cartons and walked out the door. Harry paused for a moment to look back, then cut the lights. "Good-bye, class of 1980."

Mrs. Murphy and Pewter dashed ahead of the humans, turned a few very pretty kitty circles, and waited at the door. Tucker barked at the door; she'd barreled on ahead of them.

Harry put her carton down for a second. The faint sounds of fifties music wafted down the hall from the cafeteria. She wanted to stick her head in and watch but thought the better of it. Hank came back in for another carton.

"Should we dance?" He nodded toward the music.

"No. It's their night."

"Well, I'm not flying back to New York until Monday. If you change your mind about dancing, call me." He winked, picked up

Harry's carton, and headed for the door. Harry turned to follow but thought she heard a sound on the stairwell.

The lights were out in the stairwell. She walked up a step and went over to turn them on to double-check.

A black-gloved hand came down over hers.

A man's tenor, a familiar voice, snarled, "Don't, you idiot!"

Before she could respond he drew back the side of his hand and hit her hard in the windpipe. She staggered back, choking, falling off the one step. She saw briefly the back of a man, dressed in black, a black ski mask over his face as he jumped over her. Nimbly, he ran down the hall.

Tears of pain rolled down her face; she couldn't get up. She was fighting hard to breathe.

Mrs. Murphy noticed first. *"Something's wrong!"*

The three animals tore back down the hallway, their paws barely touching the ground. They were all going so fast that when they reached Harry they spun out of control.

Harry, on her hands and knees, gasped for air. Tucker licked her face.

"I'll catch him!" Pewter took off down the hall. Once the humans saw Harry, Murphy ran after Pewter.

"Harry? Harry!" Susan came running toward Harry, the sound of footsteps receding, fading into the fifties music.

Murphy left Harry, hit Mach One, sped

past Pewter, sped past the running man, ducked into the cafeteria, pushed out a skateboard from behind the door, and pushed it so it would cross the man's path.

He never saw the skateboard. He hit it running flat out, fell down, and skidded on the polished floor. He struggled up and kept running, although his arm was crooked.

"Dennis Rablan! It's Dennis Rablan!" Murphy yelled, but only Pewter understood as she came alongside Murphy.

The two cats followed Dennis, running hard, his right arm hanging uselessly by his side. He turned, hit the doors with his left side, and escaped.

The double doors swung shut, keeping the cats inside.

"Damn!" Mrs. Murphy spit, the hair on her tail puffed, her eyes huge.

As Susan reached Harry, Tucker, hearing a second set of footsteps, bounded up the stairwell. Tucker, now on the second floor, heard footsteps thump down the far stairway. The corgi ran down the hall, reaching the top of the back stairwell as the human hit the bottom, turned right and, narrowly missing the cats, opened the doors and escaped. The cats escaped with him. He was in black sweats with a ski mask covering his face.

Within seconds Tucker was at the bottom of the stairs. With her greater bulk, she pushed a door open and followed the cats.

About a hundred yards ahead of them they heard footsteps drop over the bank; they followed as the figure ran toward the houses behind the school. He disappeared, they heard a car door slam and a car took off, heading west, no lights.

"Damnit!" Tucker cursed.

"It was Dennis Rablan," Murphy panted.

"But who was the guy upstairs?" Tucker kept sniffing the ground.

"Let's follow the tracks," Pewter wisely suggested. They followed two sets of tracks to the end of the schoolyard.

Looking down at the houses below, Murphy said, *"I would never have thought Dennis capable of these murders. I can't believe it but I smelled him. It was him."*

"Let's go back inside," Tucker said.

"We can't open the doors." Pewter sat in the cool grass.

"I can. Come on."

Once inside, they checked down the hall. Everyone was around Harry.

"Let's go upstairs and work backwards. There may be a scent up there that will help us." Pewter started up the back stairs.

The other two followed.

Tucker, nose to the ground, moved along the hall. Pewter, pupils wide in the dark, checked each room, as did Mrs. Murphy.

"English Leather." Tucker identified the cologne. *"Enough to mask the scent of an entire regiment. Odd. So heavy a scent even humans can smell it. Why advertise your presence like that?"*

"What's this?" Pewter stopped in the hall, patting at a thin, twisted piece of rope with a wooden dowel on each end.

"A garotte!" Mrs. Murphy exclaimed. *"He was going to strangle someone."*

"Think we can get Susan or another human up here?" Tucker said.

"No, they're worried about Mom and we should be, too," Pewter replied.

"We can't just leave it here." Murphy thought a moment. *"Tucker, pick it up. Drop it at their feet. When things quiet down one of the humans will notice."*

Without another word, Tucker picked up the garotte, and hurried down the stairs to Harry.

Rick Shaw and Cynthia attended to her. They had just arrived at the school. Hank, Fair, and Susan knelt down with Harry.

"It's not crushed, thank God." Cynthia gently felt Harry's windpipe.

Harry still couldn't speak but she was breathing better.

Mrs. Murphy, Pewter, and Tucker quietly walked down the stairs.

Tucker dropped the garotte at Rick Shaw's feet. He pulled a handkerchief from his pocket, bent over, and picked it up. He whistled low.

Tucker eagerly looked up at him, then turned, walking toward the stairwell.

Harry whispered—her throat felt on fire—"They chased him."

"There were two of them!" Pewter, in frustration, yowled.

Rick followed Tucker up the stairs. The dog stopped where Pewter found the twisted rope. Although it was cool on the second floor—the heat was turned down for the weekend—Rick was sweating. He knew what a close call Harry had suffered. And he also knew because Jason called in on the squad car radio that he had lost Dennis Rablan at the intersection of Route 240 and Route 250. A big semi crossed the intersection and when Jason could finally turn, Dennis was out of sight. The officer drove down Beaver Dam Road, turned back on 250 to check that out, turned west on 250, and finally doubled back on 240. No trace.

Slowly he walked down the hallway, down the back stairwell, to the doors. He pushed open the doors, accompanied by Tucker, and walked to the edge of the hills.

He knelt down; the grass was flattened. He stood up and quickly walked back to the school. He and Cynthia had locked the doors at the top of each stairwell. He walked up the stairs. The door was open, a stopper under it so it wouldn't swing back and forth. The lock had been neatly picked. He walked the length of the hall to find the other door, also propped open. It had been opened from the inside. Then he came downstairs and checked on Harry again.

Harry, sitting with her back against the wall, was pushing away a glass of water Susan wanted her to drink. She was breathing evenly now.

Rick knelt down with her. "Can you talk?"

"A little," she whispered. She told him about hearing a sound, going up a step to turn on the lights, and hearing a man's voice say, "Don't, you idiot." Then he hit hard and she fell back.

"Did the voice sound familiar?" Rick put his hand on her knee.

"Yes, but...it was just a whisper. I didn't recognize it and yet, there was something familiar. Eerie."

"Height?"

"Maybe five nine, ten, average, I guess."

"Build?"

"Average."

"And you couldn't see the face?"

"Ski mask." She reached for the water now. Susan handed it to her.

Rick stood back up, asked everyone where they were. In the parking lot, they all confirmed one another's presence, except for Susan, who waited at the doors for Harry.

"Listen to me," Rick commanded. "Say nothing of this. Harry, if you can't speak normally for the next few days, put out that you have laryngitis. Let's see if we can disturb our guy. He's going to want to know what you've seen."

"Okay."

"Next thing. Keep someone with you at all times."

"*I wish they could listen. Dennis Rablan!*" Murphy meowed, knowing it was hopeless.

"It's all right, Mrs. Murphy." Harry reached for the cat. Pewter came over, too.

"You're covered at work. Miranda is there," Rick said.

"I'll stay," Fair gladly volunteered.

"Z'at all right with you?" Cynthia, sensitive to the situation, asked Harry.

"Yes." Harry nodded.

"Do you think he was waiting in the stair-well for Harry?" Susan shuddered.

"I don't know," Rick grimly replied. "If he was up there throughout the dinner, he'd have seen who was leaving and who was staying. If he'd gone to the dinner and then come back, well, maybe he hoped his intended victim was still there." He turned to Harry and then Fair: "This is a highly intelligent and bold individual. Take nothing for granted." Rick was seething inside that he hadn't posted a man upstairs. He assumed locking the doors would do the job.

The three animals looked at one another. They knew they'd be on round-the-clock duty, too.

47

Like most stubborn people, Harry failed to realize how shock would affect her. She thought she was fine. She was happy to go home but surprised that when she walked through the kitchen door a wave of exhaustion washed over her, adding to the throb caused by the headache. She wanted to talk to Fair but couldn't keep her eyes open.

"Honey, you need to go to bed." He lifted her out of the chair into which she'd slumped.

"I'm sorry. I don't know why I'm so tired. Maybe I should take more painkiller."

"No. You've had enough."

Too wiped out to protest, she meekly let him walk her into the bedroom and fell into bed.

"I'll sleep by the kitchen door," Tucker declared.

"I'll take the front door." Mrs. Murphy chose her spot.

"Well, I'll sleep in the bedroom then. What if someone climbs through the window?" Pewter dashed to the bedroom before the others could protest.

Tracy came home at midnight, whistling as he opened the kitchen door. Fair, stretched out on the sofa, swung his long legs to the floor.

"Fair?"

"Had a good night?"

"Wonderful. I feel like a kid again. I even kissed Miranda on her doorstep." He smiled broadly, then considered Fair on the sofa. "Am I interrupting anything?"

"No." Fair walked into the kitchen, reached under the cupboard by the door, pulled out a bottle of Talisker scotch, and poured them each a nightcap. They moved to the cheerful, if threadbare, living room, where Fair told Tracy everything he could remember from the evening.

A long, long silence followed as Tracy

stared into the pale gold liquid in his glass. "We were fiddling while Rome burned, I guess. That son of a bitch was over our heads the whole time."

"Harry could have been killed." Fair put his glass down on the coffee table, first sliding a coaster under it. "And whoever it is may fear she recognized him through his voice or way of going."

"Way of going?"

"Ah," Fair explained, "a horse has a special movement and I or any good horseman, really, can identify her by her gait. A way of going. For instance, you have an athlete's walk. I might be able to identify you even if you were in costume—or BoomBoom Craycroft, that sashay."

"The sheriff's command to act as though she has laryngitis is a good one for flushing him out but not so good for Harry. She knows she's bait?"

"Of course. Rick will have plainclothes men around the post office. He's got the house covered now. There's only one drive in and out."

"Somehow that's not very reassuring."

"No." Fair picked up his glass again, holding it between both hands.

"Do you have any ideas about who, what, why?"

"No, well, not exactly. I told you Rick Shaw's idea, that this is someone who was in love with Ron Brindell. Or at least is avenging him."

Tracy emptied his glass, then leaned toward

Fair. "You know what, Buddy? I'm sixty-eight years old and I don't know a damn thing. Do people snap? Can anyone snap in a given situation? Are some weak and some strong? Are there really saints and sinners? Don't know but I do know once a person loses their fear of their own death, once they no longer care about belonging to other people, they'll do anything. Anything. My God, look at Rwanda. Sarajevo. Belfast. Kill children. Kill anything."

"Presumably those killings are politically motivated."

"Yeah, that's another load, too. Some people just want to kill. Give them a reason so they can cover up their murderous selves. The church can give them a reason, the state. I've seen enough to know there are no good reasons."

"I'm with you there."

"Whoever this is no longer cares. He's given up on people. He has nothing to lose. I also think he intended to finish off his list at the reunion and he's been thwarted. He's angry. And maybe, just maybe, he'll make a mistake."

Fair nodded in agreement. "The more I think about this reunion murderer, the more the finger points to Dennis Rablan."

"There are three left." Tracy held up three fingers.

"Two. Dennis Rablan and Bob Shoaf."

"Three. Hank Bittner."

"He said he wasn't in the locker room."

"He knows too much. Three. And there's a strong possibility one of the three is the killer."

"I'd hate to be one of those guys." Fair's deep voice dropped even lower.

Truer words were never spoken.

48

"Getting the flu?" Chris asked Harry sympathetically when she heard her voice on the phone that Sunday morning.

"Laryngitis," Harry replied.

"You do sound scratchy. I called to apologize. I chickened out. I could have at least said good-bye."

"You don't have to apologize to me. If I'd been in your shoes, I'd have melted my sneakers running—flat-out flying—out of there."

"You're not mad?"

"No."

"Anybody know anything? I mean, any clues?"

"Not that I know of but then Sheriff Shaw wouldn't tell me no matter what."

"Yes, I guess. He has to be careful. Well,

I hope you feel better. I'll see you in the P.O. tomorrow."

"You bet." Harry hung up the tackroom phone.

She and Fair finished the barn chores and had decided to strip all the stalls to fill in the low spots and places where the horses had dug out.

"You need rubber mats or Equistall." Fair rolled in a wheelbarrow of black sand mixed with loam.

"Equistall costs me four hundred and fifty dollars a stall."

"It is expensive. Our alfalfa cube experiment was a big success."

"So far. I've been able to cut back on my feed bill but everyone's getting good nutrition. Maybe a little too much," she laughed, as she indicated Tomahawk in the paddock.

"If he were a man that'd be a beer belly." Fair shoveled the sand into the stall. "Tracy was up early this morning. At least their reunion is a smashing success. They're meeting for breakfast in the cafeteria."

"Chris sure wanted to know everything. Maybe I'm being suspicious. I guess it's natural since she and Denny have been pretty close. Right now I—" A car motor diverted her attention.

"*Who goes!*" Tucker barked, running out of the barn.

Pewter and Mrs. Murphy, sitting in the hayloft, saw BoomBoom's Beemer roll down the dusty drive.

298

"Wonder what she wants?" Mrs. Murphy said.

"Fair," Pewter sarcastically replied.

"We'll soon find out." The tiger cat tiptoed to the edge of the hayloft. She stayed still as she peered down into the center aisle.

Once BoomBoom parked her car and got out, Pewter joined her.

"Harry!" BoomBoom called out.

"In here," came the reply.

BoomBoom walked into the barn, saw Harry in the aisle, and then noticed Fair as he stepped out of the stall. Her expression changed slightly. "Oh, hello."

"Hi," he said.

"Has Bob Shoaf come by?"

"No. Why would he?" Harry said.

"I thought he might stop off to say good-bye before flying back up north. He always liked you."

"BoomBoom, I don't believe a word of this. What's wrong?" Harry leaned her rake against the stall door.

Her voice shot up half an octave. "I wanted to say good-bye myself, really."

"Why don't I go inside or why don't you two go inside? Maybe you can have this discussion without me." Fair tossed a shovelful of the sand mix into a stall.

"Uh...yes." BoomBoom backed out of the barn.

Mrs. Murphy and Pewter climbed down backwards from the ladder to the hayloft. They followed the two women, who stopped at the BMW.

BoomBoom, voice lowered, said, "He left without saying anything. I thought if he was still around I'd find out what was the matter."

"He's a jock, Boom. He's used to being fawned over and getting what he wants. As long as he didn't leave money on your dresser, I wouldn't worry." Harry immediately guessed what really happened.

BoomBoom's face flushed. "Harry, you have the most off-putting way of speaking sometimes." She reached in her skirt pocket. "He left this, though." A heavy, expensive Rolex gold watch gleamed in her hand.

"That costs as much as my new truck."

"Yes, I think it does. I really ought to return the watch but I can't send it to his house, now, can I?"

"Ah...?" Harry had forgotten about Bob's perfect wife and two perfect children. She took the watch from BoomBoom's palm. Nine-fifteen. She checked the old Hamilton she wore, her father's watch. Nine-fifteen.

"One other thing, I ought to check the school. I know you and Susan cleaned up last night but I am the Chair, and I should double-check everything."

"Well, go on."

"I'm afraid."

"Great. Why come to me?"

"Because Susan is at church with Ned and the kids and because—you're not afraid of much."

Within ten minutes Harry, Mrs. Murphy,

300

Pewter, Tucker, BoomBoom, and Fair reached Crozet High.

The front main entrance was open because of the class of 1950's breakfast, the last scheduled event. The first place they checked was the gym, which was locked. BoomBoom had a set of keys. She unlocked the door. They looked around quickly. Everything was fine.

"I'm going back upstairs," Tucker said. *"Maybe I missed something in the dark."*

"I can see in the dark. I didn't see anything," Pewter said.

"There was a lot going on." Tucker headed up the stairs.

Pewter followed. Mrs. Murphy stayed with Harry as the humans checked the hallways and garbage cans.

"You all cleaned up everything. I don't have anything to do," BoomBoom said gratefully.

"Murphy!" Pewter howled from the top of the stairs.

Murphy hurried up the stairs, met Pewter and raced with her as she flew over the polished floor to the classroom next to the back stairwell.

Tucker sat in the classroom. The window was open. The blinds, pulled all the way to the top, had the white cord, beige with age, hanging out the window. That wasn't all that was hanging out the window.

Mrs. Murphy jumped to the windowsill. Bob Shoaf, tongue almost touching his breastbone, hung at the end of the venetian blind cord.

"Should I get Mom?" Pewter asked.

"Not yet." Mrs. Murphy coolly surveyed the situation. *"The humans will track up everything. Let's investigate first."* She asked the dog, *"Anything?"*

"English Leather fading—and Dennis's scent."

Pewter jumped up next to Mrs. Murphy. *"His face is—I can't describe the color."*

"Don't worry about him." Murphy noted that the end classroom jutted out by the stairwell. The windows in a row could be seen from the road out front but the back window, set at a right angle to the others, was hidden from view. Bob probably wouldn't have been found until sometime Monday if they hadn't come upstairs. The frost preserved the body but even without a frost the humans wouldn't have smelled him for twenty-four to forty-eight hours, depending on the warmth of the day. She also noticed that rigor had set in. Nothing lay on the ground below.

The three animals prowled around the classroom. They walked the windowsills, checked under desks, sniffed and poked. Then they split up. Mrs. Murphy walked to the far stairwell. Tucker and Pewter checked the stairwell closest to the classroom.

They met in the downstairs hallway. No one had found anything unusual.

"Do you think the killer would have done this to Mom?" Tucker asked.

"No. But I think he would have killed her if she'd gotten too close. I know he would. But he wasn't hanging when she was attacked. Whoever

did this in the wee hours of the morning hauled him back here. That's a lot of work." Mrs. Murphy spied the humans coming out of the cafeteria, each one eating a muffin from the class of 1950's breakfast.

"*They'll wish they hadn't eaten,*" Pewter sighed.

"*Well, let's get them upstairs.*" Tucker thought she'd pull on Fair's pants leg.

"*BoomBoom is going to have a terrible time explaining that watch.*" Murphy headed toward the group.

49

All hell broke loose. The media from all over Virginia, Washington, and even Baltimore played up the murders. The attention was fueled by the fact that Rex and Bob had been killed on a weekend when news was especially slow and Bob had been a big sports celebrity.

Crozet, overrun by vans adorned with satellite dishes, pulled tight the shutters on the windows. Few chose to talk but among themselves the agreement was that the media was correct in dubbing these events the Reunion Murders.

The reporters waited outside the various

churches, trying to nab the faithful as they emerged from late-morning services.

Public buildings were closed. The reporters were out of luck there but they hit up the convenience stores, including Market Shiflett's. The reporter from Channel 29, having done her homework, knew that Market was a member of the class under siege. Being quite pretty, she managed to extract a comment from him, which was played on the news relentlessly.

"The big cities have lots of nutcases. Guess it was Crozet's turn," Market said, looking into the camera from behind the cash register of the store.

Since few other quotes were available, Market made the airwaves up and down the Mid-Atlantic.

Mim Sanburne called a meeting at her house. Invited were those she considered the movers and shakers of the town. Harry and Miranda, part of the inner circle by virtue of birth and their jobs, sat with Herb Jones, Jim Sanburne, Larry Johnson, and Mim, discussing how to divert the bad publicity.

"That problem would be solved if we could apprehend the criminal," Harry, out of sorts, whispered, her voice still rough.

The older people quieted, each realizing that not being members of the class of 1980, they felt safe.

"You're quite right." Mim smoothed her hair.

50

Dennis Rablan was nowhere to be found. Rick Shaw scoured the photo shop and Rablan's house, called his parents and his friends. No one had seen or heard from him—at least, that's what they told Rick and Cynthia. He had stationed patrol cars at Dennis's home, his parents' home, and his ex-wife's home.

Standing next to the coroner, Rick hoped Dennis would open the doors to his business on Monday morning. He was sure Dennis knew something that he wasn't telling—assuming he was alive.

"This man died from a bullet to the brain. Apart from broken fingers, smashed knees, and both sides of his collarbone broken—the results of twelve years of pro football—this was a man in good health." The coroner shook his head. "I'd like to take every high-school football hero and show them what happens to people who continue to play this game throughout college and the pros. They get money and maybe fame but that's all they get."

"How long was he dead before he was found this morning?"

"I'd say the time of death occurred about four in the morning. You examined the site, of course."

"No sign of struggle." Rick hoped the embalmer at the fu-neral home would be able to get the dark color from Bob's face and he asked the coroner if that was possible.

"Usually. Once the blood drains out it will drain from the face, too, but I'm a coroner, not a funeral director." He smiled, perfectly at home with dead bodies. "If that doesn't work, I'd suggest a closed casket. There's the problem of the deep crease in the neck but if he staples the collar to the skin at the back of the neck it should stay up and not distress the family. I remember Bob's glory days at Crozet High." He peered over his half-moon glasses. "And beyond."

"Me, too." Cynthia finally spoke. Autop-sies put her considerable composure to the test.

"Those days are over now," Rick simply stated. "Funny how an entire life reduces to that final moment. Bob probably thought he could get out of it, whatever or whoever. Self-confidence was never his problem."

"Same M.O.?" The coroner pulled the sheet up over Bob's discolored face.

"Yes. More than likely he wasn't shot at the school. His body was carried to the high school and up the steps. He's no feather either."

"One hundred and eighty-eight pounds, a good weight for a cornerback. Your killer will have sore legs unless he's a weight lifter."

When Rick and Cynthia drove away, Cynthia said, "Harry, Boom, and Fair certainly had a shock. They didn't know he'd been shot between the eyes until we hauled up the body. There's that moment when you see the corpse, the physical damage—it never leaves you."

"I was surprised that BoomBoom didn't swoon. She rarely misses an opportunity to give vent to her innermost feelings," Rick wryly commented.

"Remarkably restrained." Cynthia sighed. "Considering she'd slept with the man not six or seven hours before that."

"We've got her statement. She didn't waffle. I give her credit." Rick headed back toward the department, then turned toward Crozet.

"School?"

"No. BoomBoom's."

They pulled into the driveway of the beautiful white brick home. BoomBoom's deceased husband had made a lot of money in the gravel and concrete business, a business she still owned although she did not attend to day-to-day operations. Flakey as Boom could be, she could read an accounting report with the best of them, and she made a point of dropping in at the quarry once or twice a week. She intended to profit handsomely from the building boom in Albemarle County.

A Toyota Camry was parked next to her BMW.

If anything, BoomBoom seemed relieved to see them again. Her eyes, red from crying, were anxious.

Chris Sharpton and Bitsy Valenzuela rose when Rick and Cynthia walked into the lavish living room.

"Should we leave?"

"Not yet," Rick said.

Boom offered refreshments, which they declined.

"Ladies, what are you doing here?" the sheriff asked.

"I called them," Boom said.

"That's fine but I didn't ask you." Rick smiled, as he'd known Olivia Ulrich Craycroft since she was tiny, and no offense was taken on her part.

"Like she said, she called me, she was crying and I drove over," Chris said. "I'm afraid I haven't been much comfort. I told her to take a vacation. In fact, everyone from her class should take a vacation."

"She called me, too." Bitsy confirmed BoomBoom's statement. "I asked E.R. if I could come over. He's worried about all this but he relented since Chris and I were driving over together."

"The victims are men." Cynthia leaned forward as Rick settled into his chair. "Boom-Boom doesn't appear to be in danger."

"I'd hate to be the exception that proves the rule," BoomBoom said.

Rick waited, resting his head on his hand.

First she sat still, then she fidgeted. Finally she spoke. "I know you think I know something, sheriff, but I don't." Suddenly she got up and walked upstairs to her bedroom, returning with Bob's gold Rolex watch. She dropped it into Rick's upturned hand. "I didn't steal it. He left it here last night. Can you return it to his widow? I mean, you don't have to tell. Why should she know?"

"Fine." Rick slipped the heavy watch in his pocket.

"Were you two together in high school?" Cynthia asked.

"No. We just looked at one another at the supper and there it was. People told me these things happen at reunions but it wasn't a case of some old wish being fulfilled."

"Who did you date in high school? Any of the deceased?"

"Coop, I told you all this. No. My senior year I dated college guys mostly. The dances, let's see, I went with Bittner if my boyfriend at the time couldn't come."

"And where is this boyfriend?" Cynthia scribbled.

"A vice president at Coca-Cola in Atlanta. I think he'll be president someday. As you know, I married a hometown boy, although he was eight years older than I."

"Chris, sometimes outsiders can see more than insiders. What do you think?" Cynthia asked the blonde woman, who had been listening intently.

"That I'm glad I'm not part of this." She nervously glanced at BoomBoom. "Even if you are a woman and therefore probably safe, I'd be frightened."

"Did you notice anything unusual when you worked on the reunion?" Coop turned to Bitsy.

"Uh...well, they picked on one another.

No one held much back." She smiled nervously. "But there wasn't enough hostility for murder."

"Did anyone ever discuss Charlie's illegitimate child from high school?"

Bitsy replied, "Not until Dennis lost his composure."

Chris looked Cynthia straight in the eye. "No. I didn't hear about that until later."

"You know that Dennis Rablan accused me of having Charlie's baby, but I didn't. I swear I didn't." BoomBoom frowned.

"But you know who did?" Rick quietly cornered her.

Boom's face turned red, then the color washed right out. "Oh God, I swore never to tell."

"You couldn't have foreseen this, and the information might have a bearing on the case." Rick remained calm and quiet.

Agitated, BoomBoom jumped from her chair. "No! I won't tell. She wouldn't have killed Charlie. She wouldn't. As for Leo and the others: Why? What could the motive possibly be? It makes no sense. I don't care what happened back then, if anything did happen. The murders make no sense."

"That's our job. To find out." Coop was now perched on the edge of her seat. "What may seem like no connection to you...well, there could be all kinds of reasons."

"But I thought these murders sprang from the supposed rape of Ron Brindell." Boom paced back and forth. "Isn't that what everyone's saying?"

"That's just it. No one admits to being there. Market Shiflett heard about it at school. Bittner says he wasn't there and the same for Dennis Rablan."

"What do you think?" BoomBoom asked Cynthia.

"It's not my job to point the finger until I have sufficient evidence. Right now what I think is immaterial."

"It's not immaterial to me." BoomBoom pouted, pacing faster. "You're asking me to betray a lifelong trust and I know in my heart that this woman has nothing to do with these awful murders." She sat down abruptly. "I know what you all think of me. You think I'm a dilettante. I have, as Mrs. Hogendobber so politely puts it, 'enthusiasms.' I sleep with men when I feel like it. That makes me a tramp, to some. I guess to most. You all think I take a new lover every night. I don't, of course. You think I'm overemotional, oversexed, and underpowered." She tapped her skull. "Think what you will, I still have honor. I refuse to tell."

"This could get you in a lot of trouble," Rick softly replied.

"Trouble on the outside, not trouble on the inside." She pointed to her heart.

51

Rick had been on the phone for fifteen minutes. On a hunch he had Cynthia call the San Francisco Police Department.

He decided he wanted to talk to the officers on the scene that night. Luckily, Tony Minton, now a captain, remembered the case.

"—you're sure the note was his handwriting?"

Captain Minton replied, "Yes. We searched his apartment after the suicide and the handwriting was his. Our graphologist confirmed."

"Enough is enough." Rick quoted Ron's suicide note.

"That was it."

"There were three reliable witnesses."

"And others who didn't stop. They reported a young man climbing on the Golden Gate Bridge, waving good-bye and leaping. We never found the body."

"And the witnesses could describe the victim?"

"Medium height. Thin build. Young. Dark hair."

"Yes." Rick covered his eyes with his palm for a moment. "Did he have a police record?"

"No."

"Captain Minton, thank you for going over

this again. If you think of anything at all, please call me."

"I will."

Rick hung up the phone. He stood up, clapped his hat on his head, crooked his finger at Cynthia, who was again studying lab reports. "Let's go," he said.

Silently, she followed him. Within twenty minutes they were at Dede Rablan's front door.

She answered the door and allowed them to come inside. She then sent the two children, aged eight and ten, to their rooms and asked them not to interrupt them.

"I'm sorry to disturb you again, Mrs. Rablan."

"Sheriff, I want an answer to this as well as you do. Dennis wouldn't kill anyone. I know him."

"I hope you're right." Rick reassured her, by his tone of voice, that he felt the same way. "Has he called today?"

"No. He usually calls in the evening to check on the kids. He has them next weekend."

"You met just out of college?" Cynthia referred to her notes from an earlier questioning.

"Yes. I was working for a travel magazine. Just started. A researcher."

"Dede." Cynthia leaned toward her. She knew her socially, as they took dance classes together. "Did you ever get the feeling Dennis had a secret—even once?"

"I had hunches he was unfaithful to me." She lowered her eyes.

"Something darker?"

"Cynthia, no. I wish I could help but he's not a violent man. He's an undirected one. A spoiled one. If he had a dark secret, he kept it from me for twelve years. You have to be a pretty good actor to pull that off."

Rick cleared his throat. "Did you ever think that your husband might be a homosexual?"

Dede blinked rapidly, then laughed. "You've got to be kidding."

52

Monday proved to be even more chaotic than Sunday. Print reporters snagged people at work, and television vans rolled along Route 240 and the Whitehall Road as reporters looked for possible interviews.

Harry and Miranda refused to speak to any media person. Their patience was sorely tested when the TV cameras came inside anyway, the interviewer pouncing on people as they opened their mailboxes.

"*Ask me,*" Pewter shouted. "*I discovered the garotte.*"

"*I discovered the body. I smelled it out!*" Tucker tooted her own horn.

"*You two better shut up. This is federal prop-*

erty and I don't think animals are supposed to work in post offices," Murphy grumbled. *"They don't listen. They never listen. It's Dennis Rablan— dumbbells—Dennis and someone drenched in English Leather cologne."*

"Bull! The government rents the building. As long as they don't own it we can do what we want." Pewter had learned that fact from Miranda, though she had neglected to confirm that the renter could do as they pleased. But then the federal government did whatever they wanted, pretending to have the welfare of citizens at heart. The fact that Americans believed this astonished the gray cat, who felt all governments were no better than self-serving thieves. Cats are by instinct and inclination anarchists.

"Pewter, if we appear on television, all it takes is one officious jerk to make life difficult," Murphy, calmer now, advised her.

"I'll fight! I'll fight all the way to the Supreme Court!" Pewter crowed.

"Animals don't have political rights or legal ones, either." Tucker sat under the table. *"Humans think only of themselves."*

"Be glad of it." Mrs. Murphy watched from the divider. *"If humans decided to create laws for animals, where would it end? Would chickens have rights? Would we be allowed to hunt? Would the humans we live with have to buy hunting licenses for us? If we killed a bird would we go to jail? Remember, we're dealing with a species that denies its animal nature and wants to deny ours."*

"Hadn't thought of that," Pewter mumbled,

316

then threw back her head and sang out. *"To hell with the Supreme Court! To hell with all human laws. Let's go back to the fang and the claw!"*

"Someone has." Murphy jumped down as the TV camera swung her way.

Bitsy Valenzuela opened the door, saw the commotion and closed it. A few others did the same until the television people left.

"Damn, that makes me mad!" Harry cursed, her voice actually huskier than the day before. Her throat hurt more, too.

"They hop around like grasshoppers." Mrs. Hogendobber walked to the front window to watch the van back out into traffic. The sky was overcast. "'But if any man hates his neighbor, and lies in wait for him, and attacks him, and wounds him mortally so that he dies, and the man flees into one of these cities, then the elders of his city shall send and fetch him from there, and hand him over to the avenger of blood, so that he may die.'" She quoted Deuteronomy, Chapter nineteen, Verses eleven and twelve.

"What made you think of that?"

"I don't know exactly." Miranda flipped up the hinged part of the divider and walked into the mailroom. "There's a pall of violence over the land, a miasma over America. We must be the most violent nation among the civilized nations of the earth."

"I think that depends on how you define civilized. You mean industrialized, I think."

"I suppose I do." Mrs. Hogendobber put her arm around Harry. "You could have been killed, child. I don't know what I'd do without you."

Tears welled up in their eyes and they hugged.

"The strange thing was, Mrs. H., that I wasn't scared until I got home. I was glad to have Fair there and Tracy, too."

"Tracy is very fond of you. He's..." She didn't finish her sentence. Bitsy slipped back in now that the television crew had left.

"Hi."

"Hi, Bitsy." Miranda greeted her.

"Just came for my mail."

Chris pushed open the door, said hello to everyone, then exhaled sharply. "It's like a circus out there. Do you think there'd be this many reporters if someone in town had won the Nobel Prize?"

"No. Goodness isn't as interesting as evil, it would seem," Harry said.

"Still under the weather?" Chris came up to the counter, followed by Bitsy.

"Laryngitis. Can't shake it."

"There's a dark red mark on your neck," Chris observed. "Girl, you'd better go to the doctor. That doesn't look like laryngitis to me. Come on, I'll run you over."

"No, no," Harry politely refused.

"If there's color on your neck, Harry, this could be something quite serious. You're being awfully nonchalant."

"Chris, don't tell me the seven warning signs of cancer," Harry rasped, then laughed.

"It's not funny!" Chris was deadly serious.

Miranda stepped up to the counter. "I'll take her at lunch. You're quite right to be concerned. Harry is bullheaded—and I'm being restrained in my description."

The animals watched as Chris and Bitsy left, each getting into separate cars.

"Do you think those present can keep from telling what really happened to Mom Saturday night?" Tucker worried.

"They'd better. Mom is in enough trouble as it is." Pewter sat by the animal door. She couldn't make up her mind whether to stay inside, where it was cozy, or whether to take a little walk. She was feeling antsy.

"But that's the deal. The killer will come into this post office. He'll know that Mom doesn't have laryngitis. If she pretends that is her problem, it could rattle his cage. I flat-out don't like it and I don't care what the humans say—this person will strike like a cobra. They think because there's a human with her at all times, that she's safe. Remember, this killer gets close to his victims. They aren't threatened. Then—pow!" Tucker was deeply worried. How could two cats and one dog save Harry?

Murphy, listening intently, hummed "The Old Gray Mare" under her breath.

53

Coop, alone in her squad car, rolled by the post office at five in the afternoon. She knocked, then came through the back door.

"More black clouds piling up by the mountains. The storm will blow the leaves off the trees by sundown." She bent down to scratch Tucker's ears. "I hate that. The color has been spectacular. One of the prettiest falls I remember."

"Storm's not here yet." Harry tossed debris into a dark green garbage bag with yellow drawstrings. She looked at the bag. "Silly, but I hate going out to that dumpster."

"Not so silly. Where's Miranda?"

"Next door. She ran over to get half-and-half for her coffee." Diet or no diet, Miranda would not give up her half-and-half.

"Weird."

"What?"

"It's so quiet. This is the last place I would expect it to be quiet."

"Wasn't this morning. Half the town dragged themselves in before ten o'clock but the media attention finally irritated them. What's so unusual is, there's no fear unless it's one of my classmates. Oh, people are upset, outraged, full of ideas, but not afraid."

"Are you?"

"Yes," Harry replied without hesitation. "I'd be a fool not to be. I scan each face that comes through that door and wonder, 'Is he the one?' I scan each face and wonder which one is scanning mine." She sighed. "At least we haven't gotten any more stupid mailings. That seems to be the signal."

"Any unusual conversations, I mean, did anyone call attention to your voice?"

"Every single person who came in. Chris Sharpton wanted to take me to Larry Johnson to have him examine my throat. She was the only one who wanted to get a medical opinion. Big Mim suggested a hot toddy after taking echinacea. Little Mim said pills, shots, nothing works. It has to run through my system. Most comments were of that nature. Although, I must say that I was impressed with BoomBoom. She hasn't spilled the beans—'course, I guess she has a lot on her mind."

"Indeed...but Boom has sense underneath all that fluff. She's not going to willingly jeopardize you."

"Fair calls every half hour. He's driven by four times. I'm sure his patients are thrilled."

Coop laughed. "Fortunately, they can't complain."

"No, but their owners can." Harry tied up the bag, setting it by the back door. "Any sign of Dennis Rablan?"

"Not a hair. We've checked plane departures, the train, the bus. His van hasn't turned up either."

"Coop, he could be dead."

"That thought has occurred to me." Cynthia sat down at the table, licked her forefinger, and picked up crumbs.

"You eat like a bird." Harry opened the small refrigerator, bringing out two buttermilk biscuits that were left. "Here. Miranda's concoction for today."

Just then Mrs. H. walked through the front door; the large brown bag in her arms testified to the fact that she had bought more than a container of half-and-half. "Cynthia, how are you?"

"Frustrated."

"And hungry. She's been picking the crumbs up off the table."

"I can take care of that." Miranda lifted a huge sandwich from the bag. "You girls can share. I got a salad for me, but if you prefer that, Cynthia, I can divide it." Cynthia said she'd like half of Harry's sandwich. Miranda cut the turkey, bacon, lettuce, and provolone on whole wheat in half.

"I'm glad you're here." Harry smiled at Cynthia. "You're saving me from making a pig of myself."

Chris Sharpton pulled up, stuck her head in the front door. "Did you go to the doctor?"

"Miranda took me," Harry lied.

"And?"

"Laryngitis. He said the red mark isn't anything to worry about. I bruised myself but I can't remember how."

"You take care." Chris waved to the others, shut the door, and drove off.

As Cynthia gratefully ate, Miranda put a steaming cup of coffee before her, half coffee, half cream, with a twist of tiny orange rind, a favorite drink.

"If you have any leftovers, I'd be glad to eat them." Tucker wagged her nonexistent tail.

"Pig," was all Mrs. Murphy said. Her worry soured her usually buoyant spirits.

Pewter had eaten two biscuits earlier. She was full as a tick. *"Murphy, would it do us any good to walk up to the high school? Maybe we've missed something."*

"The only thing we've missed is the boiler room and the janitor's been in there today. Besides, all the kids are back in school. No scent. I'm at a loss, Pewter. I have not one good plan of action. I don't even know where to start."

Tucker, hearing this dispiriting talk, said, *"We can read Harry's yearbook tonight. Maybe that will guide us."*

"I'll try anything." Murphy flopped down on her side, putting her head on her outstretched arm. She felt so bad it made her tired.

"Dennis?" was all Mrs. Hogendobber asked Cynthia.

"Vanished. I was telling Harry. His landlord opened the office and lab. We crawled all over it. We took a locksmith to his house. Nothing has been disturbed and he hasn't been back. Luckily, he doesn't have pets but his plants are wilting. His neighbors haven't seen him. The state police haven't seen him on the highway."

Cynthia sipped her coffee. "You think it was Dennis?"

"He's the only one left standing," Miranda replied.

"Hank Bittner," Harry reminded her. "Lucky him. He's back in New York."

"The killer had no opportunities to nail Hank," Cynthia said. "At least, I don't think he did."

Harry poured herself a cup of tea, putting a small orange rind in it, too. She couldn't drink coffee. Made her too jumpy. "Maybe he did and maybe he didn't. Rex Harnett was killed in the bathroom. He wasn't dragged there. I wasn't keeping track of when the men went to the loo but our killer was probably in there or saw Rex in there and followed him. He worked fast. How he got out without anyone seeing him makes me think he crawled through the window. After all, the bathroom is on the first floor. And he was prepared for any opportunity. It's frightening how clever and fearless he is."

"You're right about him crawling through the bathroom window." Cynthia confirmed Harry's thesis.

"You could have told us." Mrs. Murphy was miffed.

As if in reply to the cat, Cynthia said, "We can't tell you everything. Well, Boss worries more than I do. I know neither of you did it. Anyway, yes, he dropped on the other side, maybe a six-foot drop. The grass wasn't torn up, no clear prints, obviously, but the ground was slightly indented. He dropped over, brushed himself off, hid the gun somewhere, and strolled back into the gym."

"Wish we knew if he came back in before or after Dennis found Rex."

"Harry, Dennis could have done it, walked around, gone into the bathroom, and discovered the body. It would throw people off." Miranda tapped the end of her knife on the table, a counterpoint to her words.

"Why didn't you arrest him?" Harry asked Cynthia.

"Not enough proof. But Harry, go back to Hank Bittner. You said the killer didn't have an opportunity to kill Hank if he was an intended victim."

"Remember when Hank asked you if he could go to the bathroom?"

"Yes. I made him wait."

"And he did. If the killer hadn't been in the gym with us, if he'd been upstairs, or outside or in the basement, he might have known Hank was alone. Well, probably not in the basement. But from upstairs he could have listened to the sounds coming up from the hall." She held up her hand. "A long shot. Still, he might have known. If he was in the gym with us, he couldn't follow anyone anywhere. You had us all pinned down. You had secured the bathroom where Rex was killed. Your men were out in the parking lot. You'd checked out the building and the grounds while we were penned up, right? I mean, that's why you wouldn't let Hank go to the bathroom. Not until your guys were done."

"You know, Harry, you're smart. Sometimes, I forget that."

"The killer knew what was going on while we sat there. And he's smarter than we are. Now it's possible he could have run away after killing Rex and come back later. But I don't think so. You would have known. You had that school covered."

"Yes, we did."

"All right. Later we had our dinner. Dennis makes a perfect ass of himself and leaves. You knew that, too. And I'm thinking Dennis's behavior was part of a plan."

"You're right. We had a man on the roof of the grade school across the street and we had a man in the parking lot in Tracy Raz's car. We had another officer tail him, although he lost him."

"So he could have come back. He could have snuck up behind the school."

"It's possible," she agreed. "But your cats and dog ran out the back of the school. The dog barked and that alerted our man in Tracy's car. Unfortunately, he didn't put two and two together fast enough, but then he doesn't really know your animals as I do. By the time he roused himself, all he knew was that someone had run across the lawn."

"Dennis could have come back." Miranda stuck to her guns.

"It is possible but when we sent cars out to

look for his van, it was nowhere to be found on any of the roads around here."

"He could have pulled off on a dirt road," Miranda said, "or he could have used someone else's car or a closed garage."

"Yes." Cynthia put down her cup.

"When I started up the stairwell, he was waiting. I think he was waiting for Hank. He knew Dennis had left—that is, if it wasn't Dennis. He wanted the reunion to be his killing field—he set us up with Charlie and Leo. They were the overture. The reunion was going to be the big show. I swear it! And I got in the way."

"But the class of 1950 was in the cafeteria, that's what galls me." Miranda smacked her hand on the table. "Right there. He was over our heads and we never heard him. Nor did we see him come in and we may be old but we aren't blind." .

"He never left," Harry said. "He may have gotten in his car when everyone drove away but he just circled around and hid his car. He'd been up there for hours. I can't prove it but it makes sense. You had the building covered. And even if you'd walked the halls, there are plenty of places to hide: broom closets, bathrooms. He could have stood on the john. You wouldn't have seen him. I tell you, he was there all the time."

"And you believe that he was going to kill Hank Bittner." Cynthia started to rise but Miranda jumped up and refilled her cup, handing her the half-and-half.

"If the stories are true then there are two witnesses or...participants alive from that rape." Harry thought out loud. "If Hank Bittner had been killed and Dennis lived, I guess we'd have our answer." She stopped abruptly. "Dennis has a car phone. Has he used it?"

"No. We checked that, too."

"And you've called Hank Bittner, of course," Miranda pressed.

"We did. He left on the six forty-five A.M. flight for New York and showed up for work. We called again this afternoon to see if anyone from the class had called him. Nobody had. He didn't seem frightened but that could be a bluff."

"What if you bring him back to flush the game?"

"No go. He's not coming back to Crozet until we find the killer."

"Doesn't mean the killer won't go to him." Harry folded her arms across her chest. "Another thing. The gun that killed Rex and Bob. A different gun than Marcy Wiggins'?"

"Yes."

"With a silencer?"

"Exactly."

"They're illegal," Miranda exclaimed.

"So is murder," Harry said, and then they burst out laughing, relieving some of the tension.

54

That evening, Tracy Raz and Fair took turns staying awake while Harry slept. Pewter again stayed in the bedroom with Harry while Tucker rested by the kitchen door and Mrs. Murphy curled up at the front door.

At one in the morning Mrs. Murphy opened one eye. She heard the crunch of tires about a half mile away. Had she been wide awake she would have heard it earlier. With lightning speed she skidded down the hallway, turned through the living room, and soared through the kitchen, leaping over Tucker's head. The corgi, eyes now opened wide, shot through the animal door after Mrs. Murphy. The two best friends ran under the three-board fence, down over the sloping meadow, jumped a ditch and culvert, zigzagged through the protective fringe of woods by the front entrance, and came out on the paved road in time to see the taillights of a late model car recede in the darkness.

"Damn!" Tucker shook herself.

"Make that a double damn. Even a minute earlier, we might have identified the car. You can bet it wasn't someone lost and turning around. No, that was our killer all right. Coming down the driveway. Saw Tracy's car and Fair's truck."

They turned, trotting over the light silvery frost covering the ground. The storm clouds still gathered at the mountaintops. The weather in the mountains varies from minute to minute. Although it appeared in the afternoon that a storm would hit by early evening, it waited. When the winds changed, those inky masses would roll down into the valley. Deer, raccoons, fox, and rabbits scampered about, each hoping to fill their bellies before the storm pinned them down.

As the cat and dog broke into the open meadow, a low *swoosh* flattened them to the ground. Mrs. Murphy twisted her head to look upward. A pair of huge talons, wide open, reached for her.

"Ha! Ha!" Flatface called as she brushed the edge of Mrs. Murphy's fur. Then she rose again in the dark air.

"She's got a sick sense of humor," Tucker, rattled, growled.

"Flatface. Flatface. Come back," Mrs. Murphy called out to the enormous owl.

Huge shadowy wings dipped, the owl banked, then silently settled before them. Rarely were the ground animals this close to the owl, easily three times taller than they were, with a massive chest and fearsome golden eyes. When they spoke to her or were reprimanded by her, she was usually in her perch in the cupola in the barn.

Speechless for a moment, Tucker swallowed. *"You scared us."*

"Groundlings," came the imperious reply.

"Did you see the car that drove partways down the drive?" Mrs. Murphy refused to back up even though Flatface took a step toward her, turning her head upside down for effect.

"Wasn't a car. It was a van. It flashed the lights on when it turned into the driveway, then cut them off. Drove down the road with no lights. Fool."

"Did you see who was driving it?" Murphy asked.

"No."

"We think whoever is driving that van, most likely Dennis Rablan, will try to kill Mom," Tucker, ears forward, said.

"Humans don't concern me."

"She's different." Murphy puffed out her fur a bit.

Flatface swiveled her head around; a field mouse moved under the dried hay leavings. Full, she let the tiny creature pass. *"If you were a kitten I'd eat you for supper."* She let out a low chortle, then stretched her wings out wide, a sight that would have frozen the blood even of the forty-pound bobcat who prowled this territory. To further emphasize her power she stepped forward, towering over the cat and dog.

Mrs. Murphy laughed. *"Have to catch me first. Maybe I'd put pepper on my tail."*

Flatface folded her wings next to her body. She admired the sleek tiger cat's nerve. *"As I said, I don't care about humans but I like the barn. New people might change the routine. One never knows. Then again, Harry seems less human than most of them. I shouldn't like to see her killed."*

"If you see anything or if that van returns, fly down and see who is driving it. We think it's Dennis Rablan." Tucker finally spoke up.

"All right."

The wind shifted. Mrs. Murphy beheld the first inky octopus leg of the storm slide down the mountain. *"Have you had any luck catching any of the barn mice?"*

The owl blinked. *"No—and they sing the most awful songs."*

"Ah, it isn't just me then." Murphy smiled.

Flatface hooted, opened her wings, and lifted off over their heads, a rush of air from her large wings flowing over their faces as the wind from the west picked up.

By the time they reached the screened-in porch, the first tiny ratshot of sleet slashed out of the sky. It hit the tin roof of the barn like machine-gun fire. Within seconds the *rat-tat-tat* increased to a steady roar.

"Will be a hard night of it." Murphy shook herself, as did Tucker.

"Wonder where he hides that van?" Tucker shook the sleet off her fur.

"Right under our noses."

"Do you believe Pewter slept through everything?" Tucker was appalled.

"Tracy's wide awake." Murphy watched as the older man pored over Harry's high-school yearbook.

"If this is Dennis, he knows that Tracy is our lodger. He doesn't take him seriously. I think it was Fair's truck that backed him off."

"Maybe he was checking us out for later."

55

The sleet turned to ice bits which turned to snow by mid-morning. The first snow of the season arrived punctually, right on November first.

Harry felt prepared, having driven her four-wheel drive F350 dually to work.

It was also the day of Bob Shoaf's funeral in Buffalo, New York, and Rex Harnett's in Columbia, South Carolina, where his mother was living. No one had organized memorial services in Crozet. When shopping in Market Shiflett's store, Ted Smith, a fellow in his seventies, displayed a little gallows humor when he said, "Funeral. You guys need a bulldozer to dig mass graves." Market didn't find that funny.

Nor did he find it funny when he asked Chris Sharpton to the movies and she allowed as to how he was a good man but she wasn't going out with anyone from his high-school class ever again, and if she ever saw Dennis Rablan again she'd tell him a thing or two.

In a fit of loneliness he asked Bitsy Valenzuela, later that morning, if she had any unmarried girlfriends from her hometown. He'd travel for a weekend date. She very kindly said she couldn't think of anyone off the top of her head, but if she did she'd let him know.

Morose, he waved but didn't smile when Harry threw a snowball at his window. She entered the post office as Miranda hung up the phone.

"They found Dennis's van!"

"Where?"

"Yancy's Body Shop." Yancy's also specialized in painting automobiles.

"No one noticed?" Harry was incredulous.

"Yancy's on vacation, hunting in Canada. The shop's been locked since the weekend. Cynthia said they've cordoned off the place and are dusting for prints, searching for any other evidence."

"Locked, but is there anyone in town who doesn't know where the key is? Over the door-jamb. It's been there since we were kids." She unwound her scarf. "Hey, it's something, I guess."

Tracy came in, bringing them a pepper plant. "Needed something cheerful on the first snowy day."

"Tracy, I appreciate you keeping watch but really, I have the animals."

The three furry creatures smiled.

"Yes, but now you have me, too. And while it's on my mind—"

"Honey, they've found Dennis Rablan's van!" Miranda interrupted him, then told him everything she'd just heard.

Harry called Susan, who called Bonnie Baltier in Richmond. One by one the remaining senior superlatives heard the news, including Mike Alvarez in Los Angeles. BoomBoom called Hank Bittner in New York. More worried than he cared to admit, he thanked her for her thoughtfulness.

"Dennis has to be hiding somewhere close by." Pewter felt drowsy. Low-pressure systems did that to her.

"Underground." Tucker used the old term from the underground railroad days.

In a manner of speaking, he was.

56

The following day, clear in the morning, clouded up by noon. The bite in the air meant snow, big snow. Snowstorms usually did not hit central Virginia until after Christmas and then continued up to early April. Then spring would magically appear. One day it is a gray, beige, black, and white world and the next, pink, yellow, white, and purple cover the hills.

The earliest snowstorm within Harry's memory was an October snow, when the leaves were still on the branches, and the weight of the snow with the leaves brought down huge limbs throughout the region. She remembered doing her homework that night to the

335

sound of branches being torn down, screaming since the sap was still in them.

Market dashed in to get his mail. "No more toilet paper. Miranda, I put a six-pack inside your back door. People are crazy. You'd think the storm of the century was approaching." He paused. "The barometer sure is dropping, though. Ought to be a couple of days' worth or one big punch."

"I've got my snow shovel at the ready." Miranda winked.

"And Tracy to shovel it." Harry tossed a pile of fourth-class mail into the canvas cart.

"He'll do yours, too. He is a charitable soul."

"Bet the supermarket is running low on canned goods. I should have ordered more last week. But you know, I watch the weather and you'd think it was one volcano eruption, tornado, or hurricane after another. It's not weather anymore—it's melodrama. So I don't much listen."

"I go by my shinbone." Miranda reached down on the other side of the mailboxes. "Hey, almost forgot, Market, here's a package from European Coffees." She handed it over the counter, worn smooth and pale from use.

"Thanks. Oops, looks like Bitsy at the store. Better head back."

As he left, Harry waved. They'd discussed the finding of the van yesterday. There wasn't much more to say. Market didn't like being in the store alone but he had to make a living. He said he didn't think he was in danger. He wasn't part of the Ashcraft-Burkey-Shoaf "in" group but things were so crazy, how could one be sure?

"I'm going to walk about before the snow gets here. Anyone want to come along?"

"Murphy, it's twenty-seven degrees Fahrenheit out there," Pewter protested.

"I'll go," Tucker volunteered.

"You two are always showing off about how tough you are." Pewter hopped in an empty mail cart, curling up with her tail draped over her nose.

"See ya!" Both animals pushed through the dog door in the back. It hit the wall with a magnetic thwap.

Harry looked up in time to see the gray door flop back. She figured they had to empty their bladders.

Mrs. Murphy lifted her head, inhaling the sharp cold air. She and Tucker moved along, since they stayed warmer that way. They headed toward Yancy's Body Shop, a block beyond the railroad track underpass. Both animals stayed well off the road, having seen enough squashed critters to know never to trust a human behind the wheel.

They reached the closed-up shop within ten minutes.

Rick Shaw had removed the yellow cordon tape but a few pieces of it had stuck to the big double doors of the garage. They circled the concrete structure. At the back a black plastic accordion-style drainpipe protruded from the corner. A cinder block was loose next to it, the mortar having crumbled away years ago.

337

"*Can't you push it out? You're stronger than I am.*"

"*I can try.*" Tucker leaned her shoulder against the cold block. Little by little it gave way.

"*Good!*" Murphy wriggled in and turned around. "*Can you make it?*"

"*If I can push out the second block, I can.*" Tucker wedged the cinder block sideways just enough so she could flatten and claw her way under.

The light darkened with each minute as the clouds grew gunmetal gray outside. Mrs. Murphy squinted because the old odor of grease, oil, and gasoline hurt her eyes. Both animals walked over to where the van had been parked. It was easy to discern the spot since every other inch of space was crammed with vehicles in various states of distress or undress.

"*I give them credit,*" Tucker, nose to the ground, said. "*Usually they muck up the scent but it smells like only two people were here.*"

"*Tucker, I can't smell a thing. The gasoline masks everything. Makes me nauseous.*"

"*Funny, doesn't bother humans much.*" Tucker lifted her black moist nose then stuck it to the ground again. "*Dennis was here all right. There's a hint of the darkroom plus his cologne. Cold scent. I think the only reason there's scent left is the closed van kept it safe and the moisture coming up through the concrete floor held some of it, too.*" She sighed. "*I have good powers but if we had a bloodhound, well, we'd know a lot more. There's*

*also that English Leather smell—the same smell
I picked up in Crozet High, upstairs.* ”

“*Great,*” Mrs. Murphy sarcastically said, for
she was hoping that scent wouldn't be found.
Guarding against two humans is harder than
guarding against one.

Tucker looked at Mrs. Murphy, her deep
brown eyes full of concern. “*Two. Two for
sure.* ”

Murphy wanted to sit down a moment but
the greasy floor dissuaded her. “*Tucker, let's
get back to the post office.* ”

They ran back to the post office. Cynthia
Cooper's squad car was parked in the front.

As they pushed through the animal door,
Pewter bounded to greet them. “*Dennis Rablan
called! He threatened Mother.* ”

“*What?*” Tucker and Murphy shouted.

“*Yes, he called about five minutes after you left
and he said, 'Butt out, Butthead.' Then he said,
'Ron Brindell lives!' Mom called the sheriff, and
Cynthia, who was around the corner, got here in
less than two minutes, I can tell you. No one
knows where he called from but Mom said he
sounded like he was right next door.* ”

Miranda kept her eye on the door. If someone
came in she would go directly to the counter
and help if they needed her. Cynthia and
Harry sat at the table.

“He's not far, Coop. And he wasn't on a cell
phone. The reception was too clear.” Harry,
surprisingly calm, spoke. “But Ron being
alive? I don't believe it.”

“I called 360° Communications just in

case, got E.R. Valenzuela. He's checking every call within the last ten minutes."

"Can they do that?"

"Yes. The technology is amazing and evolving by the minute. They'll work backwards, from your number. Harry, go over the conversation again. In case something occurs to you, an inflection of voice, a background sound, anything at all."

Harry folded her hands on the table. "The phone rang. I picked it up. I recognized Dennis's voice immediately. His voice was clear and firm, I guess is how I'd describe it. He didn't shout or anything. He just said, 'Butt out, Butthead' and 'Ron Brindell lives' and hung up." She furrowed her brow. "Wait, he breathed out hard and I heard a clink. A metal sound but I can't tell you what really. Just something like metal touching metal."

"He knows you saw him, obviously." Coop ran her fingers across her forehead, then squeezed the back of her neck. She felt a whopper of a tension headache coming on.

"But we know Dennis is alive."

"Yes, that makes it easier. Now we have to find him. Do you think his saying 'Ron Brindell lives' is meant as literal truth or is it part of the revenge scenario?"

"I don't know. People saw Ron jump from the bridge. How could he live?"

Miranda walked back to them. "There have been a few survivors since the Golden Gate Bridge was built, but Dennis doesn't want to hurt you, Harry. I truly believe he's warning you. What 'Ron Brindell lives' means, who knows?"

Murphy yowled. *"The Old Gray Mare! I get it. Ain't what she used to be."*

"Hush, sweetie." Harry picked her up to pet her.

"Don't let your guard down!" Murphy put her paws on the table.

"Guess Dennis was Ron Brindell's boyfriend. Bittner was right."

"Oh, that's another thing." Coop spoke to Harry, then glanced up at Miranda. "Dennis called Bittner, too. Told Bittner he was next."

The Reverend Herb Jones stomped his feet, bent over to pick something up, then opened the door. "Three beautiful ladies. I've come to the right place." He turned over the soggy white envelope that he'd found on the ground outside. "Addressed to Mrs. George Hogendobber. Now Miranda, this has to be someone younger than we are. They should know that you address a widow differently. It should be Mrs. Miranda Hogendobber. The old ways let you know the important things, right off. No wonder the young waste so much time. They're slipping and sliding trying to find out the essentials." He laughed. "Listen to me! I'm getting old!"

"Not you." Miranda took the envelope.

"Must have slipped out of the door. It's been stepped on." Herb leaned over the counter as Miranda opened the note.

She read, "His power to punish is real. He is God's servant and carries out God's punishment on those who do evil." She thought a moment. "Romans, Chapter thirteen, Verse four."

"You know the Bible better than I do!" Herb complimented her.

She read the note again. "Cynthia, I think you might want to look at this. It could be a crank or it could be Dennis trying to justify himself."

"Dennis?" Herb's eyebrows raised in puzzlement.

"He's alive." Harry then told him what had just happened.

As she was filling in the good Reverend, the phone rang.

Miranda picked it up. "Cynthia, E.R. Valenzuela for you."

Cynthia listened, then hung up the phone. "Wasn't a cell phone."

"He's here," Harry said with resolution.

"There are two and one of them you can't see, I mean, none of us can see. We take him for granted!" Murphy howled.

"Here it comes." Herb called attention to the big snowflakes falling from the glowering sky.

57

"Don't drive to New York. We'll be stranded in the storm." Dennis, right hand chained to the passenger door, pleaded. His left hand was chained to his belt. His wrists were raw from the handcuffs he'd been wearing since Saturday.

Ron Brindell started the car. "You might be right about that. I'm bored, though. Hey, I'll get Harry."

"She hasn't done a thing to you."

"She saw you," Ron said. "You know. I don't care. I just feel like killing someone else from the bad old days."

"I had a ski mask on," Dennis said wearily. "Look, just kill me and get it over with. You don't care if she saw me or not. I called her and Hank. Want me to call BoomBoom and Baltier, too?" he asked. "Just kill me. You're saving me for last, anyway." Dennis held no illusions that Ron had a scrap of sanity left but he tried to reason with him.

"Why, Dennis, what a courageous thing to say," Ron replied sarcastically.

"All right then, let's drive to New York."

"I *will* get Bittner. Maybe not tonight but I'll get him."

"He didn't *do* anything." Dennis, haggard

from his ordeal, stared at the closed garage doors.

"Exactly. He opened the door, saw what was going on, and closed it. Did precisely nothing."

"In shock, probably."

"He could have gotten the coach."

"We were all kids. Kids make bad decisions. He was probably as scared in his way as I was in my way. He's a father now. Have you no pity?"

"No." Ron turned his cold eyes on Dennis. "Why should I? I was pinned down, raped— and they laughed. Called me a faggot. I was a faggot. Do you know where the word 'faggot' comes from, Dennis? From the Middle Ages, when people burned witches. The woman was tied to the stake and surrounding her were homosexual men who were set on fire first. Instead of bundles of kindling, we were the kindling. I have *no* pity."

Ron checked his watch. "Lie down. I don't want your head to show." As Dennis squinched down, Ron reached over and stuck a rag in the poor man's mouth. "You should have stood up for me, you know. You just stood there. Oh, you told them to stop. I believe you said it once. If it had been you I'd have fought. I'd have given my life for you. Now you can give yours for me. Lie down, damnit!"

Dennis didn't even look at him as he slid down as far as he could. Since Ron had threatened to kill Dennis's two children, Dennis would do anything Ron said. Meanwhile, his brain overheated, trying to find a way out. If there was no way out, then he was determined to take out Ron. But how?

Ron hit the electronic button to raise the garage door, then pulled out into the snowy darkness.

"Hi ho, hi ho, it's off to work I go," he sang as he headed through town. Everyone was snug inside, their lights shining through the falling snow.

58

Harry and Tracy buzzed around the kitchen making pea soup, a favorite winter treat. Fair called to say he'd be late. A horse at Mountain Stables had badly cut his hind leg and needed stitching up. He didn't think he'd be back for another hour and a half because he needed to swing by the office and fill his truck with supplies. He had a hunch he'd be on plenty of calls the next couple of days as people kept their horses in stalls, feeding them too much grain. Colic often followed heavy snows. Since Tracy was there he felt Harry was okay.

Tucker jerked up her head. *"Someone's coming. On foot!"*

"Tucker, chill." Harry heard nothing.

Both cats ran to the kitchen door. A towel was stretched across the bottom of it to keep out the draft.

A knock on the door surprised the humans.

"Chris, what on earth are you doing here in this weather?" Harry opened the door.

"I was coming back from Waynesboro. I did a big shop at Harris Teeter in preparation for the storm and my car died. Absolutely dead. No lights. No nothing. Do you think you could run me home in your truck? I could throw everything in the back."

"Sure."

"I'll do it." Tracy plucked his coat off the peg.

"Thank you so much." Chris smiled. "I'm sorry to bother you on such a cold night. I saw Fair's truck parked at Mountain Stables when I came down the mountain. He never gets a break, does he?"

"No." Harry smiled. "Comes with the territory."

Tracy, his hand on the doorknob, said, "Call Fair, will you?" What he really meant was, call Rick Shaw and tell him you're alone, but he didn't want to say that in front of Chris since the sheriff had told them to keep it quiet.

"I will." She waved as the two walked out the door.

Harry picked up the phone, dialing the sheriff's number. "Hi," she said, but before she could finish her sentence Chris was back in the kitchen, a gun in her hand, leveled at Harry.

"Hang up. Come outside."

Tucker grabbed Chris's ankle but she leaned over and clunked the faithful creature on her head. Tucker dropped where she was hit.

"Tucker!" Mrs. Murphy screamed.

Pewter, thinking fast, shot out the kitchen door and through the screened-in porch door, which was easy to open. Much as Mrs. Murphy wanted to lick her fallen friend's face, she knew she had to follow.

The two cats ran into the barn. Nearly six inches of snow were already on the ground and the snow was so thick you couldn't see your hand in front of your face.

Tracy Raz lay in the snow facedown, blood oozing from the back of his head.

Again the cats couldn't stop to help him. They raced into the barn, climbing up into the loft. Once there, Mrs. Murphy stood on her hind legs, pushing up the latch. They wedged their paws at the side and pushed the door open.

"If she'll come this way we can jump down on her. The height will give us force."

"And if she doesn't?" Pewter breathed hard.

"We follow and do what we can."

Simon waddled over and saw Tracy. *"Uh oh."*

"Simon, help us push a bale of hay over to the opening," Murphy commanded.

The three small animals tried but they couldn't do it. Pewter kept running back and forth from the hay bale to the loft door opening.

"Here they come!"

Chris walked behind Harry. At least she let

Harry pull on a jacket. On seeing Tracy lying in front of the barn, Harry rushed over.

"Forget him!"

"But he's..."

"Forget him."

"I take it you're not really Chris Sharpton." Harry kept talking as she knelt down and felt Tracy's pulse, which, thanks-be-to-God, was strong.

"No. Come on."

"Where's Dennis?"

"You'll see soon enough."

Murphy wriggled her rear end, then launched herself from the loft opening. She soared through the snowflakes with Pewter right behind her.

"Ooph!" Chris fell backwards as Mrs. Murphy hit her on the chest. A split second later Pewter hit her square in the face. Chris slipped in the snow, falling on her back.

Harry jumped on her.

The gun discharged.

The cats clawed and bit but couldn't do much damage through the winter clothes. Also, the humans were rolling in the snow. Harry, strong, wasn't as strong as Chris. Harry bit Chris's gun hand but Chris wouldn't drop the gun. The cats leapt off when the humans rolled back on the ground. They'd get up, slip and fall, but Harry never let go of Chris's gun hand no matter how hard Chris hit or kicked her.

"We've got to get the gun!" Pewter hollered.

Harry hung on as Chris flung her around, her feet off the ground. Harry dragged Chris down again but they struggled up. The cats kept circling the humans while Simon watched in horror, not knowing what to do.

Finally, Chris pushed Harry away far enough to hit her hard on the jaw with a left hook. The blow stunned Harry enough that she relaxed her grip. Chris hit her again. Harry let go of the gun hand as she slid back into the snow, the blood running from her mouth. The cats again climbed up Chris's legs but she barely noticed them.

She aimed her gun at Harry, who neither begged for life nor flinched. Chris fired, missing her, because Flatface had suddenly flown low overhead and scared her for an instant.

Murphy climbed up Chris's leg, her back, and reached up to claw deep into her face. Chris struggled to rise and throw off the cat. Pewter climbed up and hung on to Chris's gun hand, sinking her fangs into the fleshy part of the palm. Chris tried again to throw off the cats, slipped in the snow, and fell down, cats shredding her face and hand.

Harry scrambled and grabbed the gun as Chris flailed, screaming, struggling to her knees. Harry had gotten up and smashed the butt of the gun into her skull. Chris dropped face first into the snow. Harry kicked her in the ribs, then kicked her again, rolling her over. Chris was out cold. Harry wanted to kill her. But some voice inside reminding her "Thou shalt not kill" prevented her from her own rage and act of revenge.

She looked into the falling snow, the flakes

351

sticking to her eyelashes. Half-dazed herself, she sank to the ground.

Mrs. Murphy, on her hind paws, licked Harry's face. *"Come on, Mom. You've got to tie her up before she comes to—come on."*

Pewter licked the other side of her face.

Harry blinked and shook her head, then stood up, swayed a little but walked into the barn, grabbed a rope lead shank, and made quick work of tying Chris's hands behind her back and tying her feet up behind her, the rope also around her neck. If Chris kicked her feet she'd choke herself.

She hurried over to Tracy, who was slowly awakening. She rubbed snow on his face. He opened his eyes.

"Tracy, can you get up?"

She put his arm around her shoulder and they both slipped and slid into the kitchen, where a groggy, sore corgi wobbled to her feet.

59

Harry, Miranda, Tracy, Fair, Susan, and Cynthia sat before Harry's roaring fire in the living-room fireplace. It was past midnight but the friends had gathered together as the snow piled up outside.

Fair treated Tucker's knot on the head by holding her in his lap, applying an ice pack periodically.

"You were saved by the grace of God," Miranda, still terribly upset, said. "He sent his furry angels of deliverance." She started to cry again.

Tracy sat next to her on the sofa, putting his arm around her. "There, there, Cuddles. You're right, our guardian angels worked overtime." A bandage was wrapped around his head and one eye was swollen shut.

"Mrs. Murphy and Pewter are heroes." Harry sat cross-legged before the fire, her cats in her lap. "You know, I would never have figured this out. So much for my deductive powers."

"If it makes you feel any better, I don't think I would have figured it out either," Cynthia consoled her. "We waited for a mistake and he finally made one. Had it not been for Mrs. Murphy and Pewter, you all would be dead and Ron would be heading for New York to get Hank Bittner."

"Has he confessed?" Fair, both hands on Tucker, asked.

"Yes. He didn't expect to live. His plan was to kill Dennis and then himself after killing Bittner. He felt no particular animosity toward Harry but toward the end, the power went to his head. He chained Dennis in his basement, forcing him to cooperate. He told Dennis if he didn't help him he'd kill Dennis's children as well as others from the class of 1980. If Dennis would help—with a gun in his ribs—he'd confine himself to the locker room boys. He broke his promise, of course."

"What about the two footprints at the dumpster?" Harry asked. "Remember, an L.L. Bean chain print and a high heel. You told us about that after we pestered you."

"He had his boots on. The heel was someone else. That was the thing. He could still pass as a man, an effeminate one, if he again dressed in men's clothes. He swears he nailed Leo Burkey in the Outback parking lot. Says he came back around and got Leo in the car. As to Charlie, Ron came down the back stairs, dressed as a man, walked into the locker room and shot him. He always identified himself first. He said Charlie laughed and Leo turned white as a sheet."

"What an elaborate ritual of revenge." Tracy's head throbbed. "To fake his own death. He knew whoever jumped off that bridge would be swept to sea. They hardly ever retrieve the bodies of the people who jump or fall from the Golden Gate Bridge."

"It was a despondent man he met in a bar," Cynthia said. "They made a suicide pact, the other fellow jumped and Ron didn't. Ron wrote the note 'Enough is enough.' People were so shocked at seeing a man standing on the edge of the bridge they didn't notice another man creeping away."

"But the yearbook!" Harry stood up, brushing off her rear end. She was sore from the struggle and her left jaw, turning dark red, would soon turn black-and-blue.

"He rummaged around used-bookstores. Found yearbooks, leafing through them. He said he looked through hundreds until he found a picture of a tall, lanky dark-haired girl that would work. People don't study yearbook pictures. He knew you wouldn't scrutinize. He said he decided to live life a blonde, which would make you laugh. He somewhat resembled Chris Sharpton. He understood people in a cunning fashion. He especially understood the code of politeness. He knew people around here wouldn't pry."

"Is Chris Sharpton alive?"

"Yes. She's married for the second time and lives in Fort Wayne, Indiana. She married her high-school boyfriend, divorced him, and in a fit sold off everything they'd had together, including her high-school yearbook. The book found its way to a San Francisco used-bookshop. Sometimes those dealers buy in lots from other dealers. At least he didn't kill Chris Sharpton," Cynthia said. "Rick had our guys calling and checking everything the minute he started talking."

"Did he fake Marcy Wiggins' suicide?" Susan felt terrible for the dead woman.

"No, she really was despondent and was on antidepression medication for months. She kept her gun in the glove compartment of her car. He'd steal it, then put it back. Brazen. If she'd caught him, he'd have made up a story."

"When did he become a woman?" Miranda wanted to know.

"After college. He worked for a large pharmaceutical company, learned as much as he could about the process, saved his money, moved to San Francisco, and underwent the sex-change process there, which is time-consuming and costly. It didn't make him any happier, though. All those years he was transforming, his one motivation was to return and punish his tormentors."

"Time stopped for him." Fair removed the cold pack from Tucker's head for a moment, to the relief of the dog.

"He'll get the chair," Susan bluntly stated.

"He wants to die. His only regret is that he couldn't kill Hank Bittner and Dennis."

"What will happen to Dennis?" Harry wondered out loud. "Was he in on it from the beginning?"

"No. Dennis drove to Chris's after losing our tail. He put his van in Chris's garage—at her suggestion. Or should I say, his? He was upset from the reunion supper and wanted to talk. She lured him into sex games. He went to bed with her and that's how Chris—or Ron—got the cuffs on him without a struggle. After that Ron was always near him with a gun on him. He was up in the stairwell when Dennis hit you, Harry. They were waiting for Hank."

Cynthia shrugged. "Dennis was a coward in not fighting Leo, Charlie, Rex, and Bob in the locker room but then four against one isn't good odds. Two against four if Ron had fought back isn't good odds either, but Dennis was afraid to be discovered. He was in a sexual relationship with Ron. At least up until the rape. But you know, Dennis wasn't a coward once Chris revealed who she really was. He said he was prepared to die in order to save his children. Ron confirms that, too."

"Is Dennis gay?" Fair asked.

"I don't know. Ron was crazy about him and Dennis said at that time in his life getting laid was the most important thing in the world."

"In a way, I'm surprised more gay people don't lose it, become violent." Fair had never really thought about it.

"Statistically, they are one of the most non-violent groups we have in America," Cynthia replied. "Yet they are still utterly despised by a lot of people. It was worse in Ron's youth. That doesn't justify what he's done. And the press will make a big hoo-ha over it. Every gay leader in the country will have something to say and every reactionary will point to this as proof positive that gays are the Devil's spawn, ignoring the fact that most violent crimes are committed by heterosexual males between the ages of fifteen and twenty-five. The truth is irrelevant."

"It always has been," Susan agreed. "My husband can tell you that."

Ned Tucker, being a lawyer, had seen enough lying, cheating, and getting-away-with-it to fill three lifetimes.

"No wonder we couldn't figure out what was happening," Harry said thoughtfully. "A man consumed by revenge, turns into a woman. One life is deformed, if you can stand that word, and four men die for it twenty years later. I would have never figured out that Chris Sharpton was Ron Brindell. I'm just glad to be alive—even if I am a little dumb."

"None of us would have figured it out." Susan, too, knew she wouldn't have put the pieces together.

"Then what was all that business about the mother of Charlie Ashcraft's illegitimate child?" Fair asked. "A couple of the victims mentioned that—and, well, there was a lot of loose talk."

"That was a red herring," Cynthia replied. "But at that stage no one except the victims knew this was connected to Ron Brindell. They thought Charlie's murder might have something to do with his past lovers or his illegitimate child."

"Does anyone know who that woman is?" Harry asked Cynthia.

"It has no bearing on the case," Cynthia quickly said.

"I'd like to know." Harry shrugged. "Curiosity."

"Forget about it." Susan sighed. "It will come out in time. All of Crozet's secrets eventually see the light of day."

"I can't believe all the times I was in Chris's company and I never thought anything. Although I thought she had awfully big feet," Harry exclaimed.

Cynthia said, "He was brilliant in his way."

"Well, I owe thanks to one brave dog and two kitties who flew through the air with the greatest of ease." Harry kissed Mrs. Murphy and Pewter.

Tracy said, "And I thank them, too. Ron hit me hard on the back of the head. If he'd shot me the noise would have warned you. He would have finished me off after he killed you."

"Tracy, you came all the way back from Hawaii for your reunion. I'm sorry it was spoiled," Harry said.

"Brought me home. I'm thankful for that. I might stay awhile." He squeezed Miranda to him.

"I don't think I would have figured out that Chris was Ron." Mrs. Murphy rubbed against Harry's side as she was again seated on the floor.

"She was as nice as she could be and she didn't seem masculine or anything—except she had this little Adam's apple. I never thought a thing about it," Pewter said.

"I should have known." Tucker sat up on Fair's lap. *"Too much perfume. She masked her scent or rather lack of it. You can change forms but you can't really change scent but so much. That's probably why he doused his black sweats and black shirt with English Leather. It smells manly."*

"Well, we'd better go check on Simon." Mrs. Murphy left the room followed by Pewter and Tucker, too.

"Are you guys going potsie?" Harry asked.

"God, I wish she wouldn't say that. It sounds

so stupid. I love her, I'm thrilled she's alive, but is there any way to get her to drop 'potsie' from her vocabulary?" Tucker laid her ears back.

"Just say yes, you are, and come on," Pewter advised.

Outside, the cold bracing air felt clean as they breathed. The snow was now nearly eight to ten inches deep. Tucker ran to the barn, snow flying up behind her. Pewter and Mrs. Murphy, hopping from spot to spot since the snow was almost over their heads, soon followed.

Simon peered over the loft edge. The horses offered thanks to all. They'd been in their stalls and couldn't do anything to help.

"Thank you, Simon," Murphy meowed.

"Flatface," Pewter called up.

"Who's there?" said the enormous bird, who knew exactly who was there as she looked down from her high nest.

"Thank you," they said in unison. *"Thank you for helping to save Harry."*

"Inept groundlings!" came the Olympian reply.

Dear Reader,

Perfect revenge. I must tell. Today the thermometer soared to 105.4°F. Granted, that's hateful to man or beast but I needed a constitutional. My human thinks she knows what's best for me. The gall. I don't pretend to know what's best for her even when I do. Anyway, she wouldn't let me outside. Of course, I'm not going to befoul the rug. I used my dirt box like a civilized animal. Still, it bothered me that I couldn't do what I wanted to do when I wanted to do it. I'm sure you understand.

Later, she got all dolled up. That in itself is worthy of comment. Oh, the whole symphony of loveliness—hair curled, lipstick, mascara, a summer blouse and skirt along with sheer hose. Why do women wear nylons? To entice us, I suppose.

I hid behind the chair and when she walked by on her way to the front door, I attacked, snagged the hose, and she had a run that ruined them. The fussing and cursing did my heart good. Naturally, she was late for her date. Too bad. That will teach her to pay attention to my needs/demands.

Before I forget it. My website is www.ritamaebrown.com. We've simplified the address. Don't worry. You don't have

to waste time with her stuff. You can go right to my pages and I hope you do. You can reach me at P. O. Box 4671, Charlottesville, VA 22905.

I'd be thrilled if you'd tell me your acts of revenge—just in case.

Pewter, by the way, is on a diet. This is not improving her personality. Even the dog doesn't want to be around her but I must admit she is looking good. She got so fat there for a while that the floor shook when she waddled on it.

Hope all is well with you.

Sneaky Pie